Heart Throb
Carly Bishop

Harlequin Books

TORONTO • NEW YORK • LONDON
AMSTERDAM • PARIS • SYDNEY • HAMBURG
STOCKHOLM • ATHENS • TOKYO • MILAN
MADRID • WARSAW • BUDAPEST • AUCKLAND

To my friends at Presbyterian/St. Luke's
old and new, here and gone

ISBN 0-373-22323-4

HEART THROB

Copyright © 1995 by Cheryl McGonigle

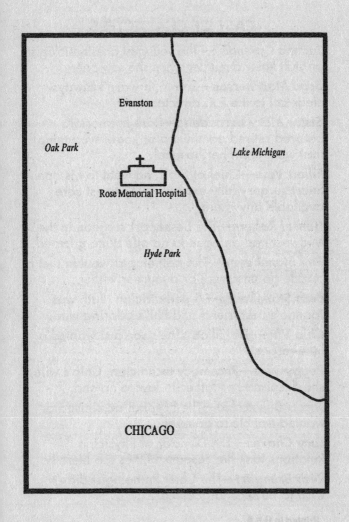

Evanston

Oak Park

Lake Michigan

✝
Rose Memorial Hospital

Hyde Park

CHICAGO

CAST OF CHARACTERS

Joanna Cavendish—The youngest anesthesiologist on staff knew a murder when she saw one.

Brad MacPherson—The truth wasn't always clear-cut to the P.R. director.

Sister Mary Bernadette—Rose Memorial's beloved retired administrator knew everything that went on in her hospital.

Elliott Vine—Chief of Staff, he went to his open-heart surgery fully expecting the finest care available anywhere....

Hensel Rabern—The best heart surgeon in the Midwest had an agenda no one quite grasped.

Phil Stonehaven—The pathologist wouldn't let a puzzle go unsolved, or a murder, either....

Beth Stonehaven—A pediatrician, Beth was Joanna's best friend and Phil's adoring wife.

Chip Vine—Dr. Elliott Vine's son just wanted a little respect.

Peggy Vine—Pharmacy technician, Chip's wife, she despised her father-in-law to no end.

Jacob Delvecchio—The hospital administrator wanted trouble to go away....

Lucy Chavez—The Director of Physician Relations took her responsibilities too literally.

Ruth Brungart—The Chief Pathologist didn't wish to be second-guessed.

Prologue

Joanna Cavendish had a reputation among the recovery-room and intensive-care nurses for sending her patients out of surgery in excellent condition. Better in most cases than her far more experienced colleagues. Patients felt no pain under her anesthesia, but they didn't come out of surgery in a near coma, either.

She sat in OR near the head of the surgical table in the cold, climate-controlled surgical suite, adjusting her monitors and anesthesia machine, listening to the hum of equipment and the conversations going on. She knew her reputation with the recovery nurses had convinced Elliott Vine, chief of staff of Rose Memorial, to choose her over a dozen others to do the anesthesia when he underwent open-heart surgery this morning.

Flattered by the opportunity, she intended to justify Vine's faith in her. At thirty-two, she was the youngest anesthesiologist on staff at Rose Memorial. The surgeon, Hensel Rabern, was old enough to be her father. He didn't trust anyone still paying off medical-school bills and he hadn't been shy about voicing his opinion. He didn't approve of Vine's choice.

Vine had insisted.

She had the chance to prove herself to the cranky, demanding Dr. Rabern this morning, to gain his respect, but the rest of the surgical team—from the two vascular surgeons assisting Rabern to the surgical resident to the nurses and techs—thought it was the worst possible luck to be assigned to this surgery. They were all far more worried about Dr. Vine's wrath should anything go even slightly wrong while he was under the knife.

"Twenty-eight, twenty-nine... You all know this had better come off picture perfect, don't you?" Rabern's scrub nurse warned, compulsively counting sponges and squares of gauze.

"If it doesn't, there'll be hell to pay," the pharmacy tech answered, unloading an armful of solutions in plastic bags.

"It's not okay to be merely competent around this joint," another nurse put in, sniffing while she adjusted the stainless-steel lights. "No one's allowed to be human. Vine would rather we were all robots."

"He is a bit of a pill, isn't he?" Joanna murmured, inventorying her own supply of medications once more. She understood Vine's attitude. In her job, mistakes could kill. She didn't allow herself any errors no matter how slight. Still, Elliott Vine was pretty tactless and overbearing.

"A pill?" the surgical resident asked, backing into the room through the swinging doors, gloved and ready to go. He picked up the conversational thread without missing a beat. "A *pill?* The man's a maniac." The resident stared down at the slack features of Vine's face. "Too bad we can't keep him like this."

Joanna smiled behind her surgical mask. No one had ever seen Vine as inanimate and peaceful as he appeared now.

"The guy's insulted or humiliated everyone on the hospital staff at one time or another," the resident went on, adding darkly, "if I were him, I'd have had my surgery somewhere else."

"Maybe" came Hensel Rabern's nasal baritone voice from the swinging doors, "you'd like to take your residency somewhere else." He shoved through, followed by the two assisting vascular surgeons.

The young resident turned and flushed to the roots of his hair. "Umm, no, sir."

"Then shut the hell up and finish the prep," Rabern snapped. He turned to Joanna, his scraggly graying eyebrows raised between his mask and surgical cap. "You get that blood mix-up figured out?"

"Yes." The tension in the suite had risen several notches, reflecting the surgeon's testiness. Joanna straightened on her stool, wondering if he expected her to elaborate.

"And?"

"And I made sure we have the proper units of blood ready." She was the one who had discovered and corrected the error—an orderly had dropped off the wrong blood cooler. It had been merely a matter of trading it for the correct cooler containing the pints of blood donated specifically for Elliott Vine by his friends and family.

The blood was her responsibility and it annoyed her that Rabern thought she hadn't already taken care of the mix-up—but since everyone was hyper about Vine's surgery, she chose not to take the question as a personal affront. "I looked at each unit of blood. Everything checks out."

"Fine. Let's get this show on the road, then." He stepped to the table between his scrub nurse and the surgical resident. "Scalpel." The nurse slapped it into his hand.

From the first incision the surgery went satisfactorily. Vine's body tolerated the procedure as well as could possibly be expected. Making the delicate repairs to the arteries in his heart, Rabern loosened up enough to joke around. The trio of surgeons rehashed the Pro-Am golf tournament of the previous weekend. Joanna monitored her equipment every few minutes—although had anything unusual or unexpected happened, the alarms on her equipment would instantly alert her.

Midway through the surgery she started two units of blood running through the filtered IV lines. One of the vascular surgeons supplied a section of healthy vein taken elsewhere, and Rabern began the repairs to the third and last artery, instructing the surgical resident as he went along. "So, Dr. Cavendish, how are we doing?" he asked.

Her monitors indicated nothing amiss. "Fine. Couldn't be better."

"Let's keep it that way."

By the end of three hours, the repairs were completed. "Show time," Rabern murmured. The moment had come to start Vine's heart beating again on its own—always tricky. If something was going to go wrong, chances were they would go wrong now. But Elliott Vine's heart cooperated and began to beat strongly.

Joanna hung two more of the six units of blood and joined in the collective sigh of relief going up around the high-tech surgical suite. They'd done it. *She'd* done it.

"Nice job, Cavendish," Rabern remarked admiringly—with the barest hint of astonishment that she really was as skilled as Vine believed. "No kidding. I mean it."

"Thanks," Joanna replied. "No kidding."

"You get Vine back to postop looking this good and I'll take a full page ad in the *Trib* taking back all the mean things I said about you."

She met Rabern's forceful milky blue gaze, instinctively mistrusting his praise. He'd waited until the vascular surgeons had gone before saying anything positive to her. And—in her experience, at least—praise and blame were just opposite ends of the same stick. If things went well you were praised—if not, you were blamed. Still, his eyes conveyed a newfound respect that was almost everything she could have hoped for.

Stripping off his gloves, Rabern backed away from the table so the surgical resident could move into place and put in the final sutures.

She hung two more units of blood, decreased the deep anesthesia medicines and noted those steps in her record book.

Thirty seconds later, Vine's blood pressure dropped out of sight.

Alarms on her equipment began wailing. Everyone went still, and idle conversation died. The phosphorescent blip of the EKG monitor struggled, then flat-lined. Vine's heart had ceased to beat.

Joanna's own heart lurched. "He's crashed, Hensel!"

"That fast?" Rabern swore. "What the hell is going on?"

"Stop the blood units and get them back to the blood bank. I want a transfusion reaction workup. Stat!" she commanded, then turned her gaze over the surgical mask back to Rabern. "His pressure just dropped out of sight. Maybe he blew a hole in his heart." If Rabern's careful stitches had broken loose inside the heart, that would explain the sudden drop in Vine's blood pressure.

"He didn't blow any damned hole," Rabern snapped. "It's got to be the blood. Get him back, damn it!"

Joanna nodded. Her concentration tripled. Ripping into packages of medications, mentally ripping through her alternatives, she fought to stimulate Elliott Vine's body back to life.

Nothing worked. She couldn't restore his circulation, his blood pressures. Rabern got panicky and turned nasty—all the angrier, Joanna thought, because only moments ago he'd been singing her praises. "What the devil are you doing, Cavendish?"

"Everything there is to do." She'd been trained to deal with this kind of unexpected physiologic disaster, but she didn't need Rabern's sudden hostility. "You'd better consider—"

"Get me the paddles," Rabern barked, interrupting to do what she'd been about to suggest. The lanky, scared resident scurried to comply. Rabern ordered the level of electrical juice, then applied the paddles directly to Vine's bare, sutured chest. "Stand clear!"

The resident sent Joanna a warning glance, as if there were something she could do to make Rabern's attempts work. She ignored him and focused on her monitors. The faintest blip took shape, then disappeared back into a flat line. "Again," she suggested.

"Clear!" Rabern delivered another shock, then glared at Joanna. "Well?"

She shook her head. "It isn't working."

Rabern swore. "Well, thanks to you, we're going to have to go in again."

Joanna met his hard, accusing glare straight on, but said nothing in her own defense. Rabern wouldn't listen in any case, and contradicting him would only make him angrier at her.

He hurled the paddles toward the resident, who dropped one of them. Rabern's scrub nurse repeated the prep of Vine's chest with the surgical iodine solution, and Rabern began the operation again.

Automatically, Joanna noted the time. Rabern worked steadily for thirty-five minutes. Nothing brought Elliott Vine back. Not the open-heart massage, not direct electrical stimulation.

Vine's heart had unaccountably given up the ghost, and no one—not even Rabern—could make it beat again on its own.

All the king's horses and all the king's men... Stunned and sick at heart, Joanna knew the entire surgical team felt the force of their patient's wrath even now in his death. Elliott Vine was dead in his own hospital, and there would be hell to pay.

Rabern flushed with rage. No surgeon was ever inclined to let a patient die on the table. Better to get them safely out of OR and let the postop nurses take the blame if the patient died. But that wouldn't happen this time.

Vine was dead on the table.

Rabern cast Joanna a scathing look, peeled off his gloves, threw them on the gray linoleum floor and stormed out. Left behind with a few stunned nurses and the surgical resident, Joanna shut off her machines.

Chapter One

A dozen hours after Rabern declared Elliott Vine officially dead, Joanna put aside her copy of the preliminary autopsy report on the end table by her sofa, and her tortoiseshell reading glasses with them. Her eyes burned from hours spent scrutinizing the tapes generated by the monitors in the OR, searching for a clue as to why Elliott Vine had crashed.

Crashed. The word was so commonly used in a hospital that it had no emotional punch left for her, but tonight it triggered the image of the mythical Icarus crashing back down to earth because he'd flown too close to the sun with wings made of wax. The image made her shiver involuntarily.

She wasn't alone. Vine's death had spooked everyone—mostly the there-but-for-the-grace-of-God-go-I variety of shock. If the chief of staff could die on the table in the course of a fairly routine surgery in his own hospital...

Wow.

As if that weren't enough, someone had called the press and now everyone in the greater Chicago area wanted answers.

Why call the press? Joanna thought for the umpteenth time. Vine might be chief of staff of Rose Memorial, but he wasn't exactly a celebrity. And at least ten percent of all patients died in open-heart surgery. But whoever had anonymously called the *Tribune* reporter and all the television network affiliates had apparently made Vine's death out to be the surgical fiasco of the decade.

Joanna was just compulsive enough herself to wish there were one clear, logical reason for Vine's death, but she knew better. Sometimes a patient's heart was just too bad to repair. Sometimes people just died.

Still, she felt compelled to search for errors she might have made. She could find nothing.

She went into her small condominium kitchen and turned on the burner beneath the brass teakettle. Using the few minutes it took to heat the water, she closed the greenhouse window over her kitchen sink against the cool night air and watered the collection of herbs growing in ceramic pots.

The teakettle whistled and her phone rang at the same time, jangling her nerves.

Lifting the teapot from the burner, she waited for the answering machine to pick up the call. Through its small speaker came the voice of Phil Stonehaven, one of the pathologists and the husband of Joanna's best friend, Beth, who also practiced at Rose Memorial as a pediatrician.

"Joanna, pick up, will you, if you're listening?"

She put down the kettle and reached for the phone. "Hi, Phil."

"Joanna, I hope I'm not interrupting anything."

He sounded tired and irritable. Joanna straightened. "No. I was just reading Brungart's preliminary report on

Vine's cause of death." She glanced at her white-faced watch. Ten-thirty at night.

"How are you doing?" he asked.

"All right, I guess." She swallowed a sudden lump in her throat. "I keep waiting for Rabern to start pointing fingers. I'm the most likely target." Might as well admit it. Phil was an old enough friend to know she kept herself pretty much under wraps. Controlled. Not allowing her emotions out. He'd only keep poking until she vented her fears.

"I've seen Rabern stomping around making an ass out of himself before," Phil said, trying to reassure her. "He should know he's a walking cliché when he does that— pointing a finger at the anesthesiologist to deflect any blame someone might want to lay at his feet. Still, you can't blame the guy. Vine died on his table."

"I know. Have you found anything new?" she asked, aware that he was reviewing Vine's autopsy at the request of the hospital administration—a sort of in-house second opinion. Phil had done a fellowship in the county medical examiner's office before coming to Rose Memorial. He was credentialed by that office to cite the official cause of death. If he agreed with the initial findings of the chief pathologist, then the hospital would be on firm ground to say there was no one at fault in Dr. Vine's death. There would be no further inquiries.

"Nothing I can point a finger at," he responded unhappily.

"Isn't that good?" Joanna asked. "For the hospital, I mean?"

"It would be, except that something here isn't clicking for me. What did you think of Brungart's preliminary autopsy report?"

Joanna poured the steaming water into her mug. Dr. Ruth Brungart was the chief pathologist, dour faced, humorless and the butt of countless Dr. Ruth jokes around the hospital.

Dunking the tea bag, savoring the scent of the chamomile, Joanna sat at her small wood-and-glass kitchen table. "A case of much ado about nothing, according to Dr. Brungart. Elliott Vine died of 'sudden cardiac death, unknown causes.' Period. End of discussion."

Phil grunted. "It's the unknown etiology part that doesn't fly. The administration hates it, not to mention MacPherson."

Joanna's hand stilled at the mention of Brad Mac-Pherson, the director of public relations at Rose Memorial. Thirty-seven, a killer soccer player in Chicago intersports club squads, he'd refereed a game Joanna played for the women's league, which was when they had originally met. He was into jazz and reggae and the Cubbies. Smart. He had a way with words Joanna instinctively mistrusted, but which the rest of the world seemed to appreciate.

Half of the reporters, looking for the sensational angle, were already speculating that Vine's heavy-handed reputation at Rose Memorial made him a real candidate for murder. The incident had all the makings of a public-relations nightmare for the hospital.

Jacob Delvecchio, Rose Memorial's CEO, naturally wanted somebody to make the whole mess go away. MacPherson was that somebody.

He was the man for the job. He could gild any ordinary lily. Dazzle any doubting Thomas. As far as Joanna was concerned, those skills made Brad MacPherson an emotional danger zone. She had plenty of reason to know that for herself, and it annoyed her no end that the mention of his name still made her heart throb.

But whatever their personal history, Brad MacPherson was going to need all those skills at the press conference in the morning. Especially if Phil had found any suggestion that Vine's death was not so cut-and-dried as Ruth Brungart's autopsy indicated.

"Phil, tell me what's bothering you."

"I'm sitting here looking at these slides and I'm saying to myself, something doesn't add up. The tissues almost suggest a generalized circulatory collapse brought on by something like an overwhelming septicemia."

Joanna frowned. The term referred to a bacterial infection of the blood—what they used to call blood poisoning. In sufficient number, certain germs produce enough toxins that the body collapses from trying so hard to neutralize the poisons. She swallowed. "Phil, how could that be? He had no fever or we would never have begun the surgery. Wouldn't that kind of infection make the body spike a temperature?"

"Most likely, yes." Phil sighed heavily. "And you would expect an abnormally high white blood cell count with such a massive infection. Vine's was actually lower than his beginning cell counts. That's why I'm puzzled. The only thing I can come up with is that one of the units of blood he received to replace the blood loss during surgery was contaminated. I've sent a sample of Vine's blood to the bacteriology lab to be cultured, but even that may be negative."

"Because even if the bacteria are all dead, the toxins they give off could still have caused Vine's death?" Joanna asked, struggling to remember her microbiology courses.

"Yes. Of course, there's always the possibility that somebody slipped Vine a gram or two of strychnine," he joked dispiritedly. "I ordered a full toxicology screen, anyway. Brungart went ballistic. She doesn't want to be second-guessed, and she thinks ordering a full toxicology screen is the same as admitting there may have been some other cause of death."

He sighed heavily again, and Joanna could almost see him shoving his wire-rimmed glasses up onto his balding head in frustration.

"Phil, are you really questioning whether or not Ruth's conclusions stand up, or are you playing intellectual 'chicken' with yourself?"

"I don't know," he said dismissively, hammering away at his keyboard. "But I intend to find out. Check in with me in the morning, will you? Let's say 6:00 a.m.—in case I've come up with anything." He broke off and she heard the telltale squeak of his chair coming upright. "What the devil?"

She heard him muttering beneath his breath, talking to himself. "Joanna, I have to go. Talk to you in the morning, okay?" He hung up the phone, breaking their connection before she could answer.

Frowning, she wondered what had made him end the call so abruptly. She thought briefly about going into his office now, but he wouldn't have hesitated to say so if he thought she needed to return tonight. She threw away the tea bag and wiped her countertop.

Taking the herb-scented mug of tea and a couple of graham crackers upstairs to her bedroom, she settled in with a novel against a soft pile of pillows.

She tried to read, but the book failed to catch her interest, not to mention distract her from Elliott Vine's death. After a few minutes, she showered and washed her hair. She worked the damp, baby-fine strands into a braid so there would be a little body when her hair dried.

She couldn't shake her uneasiness after Phil's call, but she fell into a restless sleep to the strains of a set of Simon and Garfunkel on the clock radio.

When the telephone jangled at her bedside, the sun was still nowhere near rising. Rolling over, she groped for the receiver. "Cavendish," she croaked.

"Joanna?"

Her mind protested, but her heart did a small flip-flop at the masculine, smooth-as-velvet voice. "Brad?" She swallowed and raised up on one elbow. "What time is it?"

"A quarter to five. I'm sorry I woke you."

His tone felt almost intimate to her, like a gentle caress, but even in her sleep-numbed state she registered voices in the background that meant he was only being discreet. Alarms went off inside her. "What's going on? Where are you?"

He hesitated. "In Phil Stonehaven's office."

"Phil's office?" she repeated. "At a quarter to five in the morning?"

"Yes." He gave a frustrated sigh. "The police are here. I pushed the redial on Phil's extension. I had no idea it would turn out to be you. The police want to know who was the last person—" He stopped midsentence. "Hell. Joanna, I'm sorry. I'm making a mess of this. You don't know."

Joanna swallowed and reached for her bedside lamp. Her brain must be more sleep-addled than she knew. "Don't know what?"

"I..." Brad hesitated again, which wasn't at all in keeping with his usual fluent manner. "Joanna...there's no easy way to say this. I know you were close. Phil Stonehaven is dead. He was found a few hours ago."

"Oh, my God. How?"

"By the looks of it, someone knocked him over the head with his microscope. The police were called, and it's hospital protocol that I or someone on my staff be paged in cases like this."

In cases like this? Joanna shook her head, instinctively protesting. She wanted to pinch herself, to believe she was still sleeping and that this call was part of a nightmare, but it wasn't. Brad MacPherson wasn't given to cruelty or tasteless jokes.

Her heart sank. Drawing her long legs close to her body, she planted her elbows atop her knees, too numbed, too horrified, to think straight. "Who would want to kill Phil Stonehaven?"

She heard Brad responding to comments from a female nearby, then he answered. "Apparently Phil was mugged, Joanna. Robbed, bashed over the head and left for dead. His watch is missing, and his wallet—oh, a wedding band, too."

"His wedding band?" Joanna braced the phone against her ear with her shoulder. Her thoughts were wildly disjointed. Phil was her best friend's husband. Their three kids would have to grow up without him now. It couldn't be brilliant, eggheaded, mild-mannered Phil Stonehaven who was dead.

Killed over a Seiko watch…some cash…a handful of credit cards? His wedding ring?

"Joanna, are you still there?"

"I'm coming in," she answered. "I'll be there in half an hour."

She hung up the phone, tossed aside her covers and got up, mechanically pulling her hair out of its braid, getting dressed in a pair of shapeless scrub clothes—a navy blue

V-necked top and drawstring trousers—and crepe-soled clogs.

Reality began to set in on her short drive to the hospital. There were police in Phil's office, a detective assigned. A crime scene, no doubt, already being cordoned off.

She stepped hard on the accelerator of her sedan, feeling angry and helpless. If only she'd gone in last night after Phil called, maybe the creep who'd done this would have taken off.

By the time she arrived, the cops had their hands full keeping the normal morning lab activity from contaminating the crime scene.

Forensic technicians were in the midst of vacuuming the area for evidence of the killer's presence and dusting Phil's office and microscope for fingerprints.

Her eyes were drawn to the floor of his office.

Phil's body had been removed, but the institutional gray carpet was soaked with his blood. She had seen too many grisly sights and too many autopsies for her imagination to draw a kindly blank. None of her experiences had prepared her for the brutal slaying of a man who was her friend, and her best friend's husband. Her stomach rolled sickeningly.

She turned just as Brad MacPherson walked up to her. Joanna was five-nine; Brad stood half a foot taller. He had straight, ordinary brown hair and an ordinary face— in the same way someone might say Harrison Ford had ordinary looks. Brad's eyes were a rich hazel-green, and he had a scar along his chin. And he had this raw kind of masculinity beneath all the polish that other men respected but ignored because they couldn't understand why women were attracted.

Joanna knew. Even now.

He took one look at her stricken face and steered her to the rest room across the hall, took her inside, shut the door and held her close while tears spilled down her face.

"Breathe, Dish."

She felt too queasy to object to his calling her Dish—a shortened twist on Cavendish. An endearment, he claimed. But after a few dizzying moments she felt her stomach uneasily settling.

Brad let her go and dampened a few paper towels with cold water. She reached for them, but he took her hand and drew her close to him, tucking her shoulder beneath his arm. She shook her head and started to pull away, but he didn't give her a chance.

"Hold still," he commanded softly, cupping her chin, forcing her to look into his compelling hazel-green eyes. "Take a few deep breaths."

"This is crazy." She was the doctor and he was telling her what to do.

"Do it, anyway." He mopped her face like a child's, tossed the damp towels in the trash, then blotted her face dry with the soft linen-blend handkerchief from the breast pocket of the black pin-striped suit that he was wearing even at this incredibly early hour.

The fabric carried his masculine, musky scent. She didn't want to remember it so well, but she did. She didn't want to think how well she fit against him, either. She shouldn't linger, holding tight to his lapels, resting her head against his broad chest, absorbing the heat of his body. Letting everything else slip away.

Elliott Vine was dead, and now Phil, and she shouldn't have another thought in her head. She pulled back, and Brad reluctantly let her go again.

"Are you sure you're okay?"

His voice bathed her senses. She had to remind herself how dangerous he was to her, emotionally. "Yes. Thank you." She took a deep breath and, opening the door for herself, walked back into the corridor outside Phil's office. A stockily shaped woman with short black hair and brown eyes awaited them.

"Joanna Cavendish?" she asked.

"Yes."

"Detective Laverne Dibell," Brad introduced her.

Dibell wore a rumpled brown tweed suit and sensible shoes. "Let's get out of the way of the investigators and talk for a few minutes."

Joanna led the way to a more secluded area in the corridor.

"Dr. Cavendish." Dibell leaned against the wall. "I'm very sorry. Mr. MacPherson indicated to me that you were a close friend of the victim—of Dr. Stonehaven's."

Joanna swallowed hard and glanced at Brad. His presence steadied her more than she wanted to admit. "That's right."

"Anything more than friendship there, Doctor?" Detective Dibell asked blandly.

Joanna shook her head. "It was nothing like that. Phil is married—his wife is my best friend." *Poor Beth.* Their marriage was a happy one, and despite his long hours at the hospital, Phil had been the kind of father who knew what size shoes his kids wore. "Has Beth been notified?"

"By now?" Detective Dibell checked her watch. "I'm sure she has been reached. Now we believe Dr. Stonehaven was mugged sometime between 10:00 p.m. and midnight. What time did he telephone you?"

"Ten-thirty. I had turned on my answering machine to screen calls. That way I can always be available if the hospital calls me in for an emergency surgery."

"You're a surgeon?"

"Anesthesiologist," Joanna corrected.

Idly scratching her forehead with the end of her pen, Dibell frowned. "Why did Dr. Stonehaven call you?"

"He was reviewing Dr. Brungart's autopsy on Dr. Vine. He wanted to make sure I was all right."

"Vine?" Dibell questioned, her frown deepening the crevices in her complexion, her eyes flicking between Brad and Joanna. "Let me just clarify here. You're referring to the guy—what was he—the chief of staff here? The one who died on the operating table yesterday?"

"Yes."

"Why did Dr. Stonehaven think you might not be okay?"

Joanna took a deep breath. "I was the anesthesiologist for Dr. Vine's surgery. Phil knows how tough it is to lose a patient."

"Hmm. Lots of people die on the table, don't they?" Dibell asked, including Brad in her glance.

"Not a lot," he answered. "But the press got hold of this. It makes for sensational headlines for a doctor to die under the knife in his own hospital."

"Any idea who called them?"

Brad grimaced, deepening the scar in his chin. "I wish I knew, but I don't."

"Well." Dibell shrugged. "Back to Dr. Stonehaven. Do you know where the corridor leads through the locked door at the end of his hallway?"

"To Sister Mary Bernadette's soup kitchen, I think," Joanna said. The retired, elderly, birdlike nun who had once run Rose Memorial—in the hospital's days of being

Sacred Heart—had taken on the homeless problem in the area.

"Exactly," Dibell said. "Ever any concerns for safety?"

Joanna nodded. "I remember the pathologists getting up in arms over the vagrant population having such close access to the lab with all the available syringes and needles." She hesitated. "You're thinking Phil's mugger came in that way?"

Dibell scowled at the increasing number of people walking by dressed out in lab coats impermeable to blood spills and splashes. "We found the security door unlocked. Your docs were right to be concerned."

Joanna exchanged glances with Brad. "So the theory is some junkie could have come through the soup kitchen and attacked Phil?"

"Probably not a junkie—unless he didn't realize how close he was to the lab's supply of needles."

"A vagrant, then?"

Dibell nodded. "That's what it looks like."

"But don't murderers always steal things from the victim to make it look like a mugging?"

Dibell gave a sardonic smile. "On television. In the movies. And it is a possibility we'll take into account. In real life, though, the murderer isn't usually any more experienced at stripping valuables than he is at the actual murder. It takes time. The perp gets nervous. In the rush to get away, they'll take a watch and wallet, but leave a wedding band—or some other combination of valuables."

Joanna shook her head. "You know, in all the years I've heard stories of this kind of thing around Rose, no one on staff has ever actually been mugged inside the buildings."

"There hasn't been a soup kitchen catering to the criminal element around here, either."

"I'm sure you don't mean to characterize Sister Mary Bernadette's soup kitchen as 'catering to the criminal element,'" Brad said. "It's a community service—"

"Which can still disguise the sleaze element," Detective Dibell interrupted impatiently. "Don't worry, Mr. MacPherson, I don't plan to go around bad-mouthing Rose Memorial or Sister Mary Bernadette's charity. The old girl brought me ice cream when I had my tonsils out here forty-some years ago." Dibell shifted from one foot to the other. "One more thing, Dr. Cavendish, what time did you hang up with Dr. Stonehaven?"

"You were on the phone with Phil last night?" came a voice from behind them.

Joanna turned. With all the comings and goings of lab staff and crime scene technicians, none of them had noticed Chip Vine approaching.

Always dressed as if he'd stepped out of the pages of *GQ*, his jet black hair barbered into a ponytail, this morning Chip Vine looked as if he'd slept in his clothes— except that the dark circles beneath his bloodshot gray eyes betrayed a sleepless night. He was entitled, Joanna thought. His father had been dead less than twenty-four hours.

"Your name?" Detective Dibell snapped in irritation at the interruption.

"Charles Vine. Chip. I work in HIS—hospital information services." He acknowledged Brad, then turned back to Joanna. "I just heard about Phil. I wanted to talk to him about Dad's autopsy."

"Chip Vine?" Detective Dibell repeated. "You're related to Dr. Elliott Vine?"

"My father," Chip answered, his voice shaky. "What happened to Phil?"

"The police think some vagrant—" Joanna began, only to be interrupted by Detective Dibell waving a plump hand agitatedly.

"Wait a minute," Dibell said. "You say you were looking for Dr. Stonehaven. Did you see him last night?"

"No. I went by his office. But I didn't see him. What's this all about?"

"Dr. Stonehaven was murdered." Chip paled and swallowed hard, but said nothing. Dibell went on. "You say you wanted to speak with him about your father's autopsy report. What did you think Dr. Stonehaven could tell you?"

"I was sitting around the central computer room." His jaw tightened. "I saw Stonehaven was logged into Brungart's autopsy report on the lab programs. I wanted to know what he found out."

Chip's tone seemed pretty defensive, but despite her irritation that Chip had the kind of computer access to know what Phil was doing, Joanna felt a tug of sympathy. Her mother had died unexpectedly of an especially virulent form of pneumonia three years ago. Joanna had filled the hours after her mom's death in exactly this sort of quest for reasons.

Answers.

No one who worked in a hospital could resist the impulse to know what they thought the doctors knew. The hospital grapevine knew Chip's relationship with his father was pretty rocky. Even his father's influence hadn't gotten him into medical school anywhere—only enough to get him a job in Information Systems at Rose Memorial.

Elliott Vine was no more forgiving to his son than to anyone else on staff. Less, certainly. Still, Chip had to be agonizing.

"Was Dr. Stonehaven on the phone when you went to his office?" Dibell asked.

"No. He wasn't there at all." Chip shook his head. He'd begun to look a little feverish.

"What time was that?" the detective asked.

"I can't remember what the time was. I was wandering the halls all night long, it seems like. I lost track of time."

Dibell's expression emptied again. Chip had just contradicted himself. Dibell called him on it. "You were here at the hospital all night, and even though it was important to you to see what Dr. Stonehaven might have found, you only stopped by his office that one time? Never after he was murdered?"

"That's right. I cut out after I couldn't find Stonehaven in his office." His features twisted. He was tired and confused. "Since when is it a crime to want to know what the hell happened?"

Dibell's brows raised. "What I'm wondering, young man, is why you never went back when it was so important to you to know what happened."

"I just didn't. My old man just died. I'm not being completely rational, all right? I don't know what I was thinking not to go back to Stonehaven's office again." Chip scowled and stuffed his hands into his pants pockets. Joanna had never seen him look less *GQ*, or more defenseless. His Adam's apple bobbed. "Maybe if I had, I would have scared off whoever attacked Dr. Stonehaven."

Joanna could have come in as well. Phil didn't have to be dead right now, if one or the other of them had turned up. "Chip, listen," Joanna began, touching his arm. "I know how you feel. My mother—"

"Don't patronize me, Joanna," he snarled unexpectedly. "For all I know, you're the one responsible for my father crashing on the table and Stonehouse was looking for some way to cover your pretty little ass."

She took an unconscious step backward. In a few hours, when the reality of Phil's death finally sunk into her consciousness, she'd be feeling as meanspirited and unforgiving as Chip was right now. His accusation stung, but she knew he was probably just lashing out at the first convenient target.

Brad wasn't anywhere near as forgiving. "Chip, that's enough," he said, his voice low and commanding. "You're way out of line. You need to go home and get some sleep. I'm asking you in the best interests of the hospital and your own mental health. Go home." Clearly, he wasn't only asking.

Chip's jaw set stubbornly. "Peggy and I are going to be here for the press conference," he insisted. "We'll stand behind the sudden-cardiac-death finding. It would look pretty bad for the hospital if we weren't there."

Brad nodded his reluctant agreement. It would make a far more solid impression if Elliott Vine's son and daughter-in-law, both of whom also worked at Rose Memorial, were present at the press conference.

Detective Dibell craned her short neck and watched Chip's back until he'd rounded a corner at the far end of the hall. "Interesting." She turned to Joanna. "On the one hand, he's willing to stand behind the official hospital version for the sake of appearances. On the other, he's lurking around the pathology offices waiting to find out what else is coming down."

"I wouldn't characterize it as 'lurking,'" Brad said easily.

"No. You wouldn't." Dibell smiled thinly, then turned toward Joanna. "Dr. Cavendish, what time were you off the phone with Dr. Stonehaven?"

"We were only on for ten minutes. Maybe twelve. I'd say I had hung up with Phil no later than ten forty-five."

"Were you expecting a call from him? Had he led you to believe he would be calling?"

Joanna searched her memory. "No. I knew he was going to review Dr. Brungart's findings, but he didn't specifically tell me he would call."

"Did he mention seeing anyone?"

Joanna shook her head. "No one. I had the impression he was the only one left around by that time of night. He was tired, bordering on cranky."

Dibell jotted notes in a small book, then closed the pad and put it away in her purse. "If he was tired, his reaction time would have been considerably slowed—making him all the more vulnerable to a mugger."

"Or anyone," Joanna said, sickened again by the mental image of someone crashing his microscope down on Phil's head.

Dibell turned expressionless again. "One more thing, Dr. Cavendish ... *is* there some possibility you were responsible for Dr. Vine's death? And that, being such a good friend, Dr. Stonehaven was searching for a way to cover your mistakes in the OR?"

Chapter Two

The breath rushed from Joanna's lungs. A flush began deep in her throat. Dibell's blunt question took her wholly off guard. "I... Phil wouldn't cover—"

"None," Brad interrupted, his face a mask of intentional indignation. "Dr. Brungart performed the actual autopsy, and she has no connection whatever to Dr. Cavendish."

Dibell smiled as before. "Just asking," she said, giving a cheery wave. "Have a *good* day, Doctor."

Her throat locked, Joanna watched the detective disappear into the hallway leading to Sister Mary Bernadette's soup kitchen.

Brad shook his head. "You don't have one survival instinct in your head, do you?"

Her chin went up and her lips tightened. "Of course I do—"

"Then why didn't you tell Dibell in no uncertain terms that you weren't responsible for Vine's death? It's not the same thing to say Phil wouldn't cover your mistakes."

"Not everyone is so concerned with saying things exactly the right way," she retorted. "Besides, Phil isn't here to defend himself." Her own words brought her up short, forcing her to remember. *Phil wasn't here.*

The fight went out of her. Reading her distress in her face, Brad took hold of her shoulders and shook her.

"Joanna, listen to me. You have to be very clear. You have to know in your own mind that nothing you did caused Elliott Vine's death. And when you're asked a question like that, you have to be smarter about it and a whole *hell* of a lot less emotional."

Her spine stiffened. In the entire history of their short, ill-fated affair, he had never once gotten angry with her. Never told her off or gotten in her face like this. Never cared enough to let her know he thought she was off base. She didn't trust people who wouldn't be straight with her any more than she trusted praise or Brad's gilt-edged tongue.

She hadn't trusted him. But he was angry with her now and she was just contrary enough to feel flattered that he cared at all.

"Dish, am I getting through to you, here?" he demanded.

"Stop calling me that. And, yes. I heard you, but it's not that simple."

He grabbed her hand and pulled her with him onto the elevator to the eighth floor where the physicians' private dining room was located. A large part of the elegantly appointed room was encased in floor-to-ceiling windows, affording a one-hundred-and-eighty-degree view.

To the east, the sun was rising over Lake Michigan, creating a sparse eerie forest of sailboat masts. To the south, the sun bounced off the windows of Chicago office buildings. Maybe in the light of day he could make Joanna understand.

He steered her through the deserted room to a table by the window and jerked out a chair for her. "Sit."

"Please," she said, remaining stubbornly standing.

"Please," he said stonily, his eyes narrowed dangerously. "Sit."

She complied. He sat across from her and ordered a
couple of cinnamon rolls and coffee. When the young
Thai waitress named Took Took delivered them, he
winked and smiled and reminded her that Dr. Cavendish
required a creamer all to herself.

Flattered by Brad's attention and the merest hint of a
secret between them, Took Took smiled broadly and returned with a ceramic creamer and an entire insulated pot
of coffee.

Joanna ripped off a hunk of her cinnamon roll.
"You're shameless."

"Harmless," he countered. "Harmless flirtation. People usually enjoy it, Joanna." He eyed her. "Most people." He hacked into his roll with his fork. "But then,
most people have a few nerve circuits devoted to self-
preservation, too."

"Sorry," Joanna snapped, dumping cream into her
coffee until it turned a milky brown color. "Mine are all
devoted to the truth."

"What does that mean, Joanna? Isn't it the truth that
you had nothing to do with Elliott Vine's death?"

"I told you. It's not that simple."

"Then enlighten me, because from where I sit, it is that
simple."

She pulled another strand from the cinnamon roll, but
then put it back down on her plate. "I'm really spooked
by all of this, Brad."

He could see that. "Everyone is unnerved." The wary
mood permeating the atmosphere in the hospital corridors was like the sickeningly sweet scent of ether in the
chem labs.

"But not everyone was in that operating room dispensing anesthetics." She looked straight at him, her ice blue eyes rimmed by deeper, warmer blue. Her features were pretty and delicate in a Nordic no-nonsense kind of way, and her fine blond hair flew at the first hint of electricity in the air.

"It makes me feel sick inside," she went on, "that Elliott died. I've been over it in my mind a hundred times, thinking there must have been something I could do."

"Was there?"

"No. Hensel Rabern wants to believe I could have done *something,* of course—but I can't blame him. The surgery went well, and there wasn't any reason to think Vine would crash."

"But you did everything in your power to save the man's life."

She nodded. "I believe that I did. But what if I'm wrong?"

He thought about reminding her that everyone makes mistakes, but he knew better. In some ways she was the most self-confident person he knew. She would have to be to have chosen a career that put people's lives directly in her hands. But in other ways, he suspected, the responsibility unnerved her. Chip's outburst had twisted her healthy fear into something ugly.

He watched her stirring her coffee. "Joanna, think about this. Is there any anesthesia error known to man that you don't know about? Anything that you haven't asked yourself—'could I have done this or that or the other thing'?"

Her head tilted. "No."

"Did you try everything you knew to do to bring Elliott back?"

"Yes."

"Then get over it."

Joanna sighed. "Okay. I hear you. At least, as far as my responsibility goes—"

"I'm not sure you do. You're already thinking up exceptions. Joanna, if you go into that press conference this morning acting as if you don't know you did everything humanly possible to save Vine, you'll set Rose Memorial Hospital up for a long, dragged out, unwarranted investigation."

She met his gaze directly. "What if it is warranted?"

He frowned. "What does that mean?"

"I don't think we have the whole story. Phil called me last night because he thought there may be something we were all missing—some vital piece of the puzzle."

Brad sat back. "What makes Vine's death a puzzle, Joanna? Are you saying Phil found something Brungart didn't?"

Sipping her coffee, Joanna nodded. "That's the impression he gave me. He thought, looking at the tissue slides, that Vine died of a circulatory collapse—maybe brought on by septicemia."

"Which is what?"

"Blood poisoning—caused by an overwhelming bacterial infection."

"How can you tell that by looking at a slide?"

"I don't know exactly, but something must show up in the tissues. Phil asked me to come to his office and look at a few slides."

Brad raised his brows, and she nodded. "I know what you're thinking. I haven't looked under a microscope in years. Phil knows that. He wanted me to see them, anyway, and to just brainstorm with him."

Brad drew a deep breath and sat back, considering the way this might change things. "I take it you trust his instincts on this."

"Yes," she agreed. "You'd have to know Phil to understand. He cleans up the *New York Times* crossword puzzle in about a half an hour every day. He actually has—" She stopped midsentence, then continued in a huskier tone. "He *had* a patent on a 3-D puzzle that will never be marketed because it's way too complex. If there was ever one piece of information that didn't fit, Phil was on to it."

Brad drained his cup of coffee and poured another, then warmed Joanna's. "The problem is, whatever Phil was thinking is lost to us now." He shifted in his chair. "Is it really plausible that Vine died of an infection?"

"Phil had about discarded the idea. Vine's temperature was normal, and his white blood-cell count hadn't spiked. But whatever caused it, Phil believed Vine died of a circulatory collapse." She poured the rest of the cream in the little ceramic pitcher into her coffee and stirred.

"What else could cause such a collapse?"

"Poison. Insect bites. Bee stings. Loss of blood." She'd even read a journal article describing a death the authors had attributed to ethylene oxide, the gas used to sterilize equipment and medications that couldn't be heat sterilized. "None of them are what you'd call 'likely.'"

"Can't we say, then, that whether Vine died of a simple heart attack or a circulatory collapse, no one involved in the actual surgery is at fault?"

Joanna's blond brows drew together. "Brad, I know that's what you have to say at the press conference, but—"

"What I *have* to say?" He picked up his knife and began to make creases in the white linen tablecloth with the blade. "What does that mean?"

"Only that you'll do your damage control routine—say all the right things to get the hospital and staff off the hook."

"Whoa. Wait a minute." He pinned her with his eyes. "Why is it that this sounds like something personal leftover between us?"

She began to fiddle with her fork and leftover crumbs of cinnamon roll, refusing to meet his eyes. "Nothing that happened between us has anything to do with what we're talking about now."

"Of course it does, Dish," he chided. "You're too smart to pretend otherwise, so give it up." All he had to do was look at her to know better. Her memories were written all over her face. But she thought he'd contrived every moment toward getting himself off the hook of a serious relationship. "You just reminded me all your instincts are devoted to the truth. At least a few of them know we had a great thing going together."

"*Had* being the operative word," she answered, but her fingers were trembling. She remembered.

He could feel the tension humming off her, the awareness, the wariness, the heat. The memories. He could feel himself responding to her, too. This was the way it had gone between them.

There were vitally important issues to discuss at the moment. The deaths of two important staff physicians... But at the moment, nothing seemed so vital to him as this. As Joanna and him. "Tell me why you're shaking if what we had between us isn't still there."

Her chin went up. Her neck was flushed. "Sex isn't everything."

"What's your point? That great sex—one weekend—was all we ever had?"

Her glance darted around them. "Do you know you have no social graces at all?"

"Great sex was all there was between us—yes or no," he pressed her.

Her chin raised. "Let me put it this way. If there was ever anything else you wanted, MacPherson, I didn't know about it."

He stared at her. He'd told himself if she couldn't trust the evidence that he was falling crazy in love with her, that was her loss. He'd even managed to convince himself by the end of May that he'd given up on her. After that weekend, she wouldn't see him again. Didn't trust him, or what he wanted from their relationship. But he hadn't even looked at another woman since, and now it was the end of September, so he'd been wrong. It was really his loss.

"Joanna, that's not true," he said at last.

"It's the way I felt."

"Why is it that you can't believe I have a sincere bone in my body? Yes, I'm a PR man. Yes, I can phrase things well, put things in the best possible light—"

"That's what I meant about the press conference this morning. You want to make it clear no one at Rose is at fault. You can always make things sound innocent or better than they really are, or less troubling or more sincere—"

"In other words, I'm a professional liar—and insincere at that. Whatever comes out of my mouth must be a clever lie or a spin on the truth. Even in my personal relationships."

She refused to be dragged back into that. "Brad, you know damned well that if you'd been around to represent

Lizzie Borden, it sure wouldn't have sounded like forty whacks with an ax ending up in a bloodbath.''

The creases in the tablecloth began to form geometric patterns. He didn't want to let go of what all this had to do with them and their troubled relationship, but the timing was lousy.

"Joanna, think about this. It's true that I put everything I can into the best possible light. But how long do you think my credibility would survive if I claimed no one was responsible for Vine's death if that weren't the truth?''

"That's my point. I don't think you should go on record with the kind of statement that exonerates everyone involved across the board. I think Phil was on to something—and it wouldn't surprise me if someone killed him because of what he suspected had happened in Elliott Vine's surgery.''

He sat back, bewildered by Joanna's reasoning. "Like who?''

"I don't know who." She shook her head and gave a sigh of frustration. "But in recent history, Brad, no one has ever walked in here and just knocked off a member of the staff. Doesn't that seem a little contrived to you? A little convenient that Phil was murdered at just this moment in time?''

He put down the knife. "Dibell's point is well-taken, Dish. Until Mary Bernadette started up the soup kitchen this summer, we didn't have the kind of people hanging around the hospital that might resort to mugging docs for a few extra bucks.''

Joanna waved the explanation aside. "Look at this." She held up her fingers, ticking off a list of the bizarre events. "Elliott Vine dies on the table after an apparently successful open-heart surgery. The news hits the press before Vine's body ever reached the pathology lab, and whoever called them managed to hint that there's a murderer stalking the corridors of Rose Memorial—or that, at the very least, someone is guilty of malpractice. Who did that? Who phoned the press?''

"Joanna—"

"Then, still in the same twenty-four hours, the pathologist reviewing the case gets . . . gets bashed over the head with his microscope. Damn it!'' Joanna whispered angrily, swiping at the sudden tears. "Murdered while he's reviewing Elliott Vine's tissue slides.''

She wrapped her hands around her cup. Brad reached across the table and covered her hands with his. Her fingers felt icy. He knew Phil's death had only begun to sink in for her, and the flashes of awareness struck her like a bolt out of the blue every time it penetrated her mind. She looked like hell. He wanted to comfort her, but he had to understand her clearly.

Several doctors had begun to wander in. They'd lost the sense of seclusion. He lowered his voice. "Joanna, do you know what happens when you follow that logic backward?''

She nodded. "It would mean that someone intended for Elliott Vine to die on the table.''

"And then, whoever it was had to know Phil Stonehaven wasn't going to back up Ruth Brungart's sudden-cardiac-death finding. So now you have someone smart enough to kill Vine on the table right under the noses of a crack surgical team—and smart enough to make Vine's death look so innocent that no one even suspects a murder has been committed—and dumb enough to fly into a rage and bash Phil over the head? Come on, Joanna.''

She shivered. "I know it sounds crazy.''

"Do me a favor." He tossed his linen napkin onto the table. "Don't repeat it to anyone. They'll stick you in the psych ward and throw away the key."

"All this could be one terrible coincidence after another—but I'm not buying it. And if I'm not buying it, do you seriously think there's any chance the news reporters will miss making the connection?"

He let go of her hands and massaged the knot taking form at the base of his skull. Her thinking and her intuition intrigued him—A to B was never a straight line with Joanna. He couldn't escape the simplicity, the elegance, of her reasoning. The timing of Phil's death *was* too neat.

He rolled his head. The knot in his neck refused to budge. Unless he handled this one very, very well, the media would play up the angle for the sensationalism of it all and he knew it. "The timing couldn't have been worse."

Joanna swallowed, trying not to be offended because Brad saw Phil's death as an inconvenience. Trying not to take it personally. The chemistry had always been overwhelming with her and Brad—which left her emotionally defenseless and taking things personally.

He didn't even need to look at her, didn't need to remind her.

The earthy feelings, the physical attraction between them, still throbbed.

And she was still taking things personally, just because it was Brad. Sister Mary Bernadette, whose velvet-gloved, ironhanded ways had brought Sacred Heart to such preeminence in the nation's medical community, would never have traded the life of one human being for the sake of the hospital's reputation. But the canny, birdlike old nun had recruited Brad MacPherson herself and paid him enough to entice him away from Madison Avenue.

A hospital was only as good, Mary Bernadette would say obliquely, as the public believed it to be. And in these times of fierce competition among hospitals, *good* was more a matter of style and appearances and the best PR than it was the quality of care.

The din of silverware and china, the clink of glasses as physicians came and went from an early breakfast, barely registered. Joanna could almost predict what Brad would say.

The staff and members of the board of Rose Memorial Hospital deeply regret the unfortunate death of Chief of Staff Elliott Vine, and the murder last evening of Dr. Phil Stonehaven leaves us all dismayed and in shock. Our hearts go out to their families.

The postmortem on Dr. Vine reveals, so far as can be determined, that no one involved in his care is to blame, either through neglect or malpractice.

Finally, while the police investigation is ongoing, all evidence suggests a vagrant, under the guise of a patron of the hospital soup kitchen, mugged Dr. Phil Stonehouse and left him for dead.

She pushed her empty cup away and sat back. "All I am trying to get across is that I understand that your priority is to represent the best interests of the hospital. But in this case, it's not the truth. Not all of it, anyway."

Brad sat back, as well. "Joanna, what do you want from me? Should I go on record with saying we don't care much for the timing of Dr. Stonehaven's death? That it's clear to the anesthesiologist that someone—no telling who, but trust us on this one—murdered Vine in surgery and then murdered Dr. Stonehaven—same no telling who—to cover his tracks?"

"Or *hers*," she retorted, smarting from his mocking tone. But his version had served its purpose. Her theory sounded ludicrous.

If she'd need a reminder of how very, very good he was at twisting things to suit his purposes, this was it. She had no business being disappointed, but it rankled, anyway.

Her beeper sounded. She checked the number. "It's Beth Stonehaven." Joanna felt a stab of grief for her friend, and for herself. "I have to go now." She pushed back her chair and stood.

Brad rose in the same moment. He touched his hand to the back of her arm. His hazel-green eyes filled with a compassion Joanna had never had occasion to notice before. "Please tell Beth how sorry I am."

Joanna's eyes felt prickly. Beth practiced pediatrics at Rose, but Brad knew her personally as well because the four of them had gone out together after one of Brad's league soccer games. Joanna had taken them to the Swedish café her seventy-six-year-old grandmother, Nana Bea, had opened in 1953 and still operated.

"I will," she answered at last.

He laid a hand on her cheek. "Be careful, Dish."

"Of what?"

He started to answer, but then shook his head. "Just think about what you're saying, okay?"

She nodded, took a deep breath and walked out of the physicians' dining room, her tall, lithe figure lending a feminine shape to the surgical scrubs she wore.

He watched above the crowd in the service line until her blond head disappeared through the maple doors.

He didn't want to upset her. Didn't want to get into it with her over keeping quiet about her theory. She called a spade a spade, had no patience for his shades of gray, and it wasn't likely that she would censor herself.

Joanna Cavendish wasn't the rabble-rouser sort. He knew that. She'd sooner duck out on conflict than plunge in. But her friend had been murdered and she'd have a tough time keeping quiet about it.

She wasn't used to thinking about the consequences of every word out of her mouth, either, which was what worried him most. As the chief surgeon, Hensel Rabern was ultimately responsible. If Joanna went around asking point-blank what Stonehaven knew of Vine's death that had gotten him killed, Rabern would take it for defamation of his character and slap a charge of slander against her and the hospital so fast it would make her head spin.

Watching her depart the dining room, preoccupied with considerations Joanna Cavendish hadn't begun to imagine, he hoped to God she was wrong.

Chapter Three

Joanna found Beth Stonehaven sitting woodenly at her desk in the old medical office building attached to the hospital. It was only seven in the morning. Still, the sunlight streamed in, highlighting the professional artwork on Beth's office walls. The cheery atmosphere of clowns and carousels mingled with crayon drawings mocked the morning's events.

Beth rose out of her chair and came wordlessly around her desk. Her straight, short-cropped dark hair hung limply to her jaw. Her lips tightened and her chin quivered. Her bright brown eyes were dulled with pain. She walked straight into Joanna's embrace.

"Beth, I'm so sorry."

"I know. Me, too." She clung to Joanna for a moment, then straightened. No one including Joanna had ever seen Beth Stonehaven cry. She didn't now, though moisture glimmered in her eyes. She was tough and hardy and Joanna knew she believed crying didn't solve a damn thing.

She pulled back and lifted her thin shoulders. Her pallor made a sprinkling of brown freckles stand out along with the ruby red frames of her glasses. Shoving aside a pile of patient charts in colorful folders, she leaned against her desk.

"Do you remember how excited Phil was when he got that fellowship in forensic pathology at the medical examiner's office?"

"Yeah." Joanna smiled, but she wanted to throw something. "The only time I ever saw his grin bigger was when you turned up pregnant with Kimmie."

Beth's smile wavered. Her hurting wasn't very cleverly hidden. "He was such an egghead. He thought he'd never get anyone pregnant—especially out of wedlock." She sighed and stared at the ceiling where a giant, hot-pink taffeta spiderweb hung from the ceiling. "Did you know why he came back to Rose Memorial? Why he didn't stay on at the ME's office? Because he couldn't stand the vio—" Her voice broke, but she went determinedly on. "The violence. The ugliness of people killing one another."

Though she remembered all too well Phil's distaste for the grisly, unrelentingly shocking things he dealt with in the medical examiner's office, she said nothing. Beth just needed to rail about this to someone, to get the anger out of her system.

But typically, Beth refused to wallow in emotion. She shook her head, trying to regroup, to ignore the terrible irony that someone had now killed her gentle, nonviolent husband. "How did you hear?"

"From Brad."

Her friend's brows pinched together. "Are you back together?"

"Beth, how can you even think of matchmaking now?"

She stared at her hands, at her wedding band, then looked up and shrugged. "How can I not? Misery loves company, but so does happiness, Jo. I just want you to be as happy as Phil and I are." A bolt of fresh pain streaked over Beth's plain, kindly features. "Were."

Joanna could only guess how stunned Beth felt every time she was confronted anew with the fact that Phil was really dead, even in such an ordinary conversation. "Brad sends his love, Beth," she said softly.

"Thank him for me, if I don't see him, will you?" she asked.

"Of course. If I see him."

That seemed to satisfy Beth. She took a deep breath. "So I assume Brad was called in along with the police?"

"Yes. Standard procedure, I guess, for the hospital public-relations department. When he got there, he pushed the redial button on Phil's phone."

"You were the last person he spoke to?" Beth asked.

Joanna nodded.

"I'm glad of that." Her lips flattened again in pain and she shook her head. Her gaze kept returning to her hands, clasped so tightly that her knuckles shone white. For a moment the heat of tears she would never let fall fogged her glasses. "I didn't get a chance to talk to him at all last night."

Feeling pointlessly guilty for that, Joanna sank down onto the sofa across from her friend's desk. "I'd give anything if it hadn't happened, Beth."

She dragged in a deep breath and let it go. "I just wish—" Her voice cracked on a small sob she couldn't control. "I just wish to heaven we had sound effects in life, you know?" Her large, slender, capable hands flailed with the uselessness of it all. "You know what I mean? So...so when something bad was about to happen, you'd know it. You'd have two seconds' warning. Why can't there be that? Time for a proper goodbye, damn it! Is that too much to ask?"

Joanna shook her head. It wasn't fair. Few marriages survived to a fifth anniversary anymore, never mind a fiftieth. Beth and Phil would have made it.

Joanna didn't know anyone like them. Anyone more in love—in the candid, earthy, respectful way of a man and a woman as meant for each other and familiar as a pair of old bookends. The kind of marriage Nana Bea had had with her beloved Nils. No nonsense, only a great deal of love.

But Phil was dead and Beth had been robbed of a simple, proper farewell. She wouldn't whine about it for long, Joanna knew. That wasn't in Beth's makeup—but she deserved better.

"Are the kids okay?" Joanna asked.

Beth lowered her head a moment, then looked back up at Joanna. "I haven't told them. They're probably still asleep."

Joanna nodded. Phil and Beth had the luxury of a live-in nanny. "Would it help if I came over later? To be with you when you tell them?" She couldn't imagine how you told a six- and four- and three-year-old that their daddy was dead.

Beth clamped her teeth and shook her head. "Nothing will help it, Jo. I think it would be better to be alone with them." She gave a sigh. "At least, that's what I think now. And my parents are flying in this afternoon."

She took off her glasses and polished the lenses with the hem of her skirt. Dark circles lay beneath her nearsighted eyes. "But listen. I wanted a hug from you, it's true, but the thing is I did talk to Phil last afternoon before I left. He told me he wanted to stay awhile and try to figure out what was going on with Elliott Vine dying on the table like that. I assume that's why he called you?"

"Yes."

Beth nodded. "He was really worried about you, Jo. I meant to call you myself, but the kids were up to their usual antics and I never got the chance."

Joanna smiled. "He was such a good man, Beth—but he shouldn't have worried about me so much. Things happen. I'm a big girl."

Beth stood and crossed the carpet to sit down in the rocking chair next to the sofa where Joanna was. "Phil knew that, Joanna. He wouldn't presume that you couldn't handle yourself. The thing is, Rabern had been off in a corner conferring with Brungart for over an hour when I talked to Phil. He thought if they were talking about the case, they should be including you."

Joanna felt a twinge of warning. She followed Beth's reasoning quickly. It was more than a little ominous not to be included in such a conference having to do with a postmortem. "Was Phil sure they were talking about Vine's case?"

Beth nodded. "Absolutely. He didn't like it one bit."

"Why do you suppose he didn't say something to me?"

"You know Phil." Beth shrugged. "He probably wanted to spare you the back-stabbing. But he was worried, Jo. They apparently didn't care who knew they were talking. And Rabern's posturing went beyond the usual. His attitude with Brungart was that you were most likely at fault. And it wouldn't surprise him if she came up with something clearly implicating you."

Foreboding shivered through Joanna, a visceral echo of her fear and mistrust of people with hidden agendas and no honor. "Beth, are you saying Rabern was deliberately trying to influence Ruth Brungart's findings on the post?"

"In a word? Yes."

"But that's so...so unethical. I can't believe he'd do that."

"I know. And there's more. Phil said Rabern was making noises about going to Lucy Chavez to instigate a peer review."

Lucy Chavez was the director of physician relations. More often her position required kissing up to doctors, giving them whatever they needed or wanted to insure that they continued bringing their patients to Rose Memorial.

Peer reviews were in her domain, as well. She mediated disagreements between doctors—everything from spats over parking spaces to reports of "physician impairment"—the euphemism for drug and alcohol abuse among doctors.

Joanna felt sick to her stomach. Anger swamped her. There could only be one reason for Rabern to go to Lucy Chavez. "He wants my privileges pulled," Joanna said. Without them, she couldn't practice anesthesiology in Rose Memorial.

Beth gave a tight-lipped nod. "I'm sure nothing he said to Ruth Brungart was as straightforward as all that. But any time there's a discussion behind someone's back like that...it stinks, Jo. And I think Rabern's intentions were that blatant. He might never come out and directly blame you, but he can do a lot of damage by implication."

Joanna felt cold as ice. Rabern had been angry when he left the OR. He'd even made the cutting remark that it was due to her that he'd have to go back in to do a heart massage. She would never have dreamed he would try to influence the postmortem findings to cast blame on her.

It simply wasn't done. Doctors didn't go around blaming other doctors, even when there were solid, documentable reasons.

Maybe she should have known better.

"Beth, I may be being terribly dense here, but if he did influence Ruth's findings, why didn't her preliminary autopsy report reflect that? Why didn't it implicate me?"

"Joanna," Beth admonished, "you are such a babe in the woods sometimes." Beth was the product of a hard-edged blue-collar Pittsburgh neighborhood and Joanna doubted Beth had a single illusion left about mankind. "If there were actual blame pinned on someone, they'd have to report a possible homicide or reckless endangerment to the police."

Joanna swallowed. "Well, if Rabern believes that—"

"He doesn't," Beth said flatly, pushing her glasses up. "The last thing he wants is to get the cops involved—and if they ask, he'll deny any possibility that you were at fault. But that doesn't mean he won't throw you to the lions where the administration—and even your partners—are concerned. Don't you see? His whole purpose in speaking to Brungart was to make sure she kept the autopsy report as vague as possible, which makes it all the easier to insinuate that they're all covering for you."

Joanna did see. Her career could be effectively destroyed by rumors and half-truths. Her relationship with her business partners—fellow anesthesiologists—would begin to slip. They'd be uncomfortable to be associated with her, fearing the surgeons would take their business elsewhere. Anesthesiologists were dependent on surgeons to bring them their business.

A few carefully chosen words from Rabern to her partners implicating her youth or her inexperience or plain mishandling would be enough to cause the five men who had aggressively recruited her to vote her out of the partnership. Especially since it was Chief of Staff Elliott Vine who had died.

And the Rose administration could as easily pull her privileges to practice in the hospital.

But Phil had mentioned none of these things to her. He'd even tried to insulate her from Rabern's poisonous attitude. "I understand now," she murmured softly.

"What?" Beth asked.

"Phil was looking for something—anything—that would prove to everyone that I hadn't made any errors in the OR."

THE THOUGHT LEFT HER an emotional wreck. If Phil hadn't been so consumed with protecting her reputation, he would have been home in bed, reading or sharing a late-night snifter of brandy with Beth, or making love or sleeping peacefully.

Instead, he'd been sitting at his desk, puzzling out the whys and wherefores of Vine's death. And someone had killed him for it.

She had no time to indulge the anger or the grief or the guilt. She'd left Beth's office for a surgery scheduled to correct an abdominal aneurysm. The minute she safely concluded that operation, which was when she had been asked to be present for the press conference on Elliott Vine's surgery and death, she was tapped for an emergency C-section.

The administration would be unhappy. Her absence wouldn't please Brad, either. She understood his reasoning. The press would be a lot less likely to paint anyone the villain in the piece if they were presented with real people who clearly weren't villainous—earnest, capable, hardworking doctors, doing their jobs. Saving lives.

But the point was saving lives, and even if Brad required her presence at the press conference, a patient's life would always come first.

Dressed out in fresh surgical scrubs, preparing and calming the nervous patient, Joanna shoved aside all other thoughts. She got her patient safely under anesthesia as soon and as safely as possible. Her labor had been long and protracted, and the monitor on the baby had gone unexpectedly wild.

The baby was severely stressed. These emergency cesareans were always tricky, always performed at a higher level of tension. Two lives, not one, were at stake, and any anesthesia involving an unborn infant demanded her full attention.

The ob-gyn took the baby seventeen minutes into the procedure and a pediatric team swooped in to care for the infant. One of Joanna's partners, Ron Mendelssohn, came in with the pediatric nurse practitioner. Both were dressed out and scrubbed.

A flash of annoyance crossed Mendelssohn's brown eyes, but he was quick to reassure the doctor performing the C-section. Then he turned to Joanna. "Fill me in. Admin wants you downstairs to the press conference on the double."

"Ron, they'll have to wait. I can't leave this now."

"Joanna, don't argue with me," he answered in a low, urgent tone, his round, ruddy face concealed by the surgical mask. He gestured for her to move off the stool. "Your career is at stake here. Move out."

She gave an abrupt sigh, checked her machines and monitors, then complied. "I'm doing this under protest."

He nodded. "Understood. Just do it."

"Is it all right with the two of you if we proceed?" the surgeon snapped, irritated at the interruption, though it was far from unheard of for one anesthesiologist to relieve another.

"Take it easy," Ron returned easily, studying Joanna's notes. She signed off on them after answering Ron's questions and making sure the young mother was stable, then left OR 8.

She arrived at the large amphitheater, which was mostly used for Grand Rounds—lectures combined with luncheon on Friday afternoons. The talks were generally devoted to topics of interest to a broad range of physicians and house staff.

Someone in PR had ordered a continental breakfast set up outside for the gathered members of the press. They'd pretty much cleaned up everything but the coffee. Joanna poured a cup, dumped in her usual dose of cream and walked toward the door near the podium, which was open, as the doors on all sides were. She slipped inside.

Chip Vine was just concluding a talk from prepared notes. His wife, Peggy, who was a pharmacy tech responsible for inventory and delivering medications around the hospital, stood at his side.

"We understand that these things happen," Chip was saying. "It was commonly held around the hospital that my father was a tyrant, but he only wanted—and expected—his staff to do their very best. Peggy and I are convinced that he did get the best treatment possible."

A low-level hum of conversation filled the silence after Chip turned away from the microphone. Jacob Delvecchio stood to the left behind Brad, representing the hospital administration. Beside him were the surgeon, Hensel Rabern, and Ruth Brungart, who had performed the autopsy.

Sister Mary Bernadette stood to Brad's right. It was a wise decision to have her present. While she had hired Brad MacPherson to handle the hospital's public affairs, no one came close to matching Mary Bernadette's long-standing credibility in the medical community.

Brad went to the microphone at the podium and began to accept questions from the audience of reporters. It was clear from the kinds of questions being asked that Ruth Brungart's autopsy conclusions had been given, as well as the news of Phil Stonehaven's murder during the night.

Joanna's gaze fixed on Brad. The first rush of hostile questions arose from the assumption that there were things the administration of Rose Memorial was not saying. Was, in fact, hiding. Time and again he defeated the implication, conveying the information requested.

He was truly in his element. Dramatic, skilled, engaging. Charismatic. The tougher the questions got, the more adeptly he handled them. The lighting banished any and all shadows, lending him, Joanna thought, an astonishing degree of credibility.

She didn't understand why he was here. Why he was heading a troublesome PR department in a large city hospital where trouble naturally gravitated. He could have done a far better job in the White House than the press secretaries of the past several presidents, but he'd come here, and stayed.

She knew that question played into her mistrust of him. She also knew that probably wasn't fair.

His hair gleamed like the dark patina on old oak. He squinted a little now and then against the harsh glare, and the smile lines around his eyes deepened. The exquisite tailoring of his dark suit revealed his lean, muscular body as the stuff of a young and powerful Madison Avenue ad exec, but his respectful attitude and easy grins made all of that unintimidating—to everyone but Joanna, it seemed.

She shook her head. She'd be better off paying attention.

After five or ten minutes, the questions posed by the local cable news affiliate—a shrill female reporter whom Joanna recognized—began to set the tone of a witch-hunt in the making. Who was guilty? Someone had to be responsible.

The reporter was the medical specialist on the TV news staff. Rumor had it she'd repeatedly flunked her own medical boards every time she'd attempted them, and she had a huge chip on her shoulder for anyone who had ever successfully passed. In short, anyone with an MD behind their name.

"Isn't it fair to characterize Dr. Cavendish as the most inexperienced anesthesiologist on the staff of Rose Memorial?" Her Southern drawl stretched *inexperienced* to a ten-syllable indictment.

"Not *in*experienced, Ms. Vance," Brad answered, smiling easily, calling her by name, making her tone seem strident by comparison. "Only the least experienced." He gave a quick, engaging grin. "There is a difference, you know." His audience laughed appreciatively.

"But the youngest?" she insisted, alone in not finding the humor.

"Yes," Brad answered, spotting Joanna standing near the door in the same moment. "Here she is, just out of another surgery. Please, let me introduce you to Dr. Joanna Cavendish."

The amphitheater buzzed as all the reporters present craned around to catch a glimpse of her. A spotlight came on with a videocamera. Brad had taken her off guard. The harsh lights compounded the disoriented feeling. She took a deep breath and walked to his side at the podium under the glare of many more camera lights.

He stepped away from the microphone long enough to ask one thing of her under his breath.

"My way, Dish. Please, this once, don't say anything. You're here to be seen and not heard."

"A dutiful child is not referred to as Dish," she retorted in an equally hushed but acid tone.

"Smile." He gave her a meltdown sort of wink, then squeezed her elbow encouragingly as he turned back to the mike. "As I said, Dr. Cavendish was off saving lives," he said, again relying on low-key humor, pausing for the chuckles, "literally so. A very critical case of a young mother undergoing an emergency cesarean section."

He returned to a seriousness that implied her skills were not only of the highest caliber, but widely sought after. "Being that she is in such demand, I haven't asked Dr. Cavendish for a prepared statement. I'm not making her available here for questions, either, but simply to let you meet her.

"If you'll turn again to the packets I've provided, you will find the résumé and a history of every person involved in the open-heart surgery. The packet documents the very fine work done here at Rose Memorial by Dr. Cavendish. I think you'll agree with our physicians and administration that her record is as unimpeachable as any you'll find."

"C'mon, Brad," the reporter shouted in her accented voice. "Half the hospital knows Dr. Rabern was none to happy to have her."

Before Brad could respond, Rabern stepped up, his jaw thrust belligerently forward. Even without benefit of the microphones, his voice boomed to the farthest corners of the room as he pointed at Joanna. "I'm not going to stand up here and point fingers and character-assassinate this young woman. I know that's what you bunch of jackals do, but that's *not* something we do in medicine. I will not be coerced—"

"Dr. Rabern," Brad interrupted, respectfully but firmly shutting off Rabern's outburst. He must have sensed the surprise and anger welling up in her because he reminded her with a subtle pressure to the small of her back to say nothing. She concentrated fiercely on the audience so she wouldn't be caught on camera staring in her utter disbelief at Rabern's baffling betrayal.

When would she learn?

This was beyond the pale, beyond even the sort of behavior Beth had predicted from Rabern. While sounding as if he were roaring to her defense, Rabern had managed to imply—by "this young woman"—*she's too young, she's a woman, and I don't even have enough respect for her to call her* doctor. And to top it off, he'd flaunted the medical profession's arrogant insistence upon closing ranks around their own even when one of them had made serious mistakes.

The room fell silent, waiting to see if Brad could counter the impact of Rabern's remarks. Anything she said in her own defense would come out sounding as if she were protesting her own innocence too much. She knew Brad had been right, but she resented the position it put her in of standing idly by.

There was literally nothing she could do but count on Brad to handle the situation in his usual style. For once she not only needed his gilding-the-lily powers, her survival at Rose might depend on them. The irony was too thick to bear.

She wondered if he would be gentleman enough not to remind her of it later.

"Ms. Vance—Shelley," he began, moving to the reporter's given name to suggest an air of friendly familiarity, "in all candor, I believe it is safe to say Dr. Rabern had his reservations. He had never had the opportunity to work with Dr. Cavendish. And he is a vocal man. Many people knew of his reservations—none more so than Dr. Vine himself.

"Quite naturally," he went on, "everyone felt added pressure in performing open-heart surgery on our own chief of staff. But—as Chip Vine just told you—Dr. Cavendish had the admiration and full faith of his father, Dr. Vine. A patient's confidence in his physician's abilities, as you must surely know, is of paramount importance to the outcome of any treatment."

"If she's got nothing to hide here, why don't you let her speak for herself?" a near neighbor to Shelley Vance called out.

Brad shook his head, indicating he would not be browbeaten by such tactics into putting Joanna on the hot seat, but Mary Bernadette stepped forward and put a hand on Joanna's arm.

Brad stood courteously aside. Joanna suspected he had intended from the start to give way to the elderly nun whose integrity was above reproach.

Holding tight to Joanna, Sister Mary Bernadette waited until even the last murmur had faded. Too short by far to stand behind the podium, she stood beside it and spoke without the microphone.

"Dr. Cavendish is not on trial here! And I can assure you Dr. Vine would have been appalled at the lot of you," she scolded softly, her Irish lilt very much in evidence. "There is no cover-up going on here, nor would any of us condone such a thing. Rose Memorial, and Sacred Heart before that, has had professional review boards longer in existence than some of you are old, and those are the proper arenas for any such inquiries. You now know everything we know, and if there's more to be known, Mr. MacPherson here will be the first to call you back."

"But, Sister," some intrepid soul persisted, "two of your doctors are dead!"

"That's sadly true. Our small community has suffered terrible losses in the past forty-eight hours. We hope you'll kindly remember that when you put your stories to bed."

"Not only the past forty-eight hours, either!" another television network stringer hollered. "What about Miles Cornwall? What about Alexa Sabbeth and Frank Clemenza—half of Rose's top administrators are major league criminals! What about that, MacPherson? How can this hospital continue to function like that?"

The amphitheater full of reporters hummed. The noise level rose and then began to fade. For an instant, Brad's shoulders slumped, the gesture betraying his weariness. Joanna swallowed.

Her heart pounded.

In the middle of her own crisis, she realized suddenly how much Brad had had to deal with in the past few months. The HemSynon scandal. The near tragedy of Rafe and Zoe Mastrangelo's twin girls. Now this. If her own heartbeat felt erratic and pressured, what must Brad's be like?

The room grew uncomfortably more silent, until a pin dropping would have been picked up by the masses of audio equipment. She didn't know what to expect, or how Brad could possibly summon the grit to stand up for the question.

Neither did anyone else.

He stepped forward, not back, his head bowed. He squared his shoulders, took a deep breath and began speaking in a soft tone that demanded silence to be heard.

"It's true that since the reins passed from Sister Mary Bernadette's capable, inspired hands, Rose Memorial has suffered more than its share of tragedies, and far greater adversity than most.

"It's true that Miles Cornwall was murdered, that the HemSynon project was compromised, that people died because of it.

"It's true," he went on, baring Rose's soul, "that Frank Clemenza, who was otherwise a brilliant man with a dedication you rarely find, did, in fact, conspire to defraud the estate of our beloved former bishop, Vincente Rosario, and to keep Centi's rightful heir and daughter, Zoe, from her husband, who is Dr. Mastrangelo. They and their twins suffered terribly, but of course, that all ended very well. Stephi Mastrangelo is well on her way to a full recovery.

"But now we find ourselves in the limelight yet again."

He paused and took the time to meet the eyes of every reporter in the room. The effort took more than two very long, agonizingly silent minutes. Not one person so much as cleared his throat. Brad had them all in the palm of his hand.

"Whatever else you take from this room, take this," he continued at last. "Rose Memorial provides the finest medical care available in this *or any other* community. From the hit-and-run murder of Dr. Cornwall to the murder last night of Dr. Stonehaven, we have been upfront with you.

"We have admitted our shortcomings. We have coped with the personal and professional misdeeds and failures of our leaders, and we have done it all in the harsh glare of your spotlights.

"At no time have we ceased rendering the highest quality care and deep, human compassion for which we are internationally known. I ask you now to consider carefully what you report to your viewers and readers, and how you report it. You will be doing the community a tremendous disservice if you paint this venerable institution in any other light.''

The amphitheater erupted in applause. Unsmiling, Brad stepped back and linked arms with Sister Mary Bernadette. He had done the impossible. He had turned the nightmarish character of a difficult press conference into a public-relations coup.

A part of Joanna cheered and admired him, but in her private heart, in her soul where she was attracted to him like a moth to a flame, she had never feared him more. A moth never grasped that the flame would sear it, body and soul. Joanna understood.

He thanked all the members of the press for their attention and interest, then another fellow called out. ''One more question, Brad.''

He looked to the back of the room and spotted the oped guy from the *Trib*. ''Sure, Daniel.''

''I understand Phil Stonehaven was reviewing the autopsy on Dr. Vine as a favor to the medical examiner's office. Any possibility Dr. Stonehaven's death had something to do with Dr. Vine's?''

''None that we're aware of at this time,'' he answered. But the reporters were already streaming out of the amphitheater. He had pulled the punch of even that juicy connection with his speech.

In the ensuing rush, he asked over the public address that they all exit the door where the refreshments had been replenished. The Vines, Brungart, Rabern and Delvecchio departed together through another door leading back into the hospital corridors.

Brad caught Joanna and asked her to stand with him as he shook hands and dispensed charm in appropriate measures to the departing media people.

He was putting her on display, Joanna thought, a little desperately. Her chest felt as if it were on fire. Her father had done that, too. Made her stand up and be adored, the treasured darling daughter of an icon of the community. A silent princess. And even if Brad's purposes were far different, even though she understood why he was doing it, she despised it.

She gave herself a stern mental shaking. "Can I go back to work now?"

"Your schedule is cleared for the day. And I need to talk to you."

Taken aback, she didn't have a chance to ask what he knew of her schedule, or how. He broke off from her long enough to snag Daniel Feldman to one side. When the press locusts had emptied the refreshment table again and cleared out, he and Joanna remained alone with the *Trib* op-ed guy.

"So, Daniel. Did you get a chance to meet Dr. Cavendish?"

Fit and trim with a nice mustache, shorter than Joanna by several inches, Feldman gave her a sympathetic, long-suffering roll of the eyes. "Relentless, isn't he? You can dump the media-relations routine now," he said to Brad with a smirk. He turned back to Joanna. "Dish, isn't it?"

"I—" She cast Brad a withering glance. "Joanna. Please."

"Don't worry, Joanna—and call me Daniel," Feldman said, smiled shyly, offering her his hand. "We did meet once before, actually, at a league soccer game. You were there—which is when I overheard Fearsome here calling you Dish. I subbed that afternoon. But maybe you don't remember—"

"Oh, I do," Joanna answered, remembering the game clearly. Though she'd gone to a few of Brad's practices, that was the only game she'd ever seen him play. And it was that night that they'd gone to Nana Bea's for dinner with Phil and Beth. "You saved the losing goal."

Feldman grinned. "Glory days. So, what'd you need?" he asked Brad.

"One question."

"Shoot."

"Is there any specific reason you asked if Stonehaven's murder had anything to do with Vine's death?"

"Other than the obvious timing issue? Odd that a pathologist is killed while he's reviewing a highly publicized autopsy report?" Feldman folded his arms. "Something other than that, you mean?"

Joanna and Brad exchanged glances. Brad smirked. "The guy's got a mind like a steel trap, and he's playing with me."

"It's clear he's a cut above the usual intellect," Joanna answered, in the spirit of Brad's aside, regaining a shred of her equilibrium. But the outrage of Phil's death was never far from her mind. "Daniel, is there some reason you asked about a connection between Phil's death and Elliott Vine?"

"Seriously, the timing issue is just too weird for words. But the other thing is, Ruth Brungart is my aunt. I'd hate to think the old dame was trying to cover something and Phil Stonehaven was about to catch her out."

Brad frowned. "Maybe I'm being unusually dense here, but why would you think something like that?"

"Bear with me." Folding his arms, Feldman rocked up once onto his toes. "You know my wife is the society editor?"

Joanna hadn't known that, but Brad would, naturally. "She bylines under her maiden name, doesn't she? Rachel Goldstein?"

Daniel nodded. "Well, according to Rachael, Rabern's been quite the man around town. Never with the same woman twice, usually a looker. But last week he took Ruth out to dinner twice. They've known each other going on forty years. It seems a little odd that a guy like that would suddenly squire an old battle-ax like Aunt Ruth around."

"I don't see why," Joanna said.

"Don't you?" Feldman's brow raised. "Again, it's the uncanny timing. In all those forty years, Rabern and my aunt never so much as attended a medical society meeting cocktail party together. Why now? Within the week, Elliott Vine would be dead in the OR, Rabern was the surgeon and my dear old Aunt Brungart performed the autopsy."

Joanna exchanged glances with Brad, but Feldman wasn't done.

"With all due respect to your stirring speech, old man," he said, punching Brad on the shoulder, "and to Sister Mary Bernadette, the whole thing smacks of a conspiracy."

Chapter Four

"I don't get it," Brad said, looking between Daniel Feldman and Joanna. "Are you suggesting your aunt was actually covering for Dr. Rabern in her autopsy report?"

Feldman grimaced and straightened. "That's why I asked. The woman has principles, but she also has a tremendous heart that's never been appreciated."

"But there was nothing to cover up," Joanna said, shaking her head. Rabern had behaved like a twenty-four-karat bastard since, but in the OR, Joanna couldn't fault his surgery. She'd have known if anything went wrong, anything Rabern would have felt compelled to conceal. "Dr. Vine's heart started again easily. Rabern had actually closed when the problems started."

"Well," Feldman said, shrugging, "I thought it was something you might want to figure in wherever it might fit. I don't think much happens by chance. Frankly, when odd things happen in strange clumps like this, I tend to think there's something going on. But then that's just my particular take on the world. I have a suspicious mind."

Her own reasoning wasn't so very different from Feldman's deductions. She had seen a clear link between Vine's death and Phil's murder. Feldman found it meaningful that Rabern had suddenly taken an interest in Ruth

Brungart, who just happened to be the pathologist performing the postmortem exam on Dr. Vine.

Added to Phil's fears on her behalf, which Beth had relayed, and the way Rabern had betrayed Joanna in the midst of Brad's carefully controlled press conference, maybe Feldman was on to something.

"Her mind works the same way," Brad said, jerking a thumb in her direction.

Feldman gave a lopsided smile. "That's nice. Paranoia loves company. Be careful now. Hear?"

Joanna smiled. "You, too."

Brad thanked him for the information, and the two of them postured around a bit over who was the better soccer forward. Promising Brad to meet afterward for a beer the next time they played together, Feldman left.

Brad put his hand in the small of Joanna's back and began walking around to the main corridors. "Okay. Let's have it."

"Beth told me something this morning. Ruth and Rabern aren't only going out to dinner. They were closeted away in her office discussing Vine's surgery late yesterday afternoon."

They turned a corner and came upon the elevator bank. "Is that... unexpected?" Brad asked, punching the up button.

"A little. I'm not saying there's anything wrong with it, but Beth said Phil was offended by it."

"Because?"

"If they were going to discuss what had happened, it would have been more appropriate if they'd invited me. A professional courtesy." Joanna turned to face him as they stood waiting for the elevator. "I just realized I was heading back upstairs to work. Why is my schedule clear?"

His hazel-green eyes met hers. "Because your partners want a meeting at noon. You might as well go up and change back into your street clothes."

"Why didn't they tell me?"

"It's no big deal, Dish." He glared at the elevator doors. "I called over to find out where you were when you didn't show up before the press conference. Mendelssohn went to take over for you in the C-section and Crider mentioned the meeting. I said I'd give you the message." He paused, watching her, then teased. "Does it feel like a conspiracy?"

"Yes." Paranoid or not. Why was she always so ruthlessly honest about herself around Brad? Because that's what she'd wanted from him? The truth? His feelings for her to be real? Or to drive him away, him and his gilded tongue?

He was watching the clash of emotions in her eyes. She regretted being so transparent. "If I asked you nicely to stop calling me Dish, would you do it?"

"Changing the subject, are we?" He grinned. "Okay. In answer to your question, probably not. But if I had a good enough reason . . . maybe. Where the *hell* are the elevators?" They'd already waited so long that a small crowd was beginning to gather, making them move closer if only to keep their exchange private. "How about because it bothers me. Because I asked. Either one should be a good enough reason."

He looked hard at her. "Have you asked yourself why it bothers you?"

She swallowed. Her chin went up. He made her crazy. His look made her mouth water, her heart throb like a schoolgirl's. "Because it's retro, it's fifties, it's disrespectful—"

"You're wrong about that."

"—and mostly, it's not even accurate."

"Wrong again." The elevator finally came and the doors rattled open. Joanna got on and went to the back. Brad took the corner beside her. She moved to the opposite corner and the flow of passengers naturally separated them. She avoided even looking at him, but everyone got off on the fourth floor and no one else came on.

Between the fifth and sixth, Brad stepped forward and jabbed the stop button. A risky thing to do in the aging, decrepit elevator. It might never start up again under its own power. He obviously didn't care. Muscles had bunched in his jaws, and his full dark lashes narrowed around his keen eyes.

He was angry at her for the second time in less than twelve hours and she felt a perverse, potent little thrill.

"Listen, Joanna. I know you're upset. I know you lost an important patient and then, even worse, an old friend. But let's get at least one thing straight. *Dish* is not disrespectful and it is not inaccurate. Not as far as I'm concerned. I want you. I'm attracted to you. Sexually, yes, but that's not all and never was—"

"Brad, stop it, please!"

"Not a chance." He took his finger off the stop button. The elevator wasn't going anywhere.

He came toward her. His utterly masculine presence filled the old elevator car. The novels had it all wrong, Joanna thought a little desperately. It wasn't blue eyes that were piercing, it was hazel-green, hard, glittering jewel-like green at the rims of his irises. Her back was already to the wall.

He shook his head. "Not a chance," he said again. "I haven't been back around you for six damn hours, but I'm not going six more seconds without setting this much straight.

"I'm not going to stop or apologize for taking you to bed or for great sex. We went out a few times and spent one weekend together—one!—and since I found myself contemplating happily-ever-after commitments, I was pretty damned unnerved."

"You weren't thinking that at all!"

"I was."

She had no sensible reply, or even an insensible one. Her tongue was in knots and he knew it. Her expression must have betrayed her shock. Brad MacPherson talking commitment and being unnerved? Her breasts tightened. Heat flared at the base of her throat. He planted one large hand at the wall beside her head.

She always noticed hands. His were clean and strong and rawboned, sprinkled with dark brown hair. She flashed on a memory of his long sun-burnished fingers stroking her pale naked breasts, making her tighten and bead to his touch. Making the exquisite tension of desire thrum low in her body. Making her ache for him, and forget that she feared him.

She licked her lips. "Brad—"

"Shut up, Joanna—I'm going to kiss you." He crowded closer, till she could smell him, clean and male and warm. His threat hung in the air. His gaze lingered on her lips.

"Why?" She meant to refuse.

"Why? Why," he repeated a second time in disgust. "Call me crazy. I don't know. You want an explanation, but you won't believe it. Whatever I say is too bloody eloquent. You think actions speak louder than words? Fine. We'll just get this over with right now. And don't even think about pretending you want it any less than I do."

"Then do it," she snapped, lifting her hands to his suit lapels, jerking him close, daring him, hoping to make him stop.

But it was a mistake. She knew by his slow, heated smile. Still, one hand against the wall by her head trapped her in the corner. He cupped her jaw in the warm palm of his other hand. His gaze fell to her mouth. He dragged a thumb gently over her lower lip, backed up and stroked again. Again, traversing back, grazing her upper lip, as well.

She felt numb and unwilling to escape even if she were able, entranced by the friction of his thumb against her mouth, by the moisture he dragged with his thumb from the inside of her lip, down her chin, trailing onto her neck.

"Brad..."

"Be quiet." He lowered his head. His breath was warm except where the moisture evaporated against her own skin. She gave a small moan. The anticipation was what she'd tried to head off with her challenge.

"Joanna... this is as honest as it comes...."

At last he touched his parted lips to hers. Her fingers tightened on his lapels. She'd forgotten what his kiss was like. How could she have forgotten? He made heat unfurl in her, made her shiver, made her lips tingle at the slightest touch of his and ache from the taste and the need to respond.

He ignored the buzzing protests of the old elevator. He kissed her, pulled her closer, groaned, lifted her shoulders toward him, took more.

His low groan—the depth of it, the naked candor—melted her emotional defiance. She couldn't help responding, but when she began kissing him back, he separated from her, holding her chin, searching her eyes.

He took a deep breath, let her go, turned and touched the button for the sixth floor. Miraculously, the decrepit old car began to move again, proving even the wide world of temperamental inanimate objects were also all too easily persuaded by Brad MacPherson.

She stared at him. Traces of her moisture lingered on his lips.

"Listen." He rammed his hands into his pockets. His eyes fixed on her. The elevator lights glinted off his hair, and for a moment he looked as affected by the kiss as she felt. "I know there's a lot on your mind and a lot to deal with coming down all at once. I know that." The elevator car stopped and the light above the door indicated the sixth floor. "But think about this for a while, Joanna. About how you began kissing me back. Because I don't want you to remember yourself as having been sweet-talked or dazzled into anything."

He turned and walked out the parting doors. Watching his back, Joanna shivered.

"Brad, wait." He had surprised her. She had never been kissed in an elevator. Never in the hospital, and never only to make a point about a man's intentions.

He'd unnerved her. Left her trembling. The old elevator began to rumble shut before she gathered her wits. She stuck out her hand. The doors clanked and groaned but opened again.

Brad turned back. "Are you coming?"

"Yes." Determined to collect herself, to dispel the physical impact of his kiss on her, to shake off her emotional surprise at real honesty attached to his kiss—and her own confusion—she walked past him to the door leading into the physicians' locker room. "I'll see you later."

"Joanna." He caught her elbow.

Her chin went up. "What?"

His eyes searched her face. His eyebrows drew together, and he rubbed one with his knuckle. "Will you think about it?"

She had a lot to think about. His kiss—her need to kiss him back—was only one of them. "Yes."

He took a deep breath. A relieved one, she thought. "I'm going to go speak with the nursing supervisor to see if I can find out who made the initial call to the press. After that, it might be interesting to see what Ruth Brungart will say to you. Join me?"

She needed to confront Brungart. His offer to go with her was more attentive than she wanted to believe he could be. "I'll be out in a few minutes."

She turned and walked—but she wanted to run—into the lounge. She stopped briefly inside, collecting herself in the rich, peaceful ambience. The lounge was done in dark wood and burgundy pile carpet. Comfortable, expensive leather chairs and sofas were set in small groupings. Moderately expensive paintings set in gilt-edged frames graced the walls in tasteful arrangements. The room had the atmosphere of a country club. Rose Memorial was committed to the comfort of its doctors.

A surgical resident sat slumped in one of the easy chairs, staring mindlessly at a pro-golf tournament on the large-screen television. Otherwise, the lounge was deserted. Joanna murmured a greeting. The resident grunted back without looking up.

She changed quickly out of her scrubs into a set of clothes she kept on hand. She opened and eased on a new pair of panty hose, then put on a half-slip and multihued silk crinkle skirt with an eggplant purple raw silk blouse. The thought of confronting Ruth Brungart suddenly made her nerves flutter.

A touch of lipstick for courage, she decided. A touch of defiance. Ruth Brungart would see the lipstick as frivolous—but then, her clothes were bound to seem that way to Ruth, as well. She substituted a pair of pumps for her crepe-soled clogs, closed and locked her locker door, dumped her used scrubs down a laundry hatch and exited the door leading into the main hallway.

Brad stood talking to the OR nursing supervisor at the white line in the asphalt tiles where the No Street Clothes Beyond This Point was strictly enforced.

Gurneys lined the walls except where No Parking signs had been posted. The supervisor caught a glimpse of Joanna and waved. They'd always been friendly, so Iris Kensdale was already inclined to Joanna's side if push came to shove.

"Hi, Joanna. I hear Rabern is on the warpath."

"In full battle regalia," Joanna murmured. "Any idea why he's so uptight and willing to point a finger?"

"He's a jerk. Plain and simple. With years of experience at it. I was just telling Mr. MacPherson that, as far as I know, no one called the press from up here. But what I know doesn't mean much. Since we remodeled the suites last year, outside calls can be made from any operating room, the scheduling desk, the lounges, postop." She shrugged. "Anywhere, really."

"I know," Joanna agreed. "How's Hammond?" she asked, wondering about the resident who had been the target of Rabern's sarcasm.

"Rattled. He'll be fine, though. Look, I've got to get back to work, but, Joanna, call me, will you, if you need anything?"

"I will—and thanks."

"Thanks for your time, Iris," Brad added. "I'd appreciate it if you'd put out the word again—no one should be contacting the press on their own, or answering questions. Will you refer any contacts to my office?''

She agreed to both requests, then turned to go back to the surgical desk with a parting reassurance to Joanna.

Brad gave Joanna's change of clothes an appreciative eye. "You clean up really well, Cavendish."

"Thank you so much," she returned.

"Ready to confront the old lioness in her den?"

She lifted her shoulders. "I'm not sure what it will accomplish, but I think she owes me five minutes, at least."

They began to walk back out to the main corridor to the rickety set of elevators. "Are you comfortable with me tagging along?"

"Of course." She hesitated, uncertain why she'd been so quick with that answer. But the truth was, she'd welcome the company. "I don't know if Brungart will be as frank as she might have been if I went alone, though."

"That's probably just as well. She shouldn't be saying anything to you that she wouldn't say for the record. And I briefed her earlier—before the press conference. She's not a stupid woman. Brungart knows she's better served if she's up-front with me."

They took the six flights of stairs down rather than wait on elevators. Brad opened the door at the first floor for Joanna, and she turned in the direction of the pathologists' offices. The scents of formalin and acetone wafted down the hallway. The door to Phil's small office was closed and locked, marked with a police tape warning Keep Out—Crime Scene.

The closed-off room and forbidden entry raised the specter of Phil's murder again. Why he'd been killed. Who had done it. Joanna swallowed hard and kept going.

Ruth Brungart's office was the last one along the hallway, a coveted corner. Her door was only partially closed and she sat at her desk facing the east window.

Joanna knocked softly. "Dr. Brungart, could we speak with you for a moment?"

She turned in her chair, her long steel gray hair pinned up in a French roll. Her lips clamped shut, puckering the wrinkles like poles in a stockade around her lips. "I don't know what's to be gained, but I suppose you'll insist. Come in and shut the door."

The office of the chief pathologist was sunny and uncrowded, the largest in the lab. Twice the size of Phil's, which seemed a cubicle in comparison. The carpet was a regulation gray Berber, but there were personal touches. A very old jade plant trailed thick branches on the windowsill. Her framed diplomas and certifications hung on the walls along with crayon drawings much like the ones Beth Stonehaven's small patients colored for her.

"Grandnieces and -nephews," she explained curtly, seeing they had attracted Joanna's eye. She turned in the swivel chair and indicated they should sit on the sofa opposite her. "What do you want?"

"Dr. Brungart," Joanna began, "I know that Phil Stonehaven was having some problems reconciling things he found on the autopsy slides with what you reported officially."

"That may be true. I don't know."

"Why is that, Ruth?" Brad asked.

"We didn't talk while he was working."

"But he said you were very angry to learn he had ordered toxicology screens done—"

"I was angry. I still am. But I learned of it through the pathology secretaries, not because I spoke to Phil." Her chin quivered a moment, and Joanna suspected it had upset her more than she would ever admit that one of her staff had been murdered.

She went on after a few seconds. "It would have been unethical and inappropriate of me to speak with Phil since the administration and the ME's office expected an unbiased second opinion. I left at 6:00 p.m. I'm given to understand he was still working when he was attacked."

Brad sat back and crossed an ankle over his knee and spoke casually for a few moments about the double tragedy, then asked, "Were you able to speak with Dr. Rabern about Dr. Vine's case?"

"Yes. At length."

"Did you think it was ethical and appropriate to be speaking to the responsible surgeon—before you issued your findings—at such length? And in the absence of the case anesthesiologist?"

Color rose in Brungart's pale, wrinkled cheeks. "No. I wouldn't say that was, strictly speaking, ethical."

Joanna was nearly as stunned as Brungart appeared by Brad's direct challenge, but she saw right away that his unexpectedly blunt, head-on query quickly secured for him the woman's grudging respect.

"On the other hand," Brungart went on, "my conferring with Hensel Rabern had no impact whatsoever on Phil's review of the case. Pathology is not an exact science, much as we would like it to be, and it's therefore all the more vital to be able to offer up independent opinions."

Brad cleared his throat. "Isn't it true that Rabern wanted input as to your findings? It's already on the grapevine that he didn't particularly care who knew you were conferring, or who knew he believed Dr. Cavendish had screwed up, either."

Brungart sat back in her chair and sighed. She folded her hands in the lap of her gray wool skirt. "Dr. Rabern was very upset. It was, after all, our chief of staff who expired in that operating room. Dr. Rabern made remarks he shouldn't have made that may have been overheard in the wrong quarters."

"But he did it again this morning, Dr. Brungart. In the press conference," Joanna said.

Brungart's lips thinned. "Nothing Dr. Rabern said this morning implicated you, young woman! In fact, he came very vociferously to your defense."

Joanna swallowed a sharp retort. *Young woman* was how Rabern had referred to her, as well. "I don't agree, Ruth."

"Then you've lost all objectivity," she snapped.

"Dr. Brungart, let's not insult each other's intelligence," Brad said before Joanna could spit out the retort this time. "I don't believe that and neither do you. Rabern's remarks implied the medical community would close ranks around her—one of its own—no matter what she'd done. Which is not the same thing as making it clear that he did not hold her accountable for Dr. Vine's death."

The chief pathologist drew a deep, frustrated breath, her face pinched and drawn looking. "I'm sure he didn't intend any harm."

"I'm not so sure," Brad said, still speaking more bluntly than Joanna would have believed possible of him. "Did you find any evidence that Dr. Rabern was in any way responsible for Dr. Vine's death?"

"No. None whatever."

"Or any that I was at fault?" Joanna asked.

"You must realize, I didn't conduct the autopsy with a criminal investigation in mind—but again, no. I found nothing conclusive of any malpractice."

Joanna felt a small measure of vindication at Brungart's admission. "Dr. Brungart, I'm sure you know Phil Stonehaven was a friend of mine. Beth is my best friend. Phil knew Rabern had been hanging around here and was inclined to point a finger in my direction—and he may have been going overboard himself looking for proof that Dr. Vine's death wasn't my responsibility."

"Then he was out of line."

"Phil would never step out of line," Joanna fired back. "He would only report what was conclusively true and you know it. But the point is—"

"Dr. Cavendish," Brad interrupted in a warning tone. She knew he saw where she was headed, and that he knew she was about to ignore his advice about keeping her theory concerning Phil's death to herself. "The point is there is no conclusive proof."

She met his glance, and saw that he was trying to warn her discreetly of something else.

Then it struck her. *No conclusive proof.*

She could tell Brungart that Phil had been on to something else entirely—something that did not fit her sudden-cardiac-death finding, but she had no proof. She might even go so far as to say Phil had been murdered because he had suspected Vine's death was not blameless, but again, she had no evidence of that.

Brad's waring made her realize that no one else knew Phil had been close to identifying why he found anything amiss at all in Elliott Vine's death. From Ruth Brungart's point of view, if Phil truly believed she had missed a critical finding, she was the one he should have spoken to, not Joanna. Had he not been looking out for her, she realized, she would certainly have been near the end of the list of anyone he told.

She had to face the facts. Phil had revealed his doubts to her and he had gone so far as to suggest that Elliott Vine's tissue slides resembled anaphylactic shock. But without proof, which even Phil had not positively uncovered, bringing it up to Brungart could only damage Phil's reputation and destroy Joanna's own credibility.

Brungart grew annoyed at the silence. "Is there a point to be made here?"

"Yes," Brad answered, taking up the question smoothly. "Did Dr. Rabern know that your findings exonerated everyone on the surgical team?"

She frowned. "Well, of course he did."

"Then, Dr. Brungart, can you think of any reason why Rabern spoke out the way he did?"

She sat thinking a moment, considering, it appeared to Joanna, what she could say in defense of such indefensible remarks. Brungart seemed to come to a conclusion she wasn't happy with but couldn't avoid. "Hensel is very nervous."

"Why?" Joanna asked. "He is no more to blame than I am."

"He is in no way responsible. I will admit his behavior this morning was ill-advised, but you must understand. Dr. Rabern is a pillar of the community, an icon, at the pinnacle of his career. Still, he is forced to look now more to the past than to the future."

She cast Joanna a patronizing glance. "You have no idea what it is to wake up one morning and realize that you are approaching the end of everything you hold dear. Your life. Your career. The last thing such a powerful, respected man wants is the whisper of a scandal to besmirch his hard-earned reputation. And the truth is,

Elliott Vine put Dr. Rabern on the spot by asking him to perform the surgery at all.''

Brad sat back and stretched out his arm along the length of the sofa. ''I'm afraid I don't understand.''

Brungart's face closed up. ''Ask Lucy Chavez—our esteemed director of physician relations.''

Chapter Five

When they left Ruth Brungart's office, Joanna was already five minutes late to the noon meeting of her partners.

Although her partners, all of them men, would have preferred Brad's input to a delicate situation, Joanna hadn't wanted him in the meeting with her. It wasn't a major surprise. If she was going to be raked over the coals, it would be easier to take without him around to hear it.

But Joanna was visibly shaken even before she went in. Not so much from a sense of impending professional doom, Brad thought, but because of what she knew but couldn't prove.

Phil Stonehaven had let her know Elliott Vine's death was likely not as simple as Ruth Brungart's report claimed. Because of Phil's murder, Joanna was alone in believing Vine's death wasn't a sudden cardiac death, and the fact that Phil had died even giving lip service to the possibility meant Vine's death wasn't innocent, either.

But she couldn't prove it.

Standing at the floor-to-ceiling windows in his office, Brad jerked at the knot in his tie and worked loose the top three buttons of his shirt. The windows looked out over the thick stand of trees separating the hospital and office buildings from Lake Shore Drive and the wavering gray-blue expanse of Lake Michigan on the other side.

Joanna was now in a terribly precarious position. He understood her anger and frustration and uneasiness. No one had come out and accused her of any fault in Elliott Vine's surgery and subsequent death. But she was hanging out there every bit as much as if the accusation had been made.

And if she started calling foul play, intimating that someone else had literally murdered Vine on the table—without a shred of corroborating evidence—she would be pilloried. In the press, in the hospital, in her career.

Frustration gnawed at his conscience as Sister Mary Bernadette knocked at his door, poking her head in.

He turned and asked her in, self-conscious as usual at the size and opulence of his office compared to Mary Bernadette's. Her office was little more than a cell, so even the most tasteful, conservative surroundings seemed lavish. He knew she gave it no thought at all.

He knew she thought he deserved everything Rose Memorial could conceivably give him, but the truth was, he owed her. Big time.

She opened the door wide and closed it behind her, moving at a pace he associated with children, except that she seemed to glide along, her old-fashioned black nun's habit flowing behind her.

"My dear boy." She stood tiptoed to kiss his cheek as he leaned over to receive what amounted in his mind to a blessing from her. "I just saw Joanna Cavendish leaving. She seemed quite...disturbed. I'd like to know what's going on. From a reliable source and not the grapevine, howe'er reliable it may be at times."

Brad nodded and sat down with Mary Bernadette, in the club chair placed at a conversational angle to the sofa. The late-afternoon sun slanted in. He could smell the bleach on Mary Bernadette's hands, and knew she'd probably come from the soup kitchen.

"There's more here than meets the eye," he admitted. "The situation is already very complicated, and Joanna's caught in the middle of it."

Mary Bernadette's canny old brown eyes sharpened with keen interest. "Go on."

He got up to pour them both a glass of ice tea from his small bar refrigerator and then began to describe to Sister the scope of the dilemma. Vine's death, Phil Stonehaven's call to Joanna, his murder, the timing that had led Joanna to speculate neither death was what it seemed on the surface, ending with Ruth Brungart's defense of Hensel Rabern's inappropriate remarks.

"Convenient, isn't it, how Joanna is constrained from mentioning any of this for fear of it sounding as if she's trying to divert the blame from herself?"

"Isn't it?" He'd been afraid that Joanna would find herself named in a libel suit if Rabern got his nose pushed far enough out of joint, but he'd effectively preempted her accusations.

"The tricky thing is, Mary Bernadette, Joanna's theory of what happened is based on the notion that someone intended to kill Elliott Vine on the table. I can't believe it's even possible to do that without it being obvious to everyone there—short of the oxygen lines being hooked up to some poisonous gas, or injecting a fatal dose of medicine."

"Which were both under Joanna's sole control," Sister mused.

Brad nodded dispiritedly and stared a moment at his hands. "The hell of it is, the whole nightmare would probably blow over by this time next week. The press might even buy into my portrait of Rose as a beleaguered but upstanding institution. But I can't see Joanna letting go of it. Vine's death was one thing, and no matter what Phil thought, it will probably go down as a terrible mischance. But Phil Stonehaven was her friend and her best friend's husband, and Joanna isn't buying the mugging theory."

Sister Mary Bernadette straightened. "Well, she shouldn't, either," she declared, starch backing her brogue. Her chin lowered and she looked up at him from beneath the headpiece of her wimple. Her look was commanding. Nothing anyone with two grains of sense would ignore. "You're going to have to help her prove otherwise, y'know that, don't you?"

This was the formidable Sister Mary Bernadette Reilly calling in her marker. It was none too subtle, either, except that only Mary Bernadette knew how remarkably similar the circumstances were between the proverbial jaws she'd snatched him from and the pair she expected him to save Joanna from.

The old girl knew he'd do it, too. "Delvecchio will have my tail end in a sling if word of Joanna's theory gets out— or that I've signed onto her soapbox."

"This is no ordinary soapbox," she chided. "Two fine men are dead, and the deeds are as dastardly as they come. You leave Jacob to me, and get on with assisting that equally fine young woman in ferreting out the murderers."

Brad nodded. He hadn't seen Sister Mary Bernadette on such a crusade since she'd saved his bacon, but he had reason enough to trust her instincts, which confirmed his own. There was an excellent chance Joanna was right on the money with her thinking. But he had the image of the hospital to think about, as well. "Unraveling this could damage the reputation of Rose Memorial beyond repair."

She shook her head vigorously. "I disagree. Even if it becomes known, which I suppose it eventually must, the public would far sooner forgive us the scandal of a double murder than for harboring, nay, succoring a madman in our midst."

She was right. Absolutely, without question, this was a risk the hospital must take. Bad publicity was one thing. Allowing a killer to continue stalking the corridors was untenable. Brad pitied Jacob Delvecchio should he cross Mary Bernadette in this. But he didn't know what had so goosed the old nun to such a stance.

"Mary Bernadette, what is it that you haven't told me?"

She raised her head high. "No one from my soup kitchen murdered Philip Stonehaven."

"How do you know that?"

"Because I check the door leading into the pathology offices myself, every night before I retire. I promised to do that when the hue and cry went up in the first place about vagrants so near to the staff. I promised, and meant it, and that door was locked at 10:00 p.m., just as it has been every night since I opened."

Brad knuckled his tired eyeballs. "I assume you told the police? Detective Dibell?"

"Naturally. But their forensics evidence suggests there were footprints leading to and from the kitchen. That's all very well and good," she snapped, "but they could as easily have been made after the murder was committed as before. Laverne Dibell has settled for the most likely scenario, but I don't believe it. I *won't* believe it.''

He hoped Mary Bernadette wasn't deluding herself. She wasn't the sort. She knew the way the world turned. She knew what darkness lurked in the hearts of men, and he didn't think she could be fooled. But she was growing old and, in his heart, Brad knew it was still possible that her emotional investment in her charity kitchen soup might cause her to miss the handwriting on the wall.

He wouldn't insult her by mentioning it, although knowing her, she knew he had to keep the possibility in mind.

''Well, I'll be leaving you now so you can get on with it,'' she said after a few moments of silent contemplation.

''Before you go, Mary Bernadette, could you tell me one thing?''

''If I can.''

''Joanna and I went to talk with Ruth Brungart. She said flat out that Elliott Vine had deliberately put Hensel Rabern in a difficult position by asking him to do Vine's surgery in the first place.''

Mary Bernadette frowned. ''If you're askin' my opinion of Dr. Brungart, my impression is that she's a strong, intelligent, dedicated woman. But if you're askin' me what she meant by that, I couldn't tell you. I don't know.''

''Well, we didn't, either, so we asked.''

''What did she say?''

''To ask Lucy Chavez. 'Our esteemed director of physician relations,' she said.''

Mary Bernadette's brow puckered beneath her wimple. ''There are few things about Rose Memorial in recent times of which I disapprove. Lucy Chavez is one of them.''

Brad sat up and paid her his whole attention. Nothing much went on in the hospital environs that escaped Sister's attention. "Why is that?"

She made a moue with her fragile old lips. It was distasteful to her to speak ill of anyone. Mary Bernadette infinitely preferred to take her complaints straight away to their source. But this was purposeful, not idle, gossip, and Brad saw in her eyes the decision to speak her peace.

"Lucy Chavez is a beautiful and talented young woman. But I believe she takes her physician-relations position far too literally, and far too often."

HE FOUND JOANNA at the practice field, still in the crinkly skirt and purple silk blouse she'd changed into before their meeting with Brungart. She'd taken the back of the skirt up through her thighs and tucked it in at the front of the waist. It was a totally practical, silly, endearing thing to do.

He didn't find her half so endearing as alluring. The sight of her bare legs, looking coltishly thin encased in the billowing trousers she'd fashioned from her skirt, made his mouth water.

He pulled up across the street from the park and shut off the engine of his Bronco. He sat watching her, bare legged and barefoot, keeping the soccer ball ahead of her with intricate steps, moving down the field, following, dodging left and right.

He rolled down his window, unbuttoned the rest of his shirt, stripped the tails from his pants and the knot from his tie, then hitched himself comfortably back in his seat, one foot on the dashboard. Settling in. Watching Joanna take shots at the ball that told him volumes about her mood.

He'd expected as much.

After Mary Bernadette left, he'd spoken to the headmaster of the boys' club Joanna had been invited to join— the senior-most partner in the group of anesthesiologists who had hired her. It sounded as if the partners were pretty well divided down the middle. Half of them wanted to string her up and be done with the potential nasty economic downturn in business from the surgeons.

The other half were so pissed at Rabern they wanted to convene a posse for *him*. If he got away with this, the sentiment went, with this outrageous, dirty-pool, below-the-belt bull, then they'd as soon walk out as bow and scrape.

But the result was, the partners were at one another's throats. According to Mendelssohn, Joanna had walked out of the meeting and he couldn't blame her.

Brad had called her town house, but gotten no answer. He'd gone by, but she wasn't there. She could have gone off shopping or taken in a movie to distract her mind or half a dozen other things he hadn't even thought of, but he'd decided to check out a couple of soccer fields on the off chance that he'd find her there.

It's what he'd do with the tension. Work it out. But he'd never seen a woman kicking a soccer ball around in bare feet and her silk skirt tucked between her legs.

She moved with a fluid, unselfconscious grace not common in women with her height. Brad attributed that to Joanna's grandmother, her Nana Bea, who was regally tall even at her age. The heat alone would have made Joanna's skirt cling to her long legs, the blouse to her torso. The heat of her own exertion made the clinging certain. The colorful silk molded to her bottom. The purple blouse cleaved to her breasts.

He shifted in his seat and watched her for a while, then looked down at his thumb, drumming restlessly on the center of the steering wheel, thinking about what he was doing.

Joanna Cavendish was under his skin, and if he were as truthful as she demanded, he'd have to say he'd never quite been rid of her. Now the woman was festering in his soul again like a splinter he couldn't pull. And she was in trouble. And this wasn't the most convenient time, when her best friend's husband lay in a morgue, to be courting her again.

He'd kick the ball around a little with her to let her work off the angry energy, but then they would both have to focus on the threat of serious danger to her when Stonehaven's murderer realized Joanna Cavendish wasn't going to let sleeping dogs lie.

He took off his own shoes and socks, rolled up the window, got out of the Bronco and locked it up. He crossed the field at an angle to Joanna, and was straight behind her, maybe ten yards back, when she took a goal shot that flew over the box.

She stood with her hands on her hips. Frustration came from her in waves.

"A little more finesse, Dish. A little less leg," he said, kneeling to roll up his pant legs.

"Finesse?" She turned as he stood, and laughed when she saw him.

"What's so funny?" he demanded.

"Your shirt is hanging open and your tails are all wrinkled. Your tie...your...knees."

She stopped laughing and started staring at his chest, at the tie hanging next to his bare skin. He probably did look ridiculous, but he knew he had her. "Finesse. Try it."

The color heightened in her cheeks.

His turn to laugh. He kept it to a wiseass grin, feeling the tension radiating from her diminishing by slow degrees. He backed away to go get the ball from fifteen feet behind the box. "Picture the trajectory of the ball," he called, drop-kicking it back to her. "You just have to come at it with more of your shin and a little less power. Try it."

She put the ball down, backed off aways, then ran at it, kicking so her shin cushioned the impact from above, cutting the arc down. A near-perfect kick, but he blocked the goal and sent the ball back to her.

"Better. Again."

He goaded her in to working at getting the ball past him several more times, then played one-on-one with her for a while. Breathless after a long back-and-forth battle for control of the ball, from running into each other, Joanna pulled her skirt down and sank to the grass, watching him deliver a deadly fast goal.

"Show off," she muttered darkly, but he thought she must be too tired to keep the admiration out of her voice. It was almost dark. Her lips curved in a brief smile, but he couldn't see if the humor reached her eyes. "What are you doing here, MacPherson?"

"Besides coaching your soccer game?"

"Yeah. Besides that."

"Checking up on you." He sat down on the grass beside her and pulled his tie off. "I ran into Ron Mendelssohn on my way out of the hospital."

She pulled her right foot near to her body and began idly massaging the sole of her foot. "What did he say?"

"How it went in the meeting with your partners. That you walked out, and why. That he didn't blame you."

She nodded and drew a deep breath, watching the sun sink below the horizon. "Did he tell you they went to Vine to try to convince him Mendelssohn should do the anesthesia, and not me?"

Her head tilted, but it was so dark now that Brad couldn't see the expression in her eyes. "No. He didn't tell me that."

"He says now it was to protect me against exactly this sort of fallout."

"Do you believe him?"

"Yes." She gave a sigh. "Ron Mendelssohn is a good man. An honorable man. He didn't even have to tell me that they'd gone to Vine. The strange part is, he's as paranoid about the whole thing as Daniel Feldman. Ron thinks it was a setup from the start—even that Vine asked me to do the anesthesia."

"I don't get it."

She shook her head. Her fingers were still at work on the bottom of her foot. "I don't, either. A setup for what purpose? He knew he was going to die on the table, so he picked the rookie partner to take a fall? It doesn't make sense at all."

Brad couldn't put any rhyme or reason to it, either. Couldn't believe Elliott Vine had planned his own death, or even in the remote possibility that he had, that he'd intended Joanna to take the blame.

"What's wrong with your foot?"

"I must have stepped on a twig."

He reached out and followed her calf with his fingers down to her injured foot. "Let me have it." Matter-of-factly, a great deal more nonchalantly than he felt about touching her, he took her foot and rested it on his thigh.

"Brad—"

"Relax. It's no big deal." It *did* feel like a big deal, but he didn't want to make her skittish. "Mary Bernadette came to see me. She says there's no way anyone came in through the soup kitchen to murder Phil. She checks the lock every night at ten sharp.

"And it was locked then?"

"Yes."

"So whoever really killed Phil left the door ajar deliberately to make it look like the murderer had come through the soup kitchen."

"And went to the trouble of making sure dirt was tracked in and out," he added.

The streetlights along the rim of the park came on. They'd be lucky if they weren't caught in the middle of the sprinkler coming on, as well. She sat a moment, trying to relax and enjoy Brad's strong fingers stroking the bruise on the sole of her foot, easing the throb.

"I've been trying to work out why all this bothers me so much while I was kicking the ball around. I mean, aside from the obvious." Aside from the threat to her career, her reputation. Most of all, aside from the loss of a friend. Something else nagged at her, wouldn't let go.

"And?" he prompted her, his attention focused.

"I decided the reason is, all this stuff—this...commotion, the insinuations flying around—all of it feels like one huge diversion."

"From what?"

"From the real point. Don't you see? Elliott Vine died, yes. And maybe Rabern is feeling old and vulnerable and cranky. Maybe he was squiring Ruth Brungart around because she's been around long enough to understand that about him. Maybe he really does think I'm young enough that my career will snap back from this. But, as Ruth Brungart put it herself, it's all much ado about nothing. The point is, Phil was murdered."

Brad said nothing for a few moments. "You may be right. I think Brungart was frankly surprised that Rabern spoke out like that."

"Exactly. Rabern was angry when he left the OR, and he made a few smart remarks, but it should have blown over. So what happened to make him come out swinging?"

Brad pinched the bridge of his nose. "Somebody knocked off Phil Stonehaven."

Joanna straightened, drawing back her foot. "You don't think—"

"That Rabern killed Phil himself?" He shrugged and began rolling his pant legs down. "Why not? It makes about as much sense as the rest of this. Especially if we assume that Phil knew something about Vine's death that would incriminate Rabern—or implicate him in some way."

She wanted to laugh at how farfetched it all seemed, but none of this was remotely amusing. "Brad, this is too crazy. Who would believe it?"

"No one," he answered, grimacing. "Certainly not Detective Dibell." Although she'd asked if Phil could have been searching for a reason to exonerate Joanna, Detective Dibell believed—and had the physical evidence to back up—the vagrant intruder theory.

"So what we're saying here is that the premier cardiac surgeon of the Midwest murdered a pathologist to keep his deep dark secret deep and dark?"

Brad didn't laugh, either. A shadow of worry passed over his strong, masculine features. "It's a stretch. But the question remains. Why is Rabern making such a stink? If you're right, he's doing it to cloud the picture, to take the attention off Phil's murder."

Joanna took a deep breath and let it go. "I can't let that happen. I owe it to Phil to find out what happened. To find whoever killed him—and Mendelssohn agreed that they would all cover my schedule for the next week or so."

Brad stood and offered her a hand up. He understood how she felt, but he couldn't let her play with fire alone. "C'mon, Dish. Let's go feed our faces."

She accepted the help getting up, then collected her shoes and stopped him by stepping in his path. "What is it you're not saying, MacPherson?"

"I'm worried about you trying to expose Phil's murderer." He reached out to tuck her hair behind her ear. "Promise me you'll keep quiet about this? That you won't go off and do something half-witted. Phil is dead—"

"I'm never half-witted," she retorted. Her first thought was that he would try to cover the murder, the truth for the sake of the hospital, but she felt suddenly guilty for it. And there was serious concern for her in his eyes. "What is it?"

"I want your promise that you'll be careful. That you won't take any unnecessary chances like poking sticks at wild animals."

Understanding splintered into her consciousness. If she persisted in trying to learn what Phil Stonehaven had known, or at least suspected, whoever had brutally murdered her friend would have to consider her next.

"Sure," she answered flippantly, because she had the sense to be a little scared. "But how do I be careful of a cold-blooded murderer?"

Chapter Six

Come home with me....

He knew she'd refuse. Knew she wasn't nearly ready to even consider the offer. "Let me see you home. We'll pick up some take-out and eat at your place."

"Brad, I'll be okay. I'm sure I'm not in any danger tonight."

"Well, I'm not so sure." He began buttoning his shirt. "Humor me. Please. In the morning I'll come by and give you a lift back here to get your car."

It was too dark out now to see the expression in his eyes, but she didn't really need any cue but the firmness in his voice to know it was useless to argue. "All right. But I have to make an early night of it."

"The little tofu joint around the corner from your place?" He unlocked and opened his passenger door for her. He reached in and grabbed his shoes and socks from the seat.

"It's Japanese cuisine, and you don't have to eat tofu." But she didn't want to go there. Old Kirimatsu was mad and not speaking to her since she'd stopped coming around with Brad. If they came in together now, the ancient Japanese man would rub his hands as if he was on a hot roll with the dice. "We could just as easily call for pizza."

"Nope. Kobe An, it is," Brad said, switching on the engine.

"Fine." Joanna threw up her hands. "Have it your way. But you're paying, and I want abalone."

Brad grinned. "You think expensive tastes are going to drive me away?" He shook his head. She raised her brows. "Think again, Dish."

He parked at the corner between her place and Kobe An so they could walk on to her town house from the small restaurant. Simply glad to see Brad, Kirimatsu wasn't so bad, but he didn't have any abalone. Joanna settled for a noodle dish, and Brad for vegetables and a white fish the old man was happy enough to simply broil.

They walked the block to Joanna's row of town houses and carried their meal in, joking about the hunger pangs the scent of Kirimatsu's food evoked. But when they reached her small kitchen, their laughter ended abruptly.

"Oh, my God." Joanna froze. The greenhouse window over her sink was broken and the small pots of herbs had fallen and broken, as well, spilling shards of crockery and small clumps of dirt from the counter to the floor.

The hole was big enough for someone to crawl through, and the distance to the ground outside wasn't a deterrent. Someone had broken in through the only ground-floor window not visible from the street.

Brad took the carton of food from her hands and put it with his on her kitchen table, his expression grim.

"Stay here," he said, turning. "Right here." He picked up the phone and dialed 911 to report the break-in as he checked the other first floor rooms, then went up the stairs and searched there in case they'd surprised the intruder and trapped him into finding a place to hide.

Disbelieving, Joanna turned back to survey the living room. Nothing had been disturbed. Nothing had warned her. Someone had intruded into her space, but until she saw the kitchen window, she'd had no clue.

Brad was back to the kitchen inside sixty seconds and advised the emergency operator that whoever had broken in was now gone.

She swallowed hard. "There aren't too many places in a town house to hide." Numbed, feeling sick and angry and violated, Joanna stared at the broken glass shelves and clumps of dirt and herbs scattered over the counter and kitchen linoleum. At two places there were impressions made in the dirt that looked like tracks of ridges in the soles of sport shoes. "I don't suppose I should touch anything or start cleaning up," she said, forcing herself to keep it together. "What...was anything disturbed upstairs?"

"No. You should check your jewelry and valuables, but I can't see anything obvious missing. Your CD player, the TV, everything is still here. Your closet and drawers are closed—"

"Then this wasn't a robbery?"

"Not for fencing valuables," he answered grimly. "But whoever broke in had a reason. Can you spot anything at all wrong?"

"No. That's just it. I...I didn't even really *feel* that anything was wrong. Wouldn't you think I would know?" It was almost more unnerving to her that she hadn't sensed the intrusion than that it had happened at all.

She went back through the door leading to the living room. "Look at this. Even Ruth Brungart's initial autopsy report is exactly where I left it last night when Phil telephoned."

Brad frowned, scouring the light mauve wall-to-wall carpeting with his glance. "I don't think he even left the kitchen. You don't keep any prescriptions in the cabinets, do you?"

"Only some over-the-counter pain meds," she answered as he turned back to check. "Where the glasses are. And the only alcohol is that bottle of brandy we opened months ago." Brandy they had poured into snifters and warmed over candles at her dining room table.

He found the plastic aspirin and Motrin bottles undisturbed and the half-empty bottle of brandy right where Joanna had put it away, as well. "Whoever it was had only one thing in mind, Joanna. And it had to be in here." His brow furrowed in concentration, but her doorbell rang, and she went to the door. Through her peephole she saw a pair of policemen.

"Dr. Cavendish?"

"Yes." They had left on the blinking red light atop the squad car. The flashing lights stirred deeply uneasy feelings in her. Already disoriented, vague memories surfaced of the ambulance sitting outside her parents' house the night her grandfather had suffered his stroke. Already disoriented, the flash of memory robbed her wits, and she didn't think to open the door enough to let the policemen in.

"May we come in, ma'am?"

She shook off her daze and stood back, allowing them in. They identified themselves as Officers James and Wozcinski. James was black, stood at her own height and was obviously seasoned in his demeanor. The other was still taller, a big blond kid, very young. Brad introduced himself as a friend, and answered even before the question could arise that, yes, he'd been with Dr. Cavendish when she discovered the break-in.

"Well, ma'am, we're gonna check out your burglary here, but first, are you all right?"

The long answer was *no*. Someone had broken in and invaded her privacy, the sanctity of her home, but she wasn't physically harmed, and she said so. Brad showed them where the break-in had occurred, the slight tracks in the potting soil, the telling absence of any dirt beyond the kitchen.

Going through the town house with them—through every drawer, cabinet and closet—and finding nothing touched, Joanna caught the pair of policemen exchanging shrugs and silent glances several times.

Feeling alternately angry and foolish, she had to admit that her town house hadn't been hit with any intention of looting her jewelry or entertainment electronics or silverware or knives to serve as weapons—or anything else readily fenced to a pawnshop or street buyers.

"Which still leaves open a dozen or more possibilities," Officer James concluded. "And some of those are pretty harmless."

"Harmless?" Joanna wrapped her arms around her middle. Nothing had been taken. That simple fact made the break-in seem less significant to James and Wozcinski, but she felt indefinably more threatened. The intruder clearly wasn't an ordinary thief. She'd have preferred that. She could understand, at least, if she'd been robbed for money. This break-in had no apparent purpose.

"What's harmless about a break-in?" Brad demanded with less tact and more anger than Joanna had ever seen in him.

"Well," James answered, making a real effort not to seem indifferent, speaking to Joanna. "It's possible some guy broke in intending to rob you blind—but he didn't even grab a butcher knife. Might have got scared hearing you come home. It's also possible our guy breaks in intending to lie in wait for Dr. Cavendish, but beat it out of here—again, same reason. Heard you coming, knew you weren't alone."

He turned to Brad. "For my money, sir, considering everything, some kid probably knocked a baseball through the window and came in after it."

For so little cause and such minor damage—not to mention the heavy caseload of the precinct detectives—James didn't think he could even free up a crime scene unit to come over to dust for prints or take a mold of the shoe imprints through the potting soil.

They departed, expressing apologies that did nothing to make Joanna feel safer or at all certain that the break-in was so innocent as a kid's baseball sailing through the window. She had to do something, occupy her mind, keep her hands busy—or start crying. She shoved the front door closed and turned on her heel to return to her kitchen and clean up the mess.

Attracted to the light, insects were flying in, collecting in the open fixture. Brad helped her place a cardboard cover over the broken window, then sweep up the broken glass and crockery. Some of the herbs looked as if they'd survive. Joanna got out a few old plastic containers and the bag of soil to repot them.

He picked up the parsley plant and handed it to her. "You can't stay here, Dish. You know that, don't you?"

She stabbed at the potting soil to pack it around the small plant. "There wasn't time for someone to get back out that window before we came into the kitchen."

"Yeah." She set to one side the parsley plant and began spooning soil into another pot. He handed her another small clump of herbs. "So what?"

"So no one was lying in wait for me. Maybe the policemen were right. Maybe it was just—" She broke off, cleared her throat and went back to poking soil around the fragile roots of the parsley. "Maybe it was just kids and baseballs."

"Maybe." The word conveyed a skepticism along the lines of *maybe* pigs fly. "But you're coming home with me, anyway."

Her fingers stilled and her gaze jerked upward to his eyes. She couldn't think of what to say. She blinked. He raised his brows. "I couldn't do that."

His brows drew dangerously close. The hazel color in his eyes grew darker. "Why?"

Heat spread through her chest. It wasn't reasonable to feel more vulnerable in going to his place than staying here alone. "Brad, don't push me on this, okay? If you insist—"

"If I insist?"

Her chin went up. "Yes. If you insist I leave—"

He carefully put down a fragile stem of rosemary. "Because otherwise you'd stay here?"

She swallowed. "Probably."

His expression hardened. Anger crackled off him. "*That's* what I meant about being half-witted, Joanna. You can't stay here."

"I'll go to Nana Bea's, then."

"And put your grandmother in danger, as well?" he asked incredulously. "That's a good idea." He didn't bother disguising the sarcasm.

She blinked again. "Why are you so angry at me?"

"Because you don't have a lot of choices," he snapped. "Because you're sticking your head in the sand. Come on, Dish. You're too smart to ignore this. I shouldn't have to spell anything out for you."

She broke off their eye contact and tossed the spoon aside. It bounced once, clattering in the silence on the table spread with paper towels. She knew he was right, but the reason terrified her. They both suspected this wasn't a random break-in any more than it was an accident.

She drew a shaky breath and asked, just because she needed the confirmation from him. Needed to know she wasn't being ridiculous. "You don't believe the break-in was innocent, either."

"No." He gave her the last of the herb plants and grimaced. "I don't think we can afford to assume it was. Elliott Vine is dead. Phil Stonehaven was murdered." He paused, giving her a pointed look. "Someone broke in here. Whoever it was had a purpose. A reason, and we don't know if the reason was satisfied, or if they're coming back for you now that there's only a flimsy piece of cardboard barring the way."

She began sweeping potting soil into the trash, then went to get a battered old cookie sheet from the cupboard. Arranging the repotted plants on it, her movements felt shaky. Uncoordinated.

Scared.

"The only real possibility, then," she said, "is that all this has to do with Phil's murder. The only place to go with that line of reasoning is that whoever killed him considers me to be a threat." She paused. "But that doesn't make sense because I haven't said or done anything to make anyone believe that I don't think Phil's murderer was a vagrant out of Sister Mary Bernadette's soup kitchen."

He got up and scooped the layer of paper towels strewn with potting soil into the trash. "Phil called you. People know about that—Brungart, Chip Vine, probably Rabern. We don't know who else anyone of them might have told." She had begun to dampen a cloth to wipe the table up. He took it from her. "Go pack a few things, Dish. Enough to keep you for a couple of days. I'll take care of this."

She swallowed hard. She was really going to do this. Leave her own place, everything familiar and dear to her, and go home with Brad MacPherson.

BRAD SWITCHED ON the engine of his Bronco, pulled into the flow of traffic and turned on the CD player. Joanna sat in the dark Bronco on the way to his apartment overlooking Lake Michigan, clinging to the seat-belt strap crossing between her breasts.

A part of her felt cowardly and resentful that she'd been intimidated into running away by a simple break-in. She'd lived in parts of Chicago, near the university, that were considered frankly unsafe. She'd never taken foolish chances, but she'd never let herself be alarmed or daunted by all the tales of muggings and murders and rapes, either.

Staying in her town house would have been taking a foolish chance, she rationalized. But it didn't make the decision to stay with Brad seem rational at all. The last time she had been to his place was the weekend that they had made love. She didn't think she could go there now without regretting how different the circumstances were. From wishing they were different.

She found herself glancing time and again at his profile from the corner of her eye, watching the play of light and darkness on his face. His cheeks and chin were stubbled now, his eyes narrowed against the glare of oncoming headlights. Deep in thought, stopping for a red light at the last intersection before Lake Shore Drive, he shoved the gearshift into first, then reached up to close both eyes with his thumb and third finger.

An emotion welled up in her that she couldn't distinguish from tenderness. He looked so tired. He had been through hell the past month, and if he'd thought he was out of the woods before Vine's surgery, he was now back in the thick of them again.

He'd been openly angry with her again. She knew it was perverse, but the fact that he'd gotten angry made her feel as if he cared, and that she was getting more honesty from him—more emotional truth—in the past twenty-four hours than in all the weeks they had dated. She didn't trust people who stuffed their anger only to have it leak out in poisonous ways. Didn't trust men who, like her father, the superior court judge, the Honorable Harold Elson Cavendish, were consummate public glad-handers and private bastards.

She gave a small, unconscious sigh. She hadn't had one relationship with a man in her life that hadn't been poisoned from the start by her anger and mistrust of her father.

She turned away, but Brad's image reflected in her window. She could see now, maybe because she was so tired and her defenses were too ragged to cover up for her, that she'd been all too ready to lump Brad MacPherson in with men like that. Integrity meant everything to her. She could believe in a man whose truth didn't change under pressure.

She could sit here and try to convince herself that he'd have gotten equally angry with anyone "half-witted" enough to ignore their own safety, but he had made it perfectly clear that it was her he was still interested in. That he thought they had something together, something greater than the tantalizing throb of sexual attraction between them.

There was no use denying that she was attracted to him and always had been. He was gifted, persuasive, eloquent—everything she instinctively mistrusted. He could have made several fortunes in snake oil—heaven knows, there were enough modern-day equivalents. But this morning he'd turned an almost certain media fiasco into a saving grace for Rose Memorial, and he'd done it without compromise. He'd been equally convincing on her behalf.

Then, his kiss in the elevator afterward—had it only been this morning?—had set her feminine sensibilities humming.

Her awareness of him just soared. She had wanted to return his kiss and he knew it because she'd begun to kiss him back.

She didn't know how she could walk into his apartment without remembering, in spite of Phil's death and everything else going on, the night they had made love. The night the dangerous hum of awareness between them had overtaken them both.

Brad had long since turned onto Lake Shore Drive, and she felt a little shock when he pulled off directly into the parking garage beneath his apartment building. Where had her mind been? He turned into the space marked with his number, switched off the engine and released his seat belt. The garage was brightly lit for security, but his face was deep in shadows.

He turned to her. "What are you worried about, Dish?" he asked in a low voice. "That I'll make a pass at you? Or that I won't."

She darted a glance at him, then stared at her hands. "Either way, I guess."

He looked at her. She couldn't help meeting his eyes.

"Joanna." He reached out and cupped her chin. "I'm damned if I do as an unregenerate slug taking advantage of you, and damned if I don't because that's what I want."

"To be an unregenerate slug?" she asked, her wariness defeated by his humor.

The smile fled from his eyes. "Exactly."

"But then," she admitted, "that makes me one, too." She lowered her eyes. "A shameful unregenerate." When he didn't answer she took a deep breath for courage and looked back up at him. "So...what are we going to do?"

He leaned close to her. His hand threaded through her hair, cupping her nape, pulling her closer. His head tilted, his eyes closed and he kissed her, just beneath her jaw, her cheek, then her brow. The sensations poured through her, drizzling tenderness and an achy feeling. Anticipation. "We're going to wait, Dish," he pledged, "until unregenerate feels shameless."

SLEEPING IN HIS GUEST room, the feelings his kisses aroused remained with Joanna through the night. She'd been prone to bad dreams most of her life, to waking up, remembering them, reliving them. But this night, when her dreams had more than enough reason to be traumatic and frightening, when she might have relived the horror of Phil's murder or Rabern's betrayal resounding in her ears, she woke instead feeling somehow unafraid, even . . . comforted.

Finding herself alone in the early-morning silence of the penthouse apartment.

The carpeting was a thick spruce green pile, and most everything else—the sofa, the club chairs, the curtains— were patterns of the green and a silvery gray color. By day, the effect was cool. Soothing. Like an English forest glade in the rain. By night, which was what she most remembered, the subtle recessed lighting gave the imaginary glade a mystical quality.

She wandered, touching things. Brad's things. First editions of Twain and Kerouac's beat generation *On the Road,* a scarred, deeply cracked antique duck decoy, a framed signature of Mary Todd Lincoln and one of Springsteen. The moss aggie shooter atop a pile of marbles he kept in a tin his mother once used to store homemade peanut butter cookies.

She couldn't smell peanut butter now without the memories returning.

Heated memories of the weekend last May. They'd gone to a smoky little blues dive to hear one of Rose Memorial's premier surgeons, Colin Rennslaer, pair off on his oboe with a college friend, a brilliant but little known black New Orleans trumpet player. But Colin had canceled the date to admit a little girl who desperately needed a heart transplant.

Instead, a woman was singing torch songs at the campy little club—songs that made Joanna feel like crying a river for her guarded, narrow little life.

What good was all her caution doing her? Who would ever love her again if he didn't? She didn't trust Brad MacPherson. How could she? He didn't love her. He didn't know the meaning of sincerity. But he knew passion, and after the steamy, heart-wrenching torch songs, Joanna didn't care.

Their relationship wouldn't last, she knew that, but she wanted to make love with him. He'd brought her here and made her peanut butter cookies from scratch, and fed her fingers full of dough and licked the taste of peanuts from her lips while he undressed her between batches....

In the bright light of a new morning, she felt like crying a river of tears again. Her narrow little life hadn't improved because she'd refused to see Brad again after that weekend. Old Kirimatsu wasn't the only one who thought so. Nana Bea did. Beth did.

The sun reached an angle to slant through the dining room windows. She took a deep breath and pulled his thick terry robe tight around herself. He wanted to be unregenerate with her again, he wanted it to feel shameless and he wanted her to admit that wasn't everything they had going for them.

All she had to do was convince herself that she could trust Brad MacPherson.

He would be back soon from his early-morning run along the paths on the beach of Lake Michigan. He'd left her a note and bowl of cereal on the green marble breakfast bar. "Bachelor fare for breakfast," it said. "Sorry. Back soon."

She got out the milk from the nearly empty refrigerator and splashed it on the sugarcoated flakes. Brad didn't return until after she'd showered, dressed, blown her hair dry and put the finishing touches on with a curling iron.

Half-naked, wearing only running shorts and shoes, he looked as if he'd done an extra mile. Sweaty, breathing heavy. All male. Gorgeous. He hadn't shaved yet, either.

"Hey," he breathed, eyeing her in the mirror.

"Hey, yourself." It felt intimate, like déjà vu. A treasured morning ritual, but of course it wasn't. "I'll be out of your way in just a second. I need to call Beth. See how she's doing."

He came into the bathroom and mopped his chest with the towel she'd used to dry her hair. "Would you rather drive over there and see her?"

Tears pricked at her eyelids. Advance notice of the river, she thought. She daubed at her eyes with her fingertips, absorbing the moisture. "I'll ask her, but I know her mom and dad are with her by now." She began to pick up her toiletries and pile them into her makeup bag.

"Leave it out. It's . . . nice."

She hesitated. "Clutter?" she teased, striving for a light tone.

"Female things. Your things."

She didn't want to think what it meant that he found her clutter appealing. "For a change, maybe, but trust me. You'd get tired of it in no time at all."

"We'll see," he answered, snapping the towel at her bottom. "We'll just see."

She left all her things strewn where they lay and went to put on her shoes, then sat down at the breakfast bar again to call Beth. The Stonehavens' nanny answered. Beth wasn't up yet, so her mother, whom Joanna had met many times, got on the line. "Joanna, dear. Is that you?"

Tucking the phone between her shoulder and chin, Joanna got up and ran enough hot soapy water to wash the breakfast bowls. "Yes. Hi, Margie. How is Beth?"

"Brokenhearted. Exhausted. I'm hoping she'll be able to sleep a little longer...we have an appointment with the funeral home at ten. Do you know, dear, how this happened? My God, I swear I can't believe it yet. Who would want to kill Phil? Who would leave these children fatherless? What kind of animal does this kind of thing?"

Margie Higgins's voice sounded so much like Beth's, subtly altered by the edge of pain. The suffering for her daughter. The anger refusing to dissolve into hysteria.

"I don't know, Margie," Joanna answered, rinsing a bowl. She wanted to promise that she'd find out, that she wouldn't rest until she found Phil's murderer, but it seemed such an empty, meaningless gesture. What difference would it make in the end? No matter who it was, Phil couldn't be brought back.

Margie nearly echoed Joanna's thoughts, then asked, "Was there some message you want me to give Beth when she wakes up?"

"Just have her page me—anytime, okay? Whenever she wants."

Beth's mother promised to pass the message along, and then rang off. The telephone rang almost immediately after Joanna put it down. She carried it in to Brad, who was wiping the excess shaving cream from his face.

He clicked on the phone and answered, listened for a moment, then agreed to hold. "It's the hospital operator, connecting a call from the emergency room," he told Joanna.

She waited in the doorway to the master bedroom while Brad pulled on a pristine white shirt and tucked it in his pants. She could tell when the ER came on the line. He grabbed the phone from between his shoulder and ear.

"Yeah, this is MacPherson," he answered. "What can I do for you?" In less time than it took to button his shirt, his expression went from intense listening to aggravated to angry. "Was he driving? No? Thank God for small favors. Listen, Judy, get him to a private room, ASAP. Will you do that for me? Thanks. I'll be there shortly." He clicked off the phone and hurled it onto his rumpled, unmade king-size bed.

"What is it?" Joanna asked.

He pulled a solid teal green wool tie from the rack and gave a disgusted shake of his head. ''They just brought Chip Vine into the ER in a straitjacket. Drunk or stoned off his butt—or both.''

Brad pulled a small penlight from his ear out, the back and gave it the usual spread of his hand. "Okay," Brad said. "She has two or four up. How many you reckon all this adds up to be?"

Chapter Seven

The Rose Memorial emergency room was packed. Fifteen of the available seventeen beds had been assigned and the crew was clearly frantic. One of the beds was taken up with a husky orderly bleeding from the nose and a gash in his head, compliments of Chip Vine taking a roundhouse slug at him.

Brad had meant for Chip to be assigned to the psych ward in a VIP room where no one could hear him, but Judy Spence hadn't had three seconds to get the transfer accomplished. They'd been lucky to get him moved to the isolation room where patients with possible infectious diseases were assigned.

Joanna could hear Chip bellowing obscenities before she and Brad got through the sliding-glass doors leading into the emergency room from outside the hospital. Joanna gave Brad a worried glance.

"He said no one would ever know!" Chip railed from behind the closed door of the isolation exam room. "Somebody get in here and get these damn restraints off me! Hey! Anybody. I mean it. I don't have to put up with this!"

Brad didn't bother even checking with staff, but headed straight for the isolation room. Joanna followed. Chip was worse off than either of them had counted on. Wild-eyed, jerking against the restraints, swearing a blue streak, he wrenched his head around when they entered.

Gearing himself up for another outburst, Chip clapped his mouth shut when he saw Joanna and looked for a place to hide. "Get her out of here," he snarled, eyeing her with rage. "Get her the hell out of here!"

"Settle down, Chip," Brad commanded, but Joanna took a step back. The hate in his eyes was like nothing she had ever seen. He was in restraints, going nowhere, but the fact took a moment to register in her brain. If he hadn't been restrained, she would never have found the fortitude to stand in the firing line of his venomous look. She picked up the phone on the wall inside the door. "This is Dr. Cavendish. Get me security, please. Stat."

She fought for objectivity. His fingers were thick with clotted blood, probably from taking his swing at the orderly when they took him out of the straitjacket and put him into restraints. She knew within seconds of seeing his pallor, the cold sweat beaded on his forehead and the frenzied look in his eyes, his pupils reduced to pinpoints, that he might be drunk, but he'd popped some kind of pills, as well.

"He's high as a kite, Brad," she murmured, putting her fingers at the pulse point on Chip's wrist.

"Don't touch me!" he shrieked, yanking his arm back, pinching her fingers in the leather cuff.

She snatched her hand back and turned away, shivering hard, looking for the admission papers, anything to focus on but Chip's rancor. Someone had tossed the papers on the counter next to the bottle of alcohol and cotton balls, but nothing much was filled out beyond Chip's name. The hastily scrawled notes taken down by Judy

Spence were there. No medication orders appeared on the physician order sheet.

Security came on the line. "Yes," Joanna said. "This is Dr. Cavendish, in ER 5. We've got a possible overdose here. Combative and violent. Can you get someone down here?"

"You get the sam hell outta here, you hear me?" Chip snarled at her. "I'll show *you* combative!" He fought the restraints. His torso was raised up off the gurney, and the tendons in his neck stuck out thick as cord. "Don't you come near me! Get the hell away! Who put these frigging restraints on me, anyway?"

Getting right in Chip's face, Brad planted his hand in the middle of Chip's chest and shoved him back down on the gurney. "You quiet down and get a civil tongue in your head or I'll have you thrown in lockup so fast your head will spin."

"You can't do squat to me," he snarled back, "and if you touch me again, I'll—"

"You'll do what, Chip?" Brad said, shoving Chip back down again. "Sue me? Take me to the cleaners? You're drunk, you're high, you're abusive—whose word do you think they'll take, bud? Yours?"

"Damn straight they will—"

"I don't think so, Chip," Brad interrupted sternly, "but when this is all over, you're welcome to give it your best shot. Meanwhile, you can either calm down and tell me what this is about, or we *will* stick you in lockup and let you sleep it off."

Brad's tone must have penetrated the fog in Chip's brain, and he seemed to have forgotten for the moment that Joanna was in the small examination room. "You can't do that, man. I could be sick and who'll know?" he whined.

"Chip, we're not going to let anything happen to you," Brad appeased, modifying his approach to Chip's mercuric mood swing. "Just take it easy. You show me ten minutes' restraint on your own and I'll get the cuffs off of you."

Chip turned his head away in a suddenly lucid, acute embarrassment, sniffed and pouted, his lip trembling. Joanna thought the reaction indicated he might already be on his way down from whatever dope he'd taken, but she had no doubt his temper would flare again.

Brad exchanged glances with her and pulled up a stool. "Do you want to tell me why you've gone and gotten yourself in this kind of shape?" he asked.

"My old man's dead," Chip said, breathing raggedly, sucking on his lips. "And the son of a—"

"Without the obscenities, Chip," Brad warned.

He fumed resentfully at Brad. "He said no one would know. He promised things'd be fine. Well, they're not fine, are they now? He's dead, I get nothing, not one... My old man's dead and people *won't leave it alone*. She won't leave it alone," he whined, jerking his head at Joanna, refusing to look at her. He stopped, and rambled incoherently—lost, somehow, Joanna thought, in a maze of hallucinations or paranoid delusions. "Why is that? Why is it no one can ever leave me alone!"

Trying to make sense of Chip's labored, confusing outburst, Joanna remained silent, sensing that Brad's rapport with him might disintegrate if she interrupted. He posed the question she would have asked, anyway. "Who said no one would know? Know what, Chip?"

Chip just stared at Brad as if he couldn't remember anything he'd just said.

Joanna scribbled "simplify" on the back of the manila folder and held it so Brad would see her message. He read and acknowledged her meaning with a brief nod.

"Chip, buddy, who said things would be fine?"

"That he was dead?" Chip asked dazedly. "He's dead! How were things going to be fine? He *lied* to me."

Brad tried again, gently, sympathetically, letting his tone convey he was on Chip's side. "Who lied to you, Chip?"

"You know—" But a wildly suspicious sneer contorted Chip's handsome features—so badly that Joanna knew she would never look at Chip Vine again without remembering the hate-filled expression. "You're tryin' to trick me!"

Brad looked up at Joanna, a frown creasing his brow. "Chip, buddy, you're not making sense."

"Don't look at her!" Chip snarled. "She's half the damn problem. You lousy—" He jerked his chin back. "Get outta here. I don't want to talk to you. My old man's dead. That's freaking enough, isn't it?" He rattled the restraints. "It's been more than ten minutes."

"It hasn't been three minutes, Chip."

"Liar! I'm done talking to you." His eyes shot daggers of hate at Joanna. "And you. If it weren't for you—"

"That's enough, Chip," Brad warned one last time, rising from the stool. "You just keep it down, take it easy and they'll let you out of here when you're feeling better."

"I won't be feeling better," he cried. "You…you can't just leave me here! Don't leave. I want my wife. Where is Peggy? Where's my wife?" His voice was rising in pitch with every word.

Security rapped on the door and opened it. Joanna shook her head to let them know things were slightly more under control.

"I'll try to find Peggy, Chip," Brad soothed, "but get this in your head. If I hear you outside this door again, you're going to lockup."

Chip breathed hard through his mouth, fighting off tears of rage, but he said nothing, only turned his head away again in outrage and silence.

Brad joined Joanna and they shut the door behind them. She half expected Chip to start in again, but something of Brad's warning must have penetrated his rage. Or he believed Brad would lock him up. Still, it took several seconds and half a dozen deep, steadying breaths to overcome the violent effects of the hostility Chip had directed as much toward her as anyone.

"Joanna, are you okay?" Brad asked, holding her shoulders.

His touch calmed her. She took one more breath and nodded uncertainly. "I will be."

"It's quiet in there now," one of the security team said. "Is he just in a lull?"

"No telling, Jake," Brad said. Typically, he knew the names of all three security people. "Jake, Helen, Gil, thanks for coming down so quickly. I appreciate your response. I think we'll be transferring Chip to a private room at least over night. If one of you could hang around, just to make sure that happens without any further incident?"

The eyes of the guard Brad had addressed as Gil widened. "Your overdose is Dr. Vine's son?"

Brad nodded, adding a warning confident of being obeyed, "Naturally, his identity goes no farther."

"You said it, you got it," the guard answered. The other two departed through the sliding-glass door exit.

Judy Spence hurried over. "God bless you, whatever you did," she said. "I think Dr. Connell can see Mr. Vine in just a minute, but you may want to look in on his wife." She turned and pointed to a curtained station. "She's over there in bed 12. Pretty shaken up herself."

"You've admitted Peggy Vine, as well?" Joanna asked, alarmed by the mushrooming upheaval.

"Not officially," the nurse answered. "Haven't even got the paperwork going." Ted Bayless, the medical director of the ER, called for help—stat—and Judy Spence darted away.

Brad quirked an eyebrow at Joanna. "Things are pretty well going to hell in a hand basket. Any guesses as to what's going on in Chip's head?"

"He's half out of it, Brad," she answered slowly, "but I think he clammed up in there. He's very upset, delusional, obviously. And if he could, he would have taken my head off."

Brad cupped her neck, letting his thumb stroke her near her ear. "I'd have taken Chip apart before he touched you."

She swallowed hard. Chip was stoned out of his head, and violently angry, but his suspicion toward her seemed eerily focused. And as confused as he had appeared, parts of his tirade were very clear.

"I think he meant exactly what he said, Brad. He caught himself, but he was very lucid—his father was dead, someone promised him no one would know and that things would be fine, and I'm half the problem. He knew what he was saying. He backed off it. But I don't understand."

"I don't, either," Brad answered, grimacing. "But you're right. He said the same sorts of things to you in front of Detective Dibell. What I want to know is who told him no one would ever know. Know what? *How* his dad died?"

Joanna touched her fingers to her brow, trying to close out the chaos of the busy emergency room, the noise and frenzied activity going on in the lane around them. "That's the only thing that makes sense, isn't it? Of course, it may be wildly optimistic on our part to trust anything out of his mouth in his mental condition."

Brad took a deep breath and fingered the knot of his tie. "It's also possible he's too drunk or high to keep his guard up. Under the influence, people will say things they would never say sober."

"He also accused you of trying to trick him," Joanna reminded him, moving so an orderly wheeling a gurney out to the main hospital could round the corner. "He's got to be trying to keep the lid on something, or he wouldn't worry that you could trick him into saying the wrong thing." She glanced over to the curtained-off bed where the nurse had said Peggy was. "Do you think Peggy could tell us what's going on? Or if she even knows?"

"Let's go see."

Brad followed Joanna the long way around the nursing station to avoid the busy lanes. She drew aside the curtain. Dressed in jeans, a pullover and worn, dirty sneakers, Chip's wife sat on the end of the gurney chewing her nails. "Peggy? May we talk to you?"

"Why?" She turned her head quickly away, then raked through her dark blond hair, pulling it toward instead of away from her face. Already a painfully thin, petite woman, Peggy looked fragile as a starving street urchin.

Her harried, bloodshot, pale green eyes loomed in her face. "I want to take Chip home."

Joanna slipped inside the curtain.

Brad came in from the opposite side. "Chip isn't in any shape to go home, Peg—" He broke off, focusing tightly on her face. He lifted her hair back from her face. "Oh, Peggy. Did Chip do this?"

"He's upset," she snapped, cringing like a threatened turtle drawing into itself. "He's worried. And he's darned mad, and I don't blame him."

Joanna moved quickly to the other side, exchanging places with Brad, her heart already in her throat with consternation. Peggy had been trying to cover her face from view with her limp brown hair. Violently bruised, black-and-blue, her cheek was nearly split open. Blood oozed from the abrasion. The whole left side of her face was swollen and a dried cut ran into her hairline.

Joanna's stomach lurched sickeningly. In med school and during her internship she had seen far worse injuries, but none of them had affected her like this. Nothing sucked the air from her lungs or reduced her to tears with such deadly precision as a battering.

Chip Vine had hit his wife, hard, more than once if the damage to her face were any indication. Inside, instinctively, Joanna recoiled. Her mother had looked like this more times than she could remember.

Her expression must have betrayed her gut-wrenched reaction to the sight of Peggy Vine's injuries. Brad cleared his throat. "Why don't you go get a breath of fresh air," he said. "I'll wait with Peggy."

Anger began welling up in her to compete with the outrage. "I'm a doctor." She defied his gaze over Peggy's head. "I don't need a breath of fresh air." Turning, she jerked the curtain back. "Who's in charge here?" she demanded.

Dr. Ted Bayless looked up from a chart on the counter at the nurses' station. "I am. Why..." He suddenly recognized her. "Joanna?"

"Yes. Ted, do you mind if I clean this abrasion up?" It didn't matter if he did mind. Someone had to take care of this, and the ER staff had their hands filled with crises.

"Sure, Joanna," Bayless answered, taken somewhat aback. "Actually, I'd be grateful for the help."

"Fine. Somebody get me an ice pack." She turned to the small sink, scrubbed her hands and pulled on a pair of sterile gloves, then ripped open several packages of gauze and soaked them with warm, soapy water. An orderly reached in with the cold pack. Brad took it. Joanna turned back to the job in front of her.

"Peggy, listen to me." Her hands shook. The only hands-on care of patients she had done in the past few years was to perform small localized surgeries to get IVs into veins for her anesthesia medications. "No matter how upset Chip is over his Dad, he had no right to knock you around like this."

"You don't understand anything," she answered sullenly, gritting her teeth through Joanna's ministrations.

"I understand that he hit you. It doesn't matter—"

"It matters! That slug of a father of his cut us out of the will—cut Chip off without a crying dime. I'm pregnant!" she shrilled, "and the money's going to a charity foundation. How are we supposed to get by? Chip's entitled to that money! *I'm* entitled!"

She was also entitled to be treated better than a punching bag, Joanna thought fiercely. And maybe they could better afford to live if Chip didn't drop hundreds into the cocaine or the street drugs he was flying on.

Brad stroked her upper arm. "Peggy, has this happened before?"

"Count on it," Joanna muttered angrily. "Tell him instead how many times, Peggy."

She winced and cast Joanna a scathing, resentful look. "Twice, okay? But it doesn't matter. I don't want to talk about it. I just want to get out of here and take Chip home."

"Peggy, look," Brad began reasonably. "Chip is going to have to spend the night. He's in no condition to go home and he won't be for several hours."

"I'm taking him home," she insisted stubbornly. "You can't keep him here."

Peggy and Chip would know the ropes. No patient could be compelled to stay on a doctor's orders unless they were also in official custody of the police in the first place. Chip did have the right to check himself out. There was no way they could keep him short of Peggy filing charges against her husband, and the chances of that, considering Peggy's attitude, were nil.

Her insides roiling with anger over the abuse Chip had dealt his wife, Joanna wondered if this was an established routine—Chip getting high, punching Peggy in the face, getting care, refusing follow-up treatment.

In the efficiently rational, functioning part of her mind, Joanna heard Brad carrying on a conversation with Peggy, gently probing for answers, never alienating her. He was leading, slowly, surely, toward discovering why Peggy was so desperate to get Chip away from the hospital.

Joanna knew. A part of her own spirit buckled to the crushing embarrassment—having to explain and justify and make awkward excuses nobody believed. The burning humiliation Peggy must feel was as familiar to Joanna as her own mother's face.

Stoically treating Peggy's face despite all of that, Joanna tossed one soiled gauze after another into the trash and continued cleansing the abrasions and small cuts.

"Peggy, I know you're in a lot of pain, and I'm very sorry," Brad went on, shifting the cold pack from one hand to the other. "Is there something we can do to help Chip get through this? He sounded pretty irrational just now. Like he knew—"

"Brad, she's hurting," Joanna interrupted heatedly. "This is not the time to grill her."

"I'm not grilling her, Dr. Cavendish," he answered politely, though his eyes hardened, warning her. "I'm offering assistance."

"She doesn't want assistance. She wants—"

"For all this to go away," Brad interrupted firmly, "isn't that right, Peggy?"

Chip's wife closed her eyes. Weariness came off her in waves. "Yes."

Brad nodded sympathetically, then went gently on. "Help me out, Peggy, if you can. It sounds as if Chip knew his dad was going to die. Do you know anything about that?"

"That's crazy." Struggling not to move her face, Peggy squared her shoulders defiantly. Her eyes darted once between them, then to her hands. "Chip doesn't— What... exactly did he say?"

"That his old man was dead," Brad answered softly, "and that someone told him no one would know."

"He's stoned. He doesn't have the foggiest idea what he's saying!" She let out an angry huff and tossed her head when Joanna paused long enough to get a salve. "I don't know what he meant. You saw him—you saw what kind of shape he's in. He meant his father is dead. Period." She shook her head. "I want you to get him released."

"Hold still now, Peggy," Joanna warned, prepared to apply the antiseptic with cotton swabs.

Peggy flinched and sucked in a breath at the sting of the antiseptic. Her lips twisted bitterly, and the pain must have short-circuited her guard. She began gnashing her teeth, spilling out her anger. "Elliott treated Chip like such dirt, like . . . he wasn't a doctor so he wasn't worth anything. Like a *doctor* is something to aspire to. God, he was insufferable." She glared defiantly. "I hated him. He was a mean, stingy, holier-than-thou prig and I hated him."

"Peggy—" Joanna hushed her softly.

"No!" she shrilled, knocking Joanna's gloved hand aside in her outburst. "I don't care who hears me! Chip tried. Chip *groveled*. And what good did it do him? He's so upset he bashed his hand through a window and chases dope with booze. It isn't right! If I thought I could have gotten away with it, I would have killed the stingy bastard before he could change his will."

Brad's eyes narrowed, and he looked thoughtfully at Joanna. "But someone *did* get away with it, didn't they, Peggy?" he asked softly. Dangerously. "Only it was too late."

Joanna froze. Where had that come from? Peggy's head jerked and her mouth clapped shut. Tears spilled from her eyes. "I don't know what you're talking about."

"Sure you do. Chip does. Is that why he got drunk and then high, Peggy? Because he knew? Because all of a sudden, someone else suspected?"

The swab stick broke in Joanna's hand, spattering antiseptic. It was one thing to try to pry information from Peggy Vine in the guise of offering help. But it was quite another thing to badger her about what her strung-out drunken husband knew or didn't know.

She stared at Brad while Peggy doggedly denied everything. This was the second time in less than twenty-four hours that Joanna had seen him go straight for the jugular. Both times with women. First Ruth Brungart, now Peggy Vine. Brungart could take care of herself, but, beaten and bruised, Peggy Vine was in no shape to defend herself or her miserable excuse for a husband.

Joanna hurled the broken swab stick into the biohazard trash and took the cold pack from Brad. Wrapping the pack in a dry cloth, she sent Brad a scathing look while she helped Peggy apply the cold. "Do you have somewhere safe to go, Peggy?"

Chip's wife held the cold pack to her face, swallowed and reached behind her on the gurney to fetch her purse and pull the shoulder strap up her arm. "I told you I'm going home and Chip is going with me."

"Peggy, please consider letting Chip sleep it off here," Joanna said.

But Judy Spence interrupted at the edge of the privacy curtain. "Mr. MacPherson, Dr. Cavendish, there's a limo out here."

"A limo?"

"Yeah." The nurse shrugged and nodded. "For the Vines. The driver was instructed to pick them up here."

Peggy slid off the gurney and tore open the curtain. "Where?"

"Who ordered this?" Brad asked.

"I did," Lucy Chavez answered, coming from near the corridor into the main body of the hospital.

Surprised, Brad turned to face the director of physician relations. A smart, voluptuous Hispanic woman, Lucy Chavez came only to the middle of Brad's chest in height, but what she lacked in height she made up in fearlessness of anyone who would thwart her wishes.

"He can take Peggy home," Brad said, "but Chip needs restraints. He's out of control and he's not going anywhere but to a private room."

Lucy shrugged. "Sorry, Brad. Have to pull rank on this one."

Brad's brows drew dangerously close. "What rank, Lucy?"

"Dr. Rabern feels Chip Vine has been shabbily treated and demands that his friend's son and his wife be taken care of in a more fitting manner—" Brad started to interrupt, but Lucy held up a manicured hand, jeweled designs embedded in her polished talon-length nails "—*however* poorly they're able to express their grief over Dr. Vine's death. Jacob Delvecchio approved on the administration side," she went on, shooting every bullet in her arsenal of authorities. "Chip has already been escorted to the limo."

"This is not in the best interests of the hospital, Lucy," Brad warned. "He's a loose cannon—"

"Sometimes, the best interests of *people* take precedence, Brad," she retorted.

"It sure as *hell* isn't in the best interests of Peggy Vine," Joanna snapped.

"I disagree," Lucy answered disinterestedly. "More importantly, Dr. Rabern and Jacob Delvecchio disagree. This is a couple under a great deal of stress and they need only to be left alone. It's really not up for discussion. Now if you'll excuse me."

Brad's eyes darkened, the only chink in his flawless poise, the only hint that her preemptive moves angered him. "I'd like to see you in my office, Lucy," he said easily, as if there were no more at stake than a conflict over a place to do lunch. "Thirty minutes."

She gave a half smile. "Of course. Meanwhile, the Vines go home."

Joanna stared at Brad, staggered by his restraint. "This is totally irresponsible! You can't let—"

"Please," Peggy Vine interrupted, cradling the cold pack to her cheek. Plucking distractedly at Joanna's sleeve, her chin quivered. "I know you're only trying to help me, but what's done is done.... Nothing can change that. Stop interfering, Dr. Cavendish," she begged, swallowing hard, "or things will only get worse."

Chapter Eight

After Peggy walked out the sliding-glass doors, Joanna turned and walked away in the other direction without another word. Brad caught up with her near the old Sacred Heart entrance of the hospital where the original hardwood floors were dark with age and the antiquated gas lanterns had been restored.

"Joanna, wait." She was rigid with anger he only vaguely understood. He took hold of her arm.

"No. Let me go."

"Not a chance." He guided her to a hidden vestibule where two wooden benches faced each other. Above one was a stained-glass window of a quality rarely seen anymore. The sunlight streaming through the colored glass created a calming, restful effect.

She pulled away from Brad and huddled on a pew beneath the window.

He sat across from her, steepling his hands between his thighs in frustration. She looked so damnably stubborn—and just as vulnerable—that he couldn't decide whether he should take her in his arms and hold her, or shake her out of it.

He did neither. He needed to find out what had upset her so much. "Joanna. I want to understand. Help me out with this. What's got you so upset?"

She took a deep breath, trying to recover her cool. "Chip is . . . he's dangerously violent, Brad, and the more he comes down, the worse he could get. I just can't believe you let Lucy Chavez get away with spiriting them out of here. Peggy should never have left with him."

One insight after another tumbled into place. From the first, he'd thought her reaction to Peggy's bruises too strong, almost overblown. But it hit him now that the instant Joanna saw her face, everything else, including her intention to find out what Peggy might know about what had pushed Chip over the edge, had fled Joanna's mind.

The pattern fit. He'd seen Joanna do nearly the same thing with Detective Dibell, reacting emotionally first to protect Phil Stonehaven's reputation when it was her own actions that had been called into question. This time was somehow worse, more complex. More personal.

Joanna was afraid. She'd seen that kind of domestic violence before, or been the victim herself, he'd bet on it, and anger deep in his belly began to burn.

"Joanna, has this happened to you?" he asked softly.

"No." Her head tilted. Her focus seemed inward, her body stiff. "But to my mother." Her eyes lowered. "It all happened a long time ago."

"Dish, I'm sorry." He couldn't think what to say. She wouldn't want his lip service to feelings, humiliations, he barely understood. She'd lived it.

She shrugged. "I hadn't thought of it in years until I saw Peggy's bruises." She met his gaze. "Chip was not in any condition to go home. He could get violent again."

"I agree with you," he answered simply. "It shouldn't have gone down that way. But Peggy would have gone with him no matter what I said or did."

She gave a sigh. "I know. My mother would have behaved exactly that way."

He nodded, and stared a moment at his hands. A group of nursing students and their instructor passed by, and in their wake an old couple clinging to each other, making their way down the hall. It never ceased to surprise him how many personal dramas, how many tragedies and triumphs, went on in a hospital, day in and day out, no moment respecting the fact that lives were changed, that things would never be the same, for better or worse, in the next moment.

There were things going on in Joanna's eyes, too—emotions, other recriminations he still had to deal with.

"Joanna, you were angry with me long before Lucy Chavez even showed up." He needed to know why. He thought her reasons probably had something to do with her chronic mistrust of him. "I want to know why."

Her eyes darkened. "Peggy had already been through enough. She's not responsible for what Chip knew and she shouldn't be treated like that."

"Like what, Joanna?" he asked, genuinely confused.

"You were browbeating her."

He sat back as if he'd been shoved, physically stricken, *stunned* by the word, by the parallel Joanna was caught up in. How, in her mind, the way he had questioned Peggy was *browbeating*—and not very different at all from the physical blows Chip had inflicted on his wife.

His throat tightened. He felt blindsided. Deeply offended. Looking at her, at sunlight filtering through the stained-glass window in hues of oyster shell and burgundy and sapphire glinting off her pale blond hair, he knew her mother's experience had preordained Joanna's emotional response to Peggy Vine.

But it had also blinded her to the lies, and made her look at him as if he were the one who had knocked Peggy around.

"I'm sure she was in a lot of pain and humiliation," he said, ignoring the bitter taste in his mouth. "I didn't mean to add to that, and I don't believe I did. But I'm also dead sure Peggy Vine knows something she desperately wanted to keep from us. She was frantic to get Chip out of there before he talked too much. Think about what she said, Joanna," he urged. "Stop interfering, *or things will only get worse.*"

Joanna took a small, startled breath and gripped the seat of the wooden pew with one hand, subconsciously touching her arm where Peggy had plucked at her sleeve with the other. "I thought she meant that interfering would only make it worse for her with Chip, but it...that was a warning, wasn't it? To leave it alone, stop trying to find out what happened."

"Yeah." He tilted his head. "Both, maybe."

"Brad, this is just getting so convoluted! How could Chip know anything about his father's death? How could Peggy?"

"We know he was hanging around the pathology offices. Maybe he overheard Phil. Maybe Ruth Brungart told him Phil was looking deeper into the cause of death. And remember, he heard you telling Detective Dibell that you had spoken to Phil not long before he was killed."

"But that doesn't explain anything," she protested, leaping up in frustration, pacing the small floor space of the vestibule. "He kept saying he'd been promised everything would turn out okay. It couldn't have been Phil reassuring him of that!"

"No. But maybe Chip had reason to believe he wasn't going to inherit—"

"That was just Peggy's excuse," Joanna said, surprising herself, Brad thought, because even through her anger at what Chip had done to his wife, and at Brad for questioning her, at some level Joanna had recognized that Peggy was lying.

She met his eyes, and he could see that she finally got it. He had only gone after Peggy's lies and evasions. It was her husband who had beat up on her.

"Brad, I'm sorry. You know, I just—" She broke off, clearing her throat, making futile gestures with her hands. "I react without thinking sometimes. I always think it has to do with you, but . . . it doesn't, and I'm sorry."

Her apology should have helped, but somehow managed to piss him off instead. Like saying she was sorry for mistrusting everything he said and did, everything he *was*, should make it all better.

It didn't.

He admired her strength, her resolve, her loyalty to her friends. Months ago he'd fallen for her precisely because she'd refused to tumble to his charm and flattery and smooth talking, which he had had to admit to himself was an approach to women that had never failed him before.

With Joanna he discovered why other women finally left him bored and restless. She was smart, savvy, pretty . . . and as wary as they came. A constant challenge, the beloved enemy. She wouldn't let him be shallow. But Joanna's wariness had begun to wear real thin. He wanted her to know that with her he was more, deeper, *better*, than he had ever been with anyone else he had ever known.

He looked into her eyes. All he wanted was for her to believe in his integrity, but he was beginning to think she never would. She looked at the world as a dangerous place for a woman. Instinctively, he knew he couldn't give up without a fight.

Meeting her uncertain gaze, suddenly he no longer tasted the bitterness. "Apology accepted, Dish."

Her smile of relief gave him cause for hope. She took a deep breath and let it go. "Thank you."

"You're welcome."

She searched a little awkwardly, endearingly, he thought, for something else to say. "There's no possibility that we're reading too much into this, is there?"

"No." He wanted very much to ease her mind, to erase the tiny crease between her brows. To have come up with some reasonable, innocuous explanation for everything that had happened. But in her heart she knew better, and trying to shelter her from the realities wasn't going to help him win her faith. He pinched the bridge of his nose, then met her troubled blue eyes. "Chip Vine is running real scared. He knows something, Joanna."

She nodded thoughtfully. "The only real proof we have of anything wrong has to be in whatever Phil saw on those tissue slides. Do you think there's any way we can get them back from the police?"

"We can try."

He stood, but found all of a sudden that he wasn't ready to leave the privacy of the hallowed old vestibule. He offered Joanna a hand and pulled her close enough to feel the heat of her body.

He let go of her. Her scent, as subtle as English roses, made his body tighten as much as his throat. He laid a hand at her side and swore he could feel the sudden throb of her heart matching the throb of his.

"Dish," he breathed, his lips close to her ear, his body aching for a moment when wanting Joanna this badly would be more appropriate. Possible.

"Brad..." Emotion whispered in her voice. A plea. Desire.

He touched his forehead to hers. He had to get a grip. Had to go face down Lucy Chavez on a number of issues, and con the police into returning slides that had been taken as evidence in Phil Stonehaven's murder.

He would need a few wits about him. He broke off and backed away from her and gave Joanna a rueful grin. "C'mon, Dish. I've got a little frustration to work off."

She smiled back and reached for his tie, straightened the knot and laid her hand on his lapel, fussing in a female way that drove his tension higher. "Be, umm, conservative with it, okay?"

WHEN THEY REACHED Brad's office, they had a few minutes to spare before Lucy Chavez was due to show up. His secretary had a list of fifteen things he needed to do immediately. He looked them over, had her farm out ten or twelve of them to his staff and put in return calls to the other three—in addition to placing a call to Detective Dibell. When she proved unavailable, he asked for her supervisor.

Astoundingly, Joanna thought, listening to Brad's end of the conversation, Dibell's superior turned out to be someone Brad knew from a police Big Brother campaign that he had volunteered to promote in the community last year.

She shouldn't have been surprised. He made friends everywhere. This one sounded willing to bend over backward to accommodate their request to see the tissue slides Phil had been reviewing.

Brad's secretary called in to say that Ms. Chavez was waiting in the outer office, but Lucy didn't wait for an invitation. She opened the door and breezed in. "Dr. Cavendish, Brad."

"Lucy," he acknowledged, sitting behind his desk.

Joanna took one of the chairs opposite him across the expanse of his desk. Lucy took the other, crossing her legs, smoothing the skirt of her dress, preoccupied, Joanna thought, with herself.

"Tell me what I can do for you," she said. The rhythm of her native language still came through, but there was no trace of an accent in her pronunciation.

"I've heard some interesting things in the past couple of days, Lucy," Brad said, matching her businesslike tone. "About Hensel Rabern and Elliott Vine."

"Like what?" she asked, blinking as if she hadn't a clue where he was leading. Joanna didn't believe her for a second, and she knew Lucy wasn't fooling Brad, either.

He reacted as if he had no reason to doubt her. "Did you know Dr. Rabern had been out to dinner with Ruth Brungart lately?"

"No. I didn't." She gave a bored shrug. Too bored maybe. "Is this going somewhere, Brad?"

"I think so, Lucy." He sat back. "Ruth says Elliott Vine was deliberately putting Rabern in a difficult position by asking him to perform the heart surgery. Frankly, I think I've missed something. I thought you might consent to fill me in. Ruth suggested you could."

"It's no great mystery," Lucy answered, her brow furrowing enigmatically. "The two of them didn't get along. Never have. Everyone knows that. They were at each other's throats all the time."

"Over Clemenza?" Joanna asked.

"Among an entire galaxy of other things, but yes. Dr. Vine backed Frank Clemenza's administration all the way. Dr. Rabern despised him. If it weren't for me, quite frankly, Hensel Rabern would have walked out of here when Mary Bernadette retired. He intended to take his patients to University Hospital. Rose Memorial would have been out thousands of billable patients every year. *Millions* of dollars."

"So you personally convinced Dr. Rabern to stay. To keep admitting his patients here at Rose," Brad concluded.

"That's my job and I did it. Yes. And I worked my fingers to the bone doing it." She gave a smug smile. "Hensel Rabern is not an easy man to satisfy."

"University Hospital must have offered him a great deal," Joanna said. She had the most sudden, irrational itch to wipe the boastful expression from Lucy Chavez's face.

"They did. Of course they did. Their offer included upscale office space at a steep discount, accounting and billing services for pennies on the dollar. The promise of a new cardiac-care unit."

Brad picked up a pen and began working it through his fingers. "Rose couldn't have matched that kind of offer, Lucy," he said. "So why did Rabern stay?"

"Because I asked him to."

Joanna stared at Lucy's beautiful Hispanic face and hard, dark, glittering, *calculating* eyes, and suddenly she knew exactly what Sister Mary Bernadette's disapproval of Lucy Chavez was all about.

Hensel Rabern had stayed, given up millions of dollars in concessions Rose Memorial couldn't offer him, because Lucy Chavez was willing to sweeten the deal to keep him at Rose with her voluptuous body.

Lucy certainly hadn't suffered in the deal, Joanna thought. Keeping Rabern had been considered a remarkable coup, and she had secured her position at Rose Memorial. She wore clothes more expensive that anyone Joanna had ever personally known, more shoes and exquisite jewelry—gifts Rabern had undoubtedly showered on her.

"Sister Mary Bernadette must have been appalled," Joanna murmured, unaware that she had even spoken aloud until Lucy's laughter spilled out.

"Mary Bernadette is a dear, you know, and quite perceptive—but she is a dinosaur. Her day is long since past."

Brad tossed the pen onto his desk. The clattering interrupted Lucy's pleasure, and her smile disappeared. Unamused, Brad wasn't smiling in the first place. "This is all very fascinating, Lucy, really." He let his tone convey how bored he was by her self-aggrandizing revelations. "But it explains nothing. Vine and Rabern may not have liked each other, but their animosity obviously didn't extend to professional mistrust, or Vine would have chosen someone else to do his surgery. Colin Rennslaer comes to mind."

Lucy looked at Brad in utter amazement. "You really don't get it, do you? How sweet, Brad! How incredibly endearing of you not to see it!"

"See what, Lucy?" he asked, his voice ominously low.

But Joanna saw. "You reneged on your deal, didn't you, Lucy? You dumped Rabern for Vine."

Her choice of words didn't faze Lucy Chavez in the least. "Yes." She sighed and tossed her long dark hair over her shoulder. "Frankly, I was bored. Hensel Rabern is a boring man. An old, tired, *boring* man. Surgeons like Colin Rennslaer and his ilk have already surpassed Rabern's value to this hospital.

"Elliott Vine, on the other hand," she went on, "was still a relatively young man. He was a pig, of course. But then," she paused, directing her contemptuous dark eyes on Brad, "aren't you all, in the final analysis?"

To his credit, Brad didn't even blink. "Not all of us, Lucy. I think you generally find what you expect to find."

Her failure to get a rise out of him irked her. "Enough of you are," she snapped. "It was infantile of Elliott Vine to rub Rabern's nose in it. He'd already won." She sneered, not understanding how much she devalued herself by the expression, as if she were chattel to be fought over and won by childish, vain men. "But no," she went on in disgust. "Elliott Vine was twisted. He asked Rabern to do the surgery because he knew that even holding the knife, there wasn't a damn thing Rabern could do to get even with him for taking me away."

Brad straightened in his chair. Whatever else she was, Lucy Chavez had been discreet. Sister Mary Bernadette had almost certainly guessed how Lucy had convinced Rabern to stay, but the fact was that Lucy had conducted affairs with two high-profile doctors and no word of it had ever hit the grapevine.

"One more thing, Lucy. Why did Rabern want Chip out of our ER?"

She shrugged and stood up to leave. "You'll have to ask him. I'm afraid Hensel doesn't confide in me anymore."

AFTER LUCY CHAVEZ LEFT, Brad sat silently thinking for several moments. Lost in her own thoughts, Joanna was surprised when Brad began to voice his surprise.

"I understand why Vine would ask Rabern to do the surgery, but I can't figure why Rabern would agree to do it."

"I wondered, too." She shook her head. "And if Vine was really that twisted, it makes me wonder why he chose me to do the anesthesia. But the whole thing sounds like a glorified spitting contest between Vine and Rabern. Vine just upped the ante. How could Rabern refuse? To the rest of us, the choice looks like a vote of confidence. Vine simply chose the best man available. I don't think Rabern's ego would let him refuse that plum—even if his fondest wish was that Elliott Vine would drop dead first."

"Even though Vine stole his mistress?"

Joanna shrugged. "How many people knew about that? I'd bet Rabern was crying on Ruth Brungart's shoulder about it, but no one else knew."

"Maybe not, Dish. But Rabern had to be furious."

Chapter Nine

Brad leaned back in his chair and put his feet up on the black marble desktop. "So now we have motive and opportunity. Vine had not only moved in on Rabern's affair with Lucy Chavez, he compounded the humiliation by coercing Rabern into repairing his heart—handing Rabern a rare opportunity."

"What's left?" Joanna asked. "Method?" She shook her head. "I know we talked last night about Rabern being the murderer, but, well, two things bother me about the theory."

"Go ahead," Brad said, his attention trained to her observations.

For a moment she got caught up in his deep-set eyes. He seemed to pay her serious attention and managed to please himself by looking at the same time. She gave herself a mental shake for imagining his intentions.

She cleared her throat. "There must be a half a dozen ways Rabern could have sabotaged the surgery, but he had two other surgeons—very highly regarded vascular surgeons, I should add, a surgical resident and his scrub nurse—looking on. Remember? I said the same thing to Daniel Feldman. I can't imagine any way that Rabern could have botched or intentionally done anything that would result in Vine's death. Not without attracting notice."

"Nevertheless, Elliott Vine is dead," Brad said. "What's the other thing?"

"Ruth Brungart sent us to Lucy Chavez."

"She can't have approved of Rabern's liaison with Lucy. Or Vine's, either. Maybe that was her way of making sure someone knew about it so Lucy could be put on notice that her affairs with the physicians around here are unacceptable."

Joanna kicked off her pumps and began idly rubbing her foot against the other to ease the ache of the bruise on her instep. "That probably was part of her motivation in telling us. She had to know you might very well bring Lucy's affairs to the attention of the administration. But if she thought Rabern had murdered Vine on the table, she sure wouldn't have pointed us in the direction of his motive."

"Do you find it surprising that it would never occur to Ruth Brungart that Rabern would actually knock Vine off?"

"Not at all." And it wasn't her imagination that Brad's gaze was drawn now and again to her ankles. She flexed them, and stretched. He followed, then looked up.

She gave him a slow, accusing blink.

He didn't have the sense of propriety God gave a goose, or have a lick of shame, either. He blinked back at her. "I'm listening, Dish," he assured her, grinning. "I can walk and chew gum at the same time."

"Really?"

"Really. You were about to make the point that when Brungart put us on to Lucy Chavez, there was already some question in the air about how Vine died. Ergo," he wisecracked, proving his claim, letting his gaze stray wherever on her body it suited him to look, "Brungart knew Rabern could not have done the deed because even the most frivolous investigation would have revealed a compelling motive.

"Rabern, the good doctor Brungart must have reasoned," he went on, "would have known he could never get away with killing Vine, given his outrage and jealousy—a truly powerful motive. Therefore, he could not have done it. Dr. Brungart felt safe sending us to Lucy Chavez."

He sat back and gave her the exact same take-that-and-smoke-it smile that Meg Ryan turned on Billy Crystal in *When Harry Met Sally*—right after she hammed an orgasm in the middle of a deli restaurant.

Joanna burst out laughing. It was the only rational response to his outrageous delivery. He had not only made his point, he'd done it in a summation that would have made Sherlock Holmes weep.

And he'd left her feeling caressed, turned on, as if it were his hands all over her and not just his hazel-green eyes roaming her figure. "You *can* chew gum and walk at once!"

"Thank you." He acknowledged her appreciation of his exploits with a drop-dead smile.

"So what are we saying here?" she piped up, fleeing to safer—far safer—ground. "That Rabern cannot have done this?"

"I think we already knew that," he returned, relenting, letting her flee. He'd catch her again. "He had a believable motive, I suppose, but there's no way we could say that he had any real opportunity in the OR. And that doesn't even begin to address Phil's murder. Dibell would laugh us out of the county."

Joanna felt a stillness creep over her again, a kind of silence that descended each time she was reminded of Phil's death. Her grief wouldn't help Phil now. Bending in her chair, she picked up her shoes and put them back on as a means to school her thoughts. "Okay. But of everyone involved, Rabern had the best opportunity in the OR."

"Actually, Joanna, you had the best opportunity," he reminded her.

"But I didn't do it."

"Could anyone have tampered with your machine or your meds or IV fluids?"

"The machine was working perfectly," Joanna said, "even at the end. The thing is wired to alarm at the first sign of any kind of failure. As for the medications—they're just like any bottle of pills you can buy over the counter—everything is tightly sealed. I would have to be asleep to miss any tampering."

"I presume you weren't asleep."

"No. I was jazzed. This was going to be my chance to convince Rabern and all the old guard that I am every bit as capable as anyone practicing anesthesia at Rose. Or anywhere for that matter."

"Instead, you're the leading contender for fall guy." Brad got up to stretch, then came around his desk and leaned against it. "Apart from you and Rabern, then, are we saying no one had even a sliver of opportunity?"

"I can't imagine any window of opportunity," she admitted.

"Then a reasonable person would have to conclude that Vine died exactly as Brungart said he did—nothing any more sinister than a sudden cardiac death."

"Then a reasonable person would also be compelled to believe that Phil truly did die for nothing," she protested softly.

His head hung momentarily, then he looked back up at her. "Dish, this is the thing," he said softly. "I know it's attractive to believe Phil Stonehaven died for a reason. But it was a brutal murder and there isn't anything noble about it. I could make the case, as Detective Dibell certainly would, that there is no point in trying to prove that Phil was murdered because he discovered something incriminating when logically it was impossible for anyone to murder Vine in the OR."

Joanna gave a frustrated sigh. It *was* impossible to have it both ways. To know on the one hand that Phil's death wasn't just some monument to grisly timing, that it wasn't a desperate vagrant stalking the hospital corridors in search of a rich doctor to mug at the precisely wrong moment, and on the other hand, admit that no one could have killed Elliott Vine in OR 16.

Disheartened, her hands came together as if in a prayer over her lips. She searched Brad's face. She lowered her hands till her chin rested on her fingertips. "You're not making that case, are you? Not humoring me until I could accept that conclusion myself?"

"No." His eyes fixed on hers. "I'm not humoring you, Joanna. We don't know what happened. We can't prove anything. But simply because we can't fathom how Vine was killed doesn't mean it didn't happen."

Joanna gave a small nod. It seemed so farfetched, so inconceivable. But Vine's autopsy *had* set off alarms in Phil's mind. Sister Mary Bernadette was convinced that no soup kitchen vagrant had come along and murdered Phil, either. Add to that the break-in at her house... She couldn't settle for the innocuous version of either death until she could prove to herself that Phil's instincts had been wrong.

She simply didn't believe Phil Stonehaven could be so mistaken.

"I'm not giving up on this, Brad. Not unless someone as smart and trustworthy as Phil can look at the tissue slides and tell me, point-blank, that Elliott Vine's death was a simple tragic mischance. But you're the one who has to deal with Delvecchio and the rest of the administration. So if you want out—"

"I don't want out, Joanna," he chided. "I want the truth. And I want you to understand this once and for all." His eyes fixed on hers. "I am sticking my neck out, and it's not because I have your faith in Phil Stonehaven's brilliance. I don't know if Vine was murdered. Phil was. And if you're right about all this, you're next because the murderer can't afford to let you poke around until you find out what Phil knew. You'll have to forgive me if, selfishly, I'd rather you didn't die next."

Warmth flared at Joanna's throat. For the first time she believed he might truly care for her, might even love her. That she might come first in his heart, ahead of what was best for the hospital or anything or anyone else.

Her resistance to men like her father, men who could turn a phrase and twist the truth and seduce you into believing anything they wanted you to believe, was carved in granite.

Unlike men like her father, Brad was risking not only his own neck to protect her against the unknown assailant, but his reputation and his credibility—everything he stood for—because *she* wanted to believe Phil Stonehaven couldn't be wrong. That his death meant something.

She smiled. "What will you do?" she asked softly. "Delvecchio expects you to make this disaster go away, the sooner the better."

"Sister Mary Bernadette will handle Delvecchio, I have her word on that. Meanwhile, I'll be covering your back."

He intended to protect her, and he meant it, but somehow his eyes embellished his meaning.

Suddenly, ridiculously aware of him, of intentions that went far beyond the moment, Joanna blushed. Her beeper filled her awkward silence. *Little salvations,* she thought gratefully. Expecting the page to be from Beth Stonehaven, Joanna checked the LED. The number in the display belonged to Ron Mendelssohn's cellular phone.

"It's Ron. Do you mind if I call him from your phone?" Joanna asked.

"Go ahead." He shoved off the edge of his desk and went to get them some coffee.

Sitting behind the desk, she punched in the cell phone number. Mendelssohn picked up on the first ring. In the background Joanna heard the whoosh of a respirator and muted conversation. Ron had called her in the middle of some surgery.

"Ron, it's Joanna."

"Yeah. Hold on a second.... There. I'm back. Listen. George Segal gave up his regular Friday off to cover your cases, but he's coming down with the flu or some damned thing and he's begging off."

Joanna checked her watch. "Are you asking me to—"

"Yes. There's nobody else available. We're swamped. Are we going to have to start canceling, or are you up to it?"

"Of course." Irritation flared momentarily, but she knew it was unreasonable. However blunt, Ron Mendelssohn wouldn't assume she'd suddenly lost her skills or her nerve. And there was little she could do until Brad heard back from Dibell's superior officer regarding the tissue slides. "I just need to make a few calls. What time do they need me?"

"Ten o'clock, with Colin Rennslaer. He's repairing a transplant some hack sent from Nebraska."

Brad returned carrying cups of espresso. The rich scent made her mouth water. She saw that he'd added her dose of cream and accepted gratefully. "I'll be there."

"Fine. And, Joanna?"

"Yes?"

"Thanks." Mendelssohn rang off. Joanna put the receiver back into the cradle.

"Back to the mines?" Brad asked, sipping contentedly at his coffee.

"In the category of no rest for the wicked, I guess. They're apparently in a crunch upstairs."

He put his mug down on the desk beside her and stood within inches. Her pulse began to thud. His scent was a nice, intoxicating counterpoint to the espresso. His body heat began invading her and a shivery thrill raced through her. His gaze rested on her lips, then on her eyes. "Are you wicked, Dish?"

"Hardly ever," she breathed.

"Then you'll just have to work harder at deserving the reputation." He was going to kiss her.

"This isn't moving us farther along the path of shamelessness," she admonished, so close she could see the intricate patterns of green radiating out from the centers of his eyes.

"On the contrary, Dish." Leaning toward her by slow degrees, he let his eyes fall closed and then touched his espresso-warmed lips to hers.

She knew she was in some trouble, because "Dish" had begun to feel right. And because, when Colin Rennslaer waltzed into the OR only moments after Joanna began administering the anesthesia to the transplant patient brought in from Nebraska, he took one look at her, winked and grinned behind his surgical mask. "Hmm. Must be in the air. Anybody would think it was spring-time in the Windy City."

COLIN'S CASE was followed by a hernia repair and two spinal fusions, after which she thought she could leave and go see Beth. Between her second and third cases, Joanna was able to call a repairman to replace her kitchen window the following Monday, and to return Beth's call. They spoke only long enough for Joanna to learn that Phil's funeral service had been set for Sunday morning. Her plans to go see Beth and the kids and her parents never panned out.

Five o'clock on a Friday afternoon was prime time for emergencies. The typical hot appendix, the rush-hour accidents, the moms whose babies wouldn't deliver without a cesarean coupled with an ob-gyn doctor with Friday-night symphony tickets.

This afternoon was no different. Joanna pulled one of the more complicated cases—the anesthesia for a convenience store clerk wounded by a gunshot to the leg.

By the time she had cleaned up and traded in the surgical scrubs for her own clothing, it was nearly eight-thirty. Brad had called sometime in the past hour and asked the secretary to call for a cab whenever she got out of surgery. He was serious about not wanting her on her own, alone and vulnerable if Phil's assailant caught her out.

She found her ride waiting at the curbside just outside the entrance to the hospital, and climbed into the back seat for the seventeen-block trip down Lake Shore Drive to Brad's apartment.

Her day had been so ordinary, so filled with all the usual demands on her attention, that it seemed foolishly paranoid to be guarding against the possibility that Phil's murderer would try to kill her. But Peggy Vine now knew that they were, at the very least, suspicious of her father-in-law's death. Lucy Chavez knew. Brungart knew. And Phil's murderer had known, or only guessed, that he was suspicious, as well.

No, Joanna decided. Their precautions weren't foolish.

Brad had apparently instructed the building doorman to watch for her, too. Uniformed, efficient and gracious, the man opened the cab door for her, paid the driver and escorted her inside. Joanna thanked him and gave a sigh of contentment as he put her on the elevator and keyed in the penthouse floor destination.

She could definitely get used to being so well taken care of. The door to Brad's apartment stood ajar. She pushed it open into the entryway and heard the low murmur of conversation.

Stretched out in the easy chair, Brad smiled and got up when he saw her come in. Beth Stonehaven was curled up on the sofa, knees to her chest, her peasant skirt covering her legs, a glass of wine in her hand.

"Joanna." Beth sighed with relief and gave a wavery smile, but she waited where she was, transparently discreet.

Brad winked at Beth and went to properly greet Joanna. She cast her best friend a halfheartedly scathing glance, but Brad took her chin to redirect her gaze and kissed her cheek. "I'm glad you're here."

"How did you manage this?" she murmured, surprised at how intensely grateful she was for the possibility of a few hours with Beth.

He shrugged. "Beth needed to get out. You needed to be with her. I just didn't give her a choice in coming along with me."

His thoughtfulness touched her, and she had the fleeting notion that he would always be that kind of man, that he had always been, and she'd never noticed. "Thank you."

"You're welcome." He touched his index finger to his lips, then hers, and his again. "Dinner is almost on. Do you want a glass of rosé?"

"I'd love it." He went to pour her wine, and Joanna turned to Beth and took a deep breath. The scent of a rich marinara sauce tinged with garlic scented the air. "He's really quite wonderful, isn't he?"

Beth nodded and cleared her throat. "They're not common, Joanna, men like that."

"Tell me." She went to sit on the sofa with Beth. They held hands for the warmth, the connection of two women who had been through so much together. "How are you— really?"

Beth stared into her glass a moment. "Drained. Empty. Frozen in time. I don't know which really. The kids are just dazed. Lindsay is so confused. She just keeps expecting the next time the door opens it's going to be her daddy."

Feeling hopelessly inadequate to express her own emotions, either, Joanna squeezed Beth's hand. Lindsay was only three, but the sun rose and set on her father. Beth's jaw clenched in pain too deep to describe.

"Oh, Beth."

"Oh, me, is right." She sniffed. "Jo, I don't know how I'm going to live through this." Her head tilted. Her lips pursed. "I can see myself *getting* through it, I just can't see how I . . . how I'm going to live it." She took a swallow of the wine. "A day at a time, I guess. An hour at a time."

Brad returned with Joanna's wine. "We can eat anytime."

"Now would be good," Beth said, too brightly. "I didn't think I was hungry, but the marinara smells incredibly good."

Brad had set the dining room table with simple bone white china, salad, crystal water goblets, silverware—soupspoons to roll the angel-hair pasta against—and dark green tapers that flickered gently.

"Brad, this is just too nice for words," Beth said. "Was it your mother who brought you up so well?"

He grinned. "My mother would be absolutely stunned to think I had done this."

"Well, she must have done something right. Did she pick out the china?"

"No." He held out the chair for Beth. "I picked it. My mother definitely believed in a civilized dinner table."

"Amen to that," Beth murmured.

Joanna laughed. "Beth is definitely of the school that the hand that rocks the cradle rules the world."

"I am," she agreed solemnly, unfolding her linen napkin. "Motherhood is sacred."

Joanna replenished Beth's wine and Brad's, then took the chair opposite her while Brad served up the pasta and sauce from the head of the table.

Afterward, staring at the warm, waxy candles, sipping her coffee, Beth came around to explaining that she had called earlier to reach Brad about a phone call she had received late in the afternoon.

"Who was it?" Joanna asked.

"Tavish McCarter. Do you remember meeting him at our house a few years ago?"

The name stirred vague recollections in Joanna's memory. "He was at one of your barbecues.... Wasn't he Phil's mentor in the medical examiner's office?"

"Yes," Beth answered softly. "He was."

Joanna felt stricken by Beth's emphasis. There were so many ways, so many innocent remarks, to jolt her again and again with the terrible finality of Phil's death. Past-tense traps Joanna had already fallen into speaking of Phil. Traps that somehow seemed to diminish him because he was alive only in their memories now.

"Anyway," Beth continued when she had collected herself, "Tavish had just gotten off the phone with someone in the district attorney's office. They were in a real sweat over the PR director at Rose Memorial asking for the slides to be returned that Phil had been reviewing when he was killed."

"We must have really jerked somebody's chain," Brad said.

"Big time," Beth agreed, "and the request was getting bumped up the chain of command almost hourly. Some assistant DA panicked because no one could find the slides in the evidence storage bins. Phil's microscope was there, but the tissue slides were all gone."

Sipping at her coffee, Joanna put down the cup before her shaking fingers could manage to spill most of it. "Are they still missing?"

"No. Don't worry," she said, seeing Joanna's instant dread at the possibility that the slides had been lost or discarded. "As it turns out, the slides had been sent over to Tavish."

"Why?" Brad asked. "If Dibell is so convinced the murderer was a vagrant, those slides are totally irrelevant—not to mention property containing confidential patient information."

Beth nodded. "I know that—and so does Tavish. But no one knew what to do with them, and apparently Dibell asked for Tavish's impressions of the tissues—just in case her vagrant theory didn't pan out."

"Beth, that's perfect, really," Joanna said. "I would have had to take them to another pathologist, anyway. What was Tavish's opinion?"

"He's not at liberty to say, Joanna. It's all part of an ongoing police investigation, and if he talks to anyone he's 'dead meat,' in his words."

"I suppose they won't release the slides for anyone else to look at, either."

"I asked Tavish. That would also be a policy violation. He's really between a rock and a hard place with this, Joanna," she explained. "I'm sure Phil would have said exactly the same things."

Brad sat forward. "So why did he call you, Beth?"

"Because he's just sick about Phil's death. He wanted to know if I believed that knowing what was on those tissue slides would help uncover the murderer. He guessed the tissues must belong to Elliott Vine, since that's what all the media play is about."

"They must have been, Beth," Joanna said. "Phil wasn't staying that late at night going over miscellaneous cases. What did you tell Tavish?"

"That I didn't know—which was true, and it's why I needed to talk to you." She busied her hands folding the linen napkin this way and that. "I think, the way Tavish was sort of hinting around, that he could be persuaded to tell you—confidentially—what he found on the slides, *if* you could convince him that it would help you nail the lowlife that murdered Phil."

"Beth, it is that important," Joanna said, refilling her coffee from the carafe. Brad passed her the cream. "If there is evidence on those slides that Elliott Vine died of anything but cardiac failure, then it's almost a sure thing that Phil found it. He was about to put the pieces together. Someone had to stop him."

Beth appeared suddenly flustered, suddenly struck again not only with Phil's death but with the coldbloodedness of it. Uncoordinated little movements gave her away.

"Beth." Brad reached to catch her trembling hand. "If you'd rather not talk about this anymore, let's just drop it."

But Beth was tough. A little sympathy went a long ways and, as much as Joanna, she wanted Phil's life to have counted for something in his last moments. If there was any way she could help expose Phil's murderer, she would do it.

"There's not a whole lot else to say, anyway. With what you've explained to me, I think Tavish will be convinced. I'll confirm the time with him, but he told me he's always in the labs on Sunday mornings for a few hours when no one else is around. You could go there before the funeral."

"Why wait?" Joanna asked. "We could call him right now."

Beth shook her head. "He's divorced. The only time he gets to spend with his kids is the last weekend of the month, from Friday night till Sunday morning. He has to drive upstate." She glanced at her watch. "It's getting late. I'm not sure if my mother will be able to get the kids off to bed. I should go.''

"I'll take you home," Brad offered as they all got up from the table. "Just let me—"

"No. Thank you, anyway. Really. You've already been an enormous help to me. And I could use the time by myself." Tears welled up in her eyes, fogging her glasses in odd little patches. Her emotions were so bare. So fragile, Joanna thought, feeling teary-eyed herself. "Actually, I'll probably get a lot of time to myself from now on. But I'd really rather just call a cab."

"There's usually one waiting along this block," Brad said. He gathered up Beth's purse and shawl. "Let us walk you down, at least."

The ride down the elevator went too quickly, the cab was too easily hailed for the goodbyes that stuck in their throats. Beth was going home alone, and there was nothing, *nothing*, Joanna thought unhappily, that she could do to make it easier.

At the open cab door, Beth hugged Joanna fiercely. And just as fiercely whispered in her ear.

"Time is too short and too precious. Don't waste even one more night with him, Jo. For God's sake, not one more hour."

Chapter Ten

Rinsing the pot the pasta had been cooked in, Joanna felt her throat tighten with emotion again. Beth's plea kept playing in her head. Maybe it wouldn't have gotten to her so much if Beth had been able to contain her tears. Beth Stonehaven never cried.

"So tell me," she said, wiping the counter, wanting to hear his voice, wishing it was in her to follow Beth's advice with a shred of grace. "How was the rest of your day?"

"Interesting. I'll tell you about it," he said, reaching for a couple of cordial glasses. "Share a brandy with me?"

"Sure."

He opened the bottle and poured the cordials while Joanna dried her hands and hung up the tea towel. Turning out the kitchen lights, he took her by the hand through the living room and onto the terrace. Twenty-six stories up from the Lake Michigan beach, the terrace spanned the length of the penthouse. Just outside the sliding doors was a glass-top picnic table and cushioned chairs, and two lounge chairs. Wax begonias and violet plants were arranged about a small berm covered with staghorn ferns and dwarf varieties of evergreen. Brad lit a couple of outdoor candles and went to stand at the railing beside her.

There were no stars out—they were often hidden by the reflection of the city lights—but an enormous harvest moon hung in the sky. Wisps of clouds trailed across it. The cool breezes off the lake played gently with Joanna's hair. She sipped her brandy and gave a bittersweet smile. "You could almost believe all was well with the world, couldn't you?"

Standing very near to her, he drank down the brandy in a single swallow. "You're worried about Beth?"

"Yes." *Not another hour.* "But... you were going to tell me about your day."

"Yeah." He turned beside her and rested his elbows on the railing. "Let's see. The TV news guys got hold of the fact that Chip Vine had come into the ER in a straitjacket. Then Detective Dibell showed up. She's on the verge of putting Phil's murder into some kind of unsolved status."

"She's still convinced a vagrant did it? Hasn't she spoken to Sister Mary Bernadette?"

Brad nodded. "She has, but she's skeptical of Mary Bernadette's faith in the kind of person that frequents the soup kitchen. And they've rousted as many of them as they can find and come up with nothing."

"But what about the fact that Mary Bernadette made sure the door was locked?"

"The only fact Dibell is interested in is that the door was open when Phil's body was found. Other than the dirt tracked in and out, they've got no solid physical evidence."

Joanna frowned. "No fingerprints, no hairs or fabric threads?"

"Nothing on the microscope at all, according to Dibell," he said, "and no other prints that they can't rule out as belonging to pathology staff." He paused and shook his head. "Anyway, Dibell heard that your town house was broken into. Since nothing was missing or damaged other than the kitchen window, she's discounting any possibility of a connection to Phil's murder. I told her you'd come down to the station house in the morning to make your formal statement."

"But what I say doesn't really matter, does it, if Dibell is just going to shelve the whole thing?"

"No. It won't make a difference. She's got a caseload she can't handle already, and she's not going to pursue this one. As far as Dibell is concerned," he went on, explaining the detective's logic, "Phil's murderer knocked over a rich doctor, got away with a few bucks and has melted away into the crowd of ten thousand others just like him. She's just tying up loose ends so that if the case is reopened, all her ducks will appear to be in a row."

Joanna wondered why none of this surprised her, or not that so much as why the resentment she would have expected to feel never surfaced. Perhaps because even she and Brad had nothing better or more concrete to suggest. She sipped at her brandy, and watched the lights on a freighter ship twinkling as it moved farther and farther away to the interior of Lake Michigan. "We should talk to Rabern."

"He came around after lunch today—saying in no uncertain terms that he will be taking charge of the Vines and he expects my abject apologies to Chip in writing."

She smiled at his tone, but her amusement was short-lived. "Did you ask him why he agreed to do Vine's surgery? And why Peggy was in such a panic to get Chip away from the hospital?"

"Yes. He guessed immediately that Lucy Chavez had been blabbing. Said I'd been a fool to believe anything out of her mouth—and that, as far as he was concerned, he owed it to Chip and Peggy Vine to ease their grief in any way he could."

"How noble of him," Joanna said.

"Isn't it, though?" he agreed. "Then Delvecchio dropped by. Twice. Once to let me know and then to reiterate that this mess had better not escalate *one iota* more than it already has."

She could well imagine Delvecchio's frame of mind. The chief administrator was working under the added stress of Frank Clemenza's arrest and indictments in the fraud perpetrated on Bishop Rosario's estate. Clemenza had wielded enormous control and those responsibilities now weighed on Jacob Delvecchio.

Pressuring Brad despite Sister Mary Bernadette only went to point up the fact that Delvecchio believed the hospital could ill afford any more notoriety. The administrator expected that Brad would contain the damage, handling what could be handled and burying the rest from the view and attention of the public.

But already the press had hold of the fact that Chip Vine had been admitted to the ER in a straitjacket. The damage control was slipping, the repercussions haunted Delvecchio, so Delvecchio haunted Brad.

"I'm sorry. I can't imagine what it must be like."

"Don't be. It's my job. It's what I do best. And there are some gratifying moments. Stephi and Teddi Mastrangelo went home today."

"Oh, that's wonderful! But isn't it a little ahead of schedule?"

He nodded. "By a couple of days. It hasn't hit Beth yet that she missed it." He put his empty cordial glass down on the stone wall beneath the railing. "You know she took care of Stephi when Emma Harding was out of town last July."

"That's right," Joanna murmured. "She's going to be sick about missing it." But Beth would be infinitely more grateful for Zoe and Rafe's sake than selfishly disappointed. "Any other saving grace?"

"Yeah. You're here." He fell silent, watching her, his eyes fixed on her.

Dark, fearsome pleasure shivered through her. She tried to look away, but she couldn't. Equally fearsome doubts unfurled in her heart. She shouldn't waste another hour holding out against him, against the intimacy they both wanted, the kind of intimacy that might finally change and enrich her life the way Phil had forever changed Beth's life. Joanna knew that.

But knowing and acting were very different things. Maybe it was herself she mistrusted—her judgment, her ability to distinguish a man who would always honor her from one who wouldn't. The sudden insight dazed her.

How could she possibly make healthy choices when her fears were so constantly left unspoken?

"What are you doing here, MacPherson?" she blurted out before the ruthless little censor in her heart could prevent her.

His brow lifted. "As opposed to where?"

"Wherever you came from." She shrugged. The moonlight glinted off his rich brown hair. His tie was still knotted but pulled loose and the top buttons of his shirt were undone. He looked, even now, devastatingly capable of having the whole of Madison Avenue for breakfast if he chose. "Whatever you used to do."

He laughed softly. "In the vein of, what's a shark like you doing in our little pond?"

"Are you?" she asked. "A shark, I mean?"

"I used to be." He turned and rested both forearms on the railing, speaking in low, introspective tones. "I don't miss it. I thought I would, but I don't." He took a deep breath, focusing far out over the lake where the moonlight glistened off the surface in a wide, mystical swath. "Do you remember the CareAmerica scandal?"

"Of course," Joanna answered. "CareAmerica was touted to be the answer to the country's health-care crisis."

"Exactly." Brad nodded. "But most of CareAmerica's directors were naive as hell. Their early deals to accumulate health-care facilities were with the hospital variety of corporate raiders. I'd been hired to remake their image. CareAmerica was in trouble, but I made it look like the hope of the country. I was the boy genius who saved it."

Joanna had never before heard him use such a self-deprecating tone of voice. "But it did finally go under, didn't it?"

"Yes. The government regulatory investigators began an inquiry. The CareAmerica board knew they were going to come under some pretty intense scrutiny, which is when Sister Mary Bernadette came to my office."

"Mary Bernadette was on the board?" Joanna asked.

Brad nodded. "From the beginning. She believed the concept could work, and her success with charity medical care here was very highly regarded. Anyway, things had come to a head. Between us, Mary Bernadette and I came up with a plan to return ownership and control of all the hospitals CareAmerica had bought up back to the local communities. Otherwise, I'd probably be spending time in some country-club federal pen for my part in making the CareAmerica buyouts appear to be a solid investment in each community.''

"But when you came here the *Wall Street Chronicle* made you out to be a hero, the salvation of small hospitals from Chicago to New York! For Rose Memorial to entice you away from Madison Avenue was the coup of the decade.''

"Yeah." He shook his head. "I came out of it smelling like a rose. But Mary Bernadette knew the truth. If she hadn't seen it coming, or if she hadn't come to me and given me the chance to do the right thing, I'd have gone to jail. It's that simple.''

"So you came to Rose Memorial because you owed Sister Mary Bernadette?" Joanna said.

He turned toward her. "More out of respect for her. Out of knowing I'd done some decent work for a good cause, restoring those hospitals to their communities." He gave her an odd look. "You're right, Dish. I was the hero. I could have stayed in New York. I could have married another shark, had some baby sharks and never known what I was missing. Or I could come here and make a real difference in the lives of real people.''

She smiled at his imitation of Mary Bernadette's Irish brogue rolling those *r*'s for all they were worth. "She has a way about her, doesn't she?"

He tilted his head. "That she does.''

Joanna took a breath and expelled it. "Were you very close to marrying another shark?''

"Yes. But even then I knew she would never interrupt her string of feeding frenzies long enough to hatch baby sharks.''

Joanna swallowed hard. "Did you love her?''

"I thought I did." He fixed his eyes on hers. "I was wrong." Without preamble or warning he lifted her chin and pressed his lips to her mouth. "I was wrong," he murmured against her lips.

She felt inexplicably close to tears. His lips were warm and full and her cheeks and jaws ached with desire in the sizzle after the lightning-bolt sensation of his lips touching hers. He brushed small kisses over her lips, her cheeks, her brow, and she forgot to breathe and never noticed that her eyelashes were wet with tears.

"Joanna. Look at me." She dragged her gaze from his lips. "What's wrong?"

Swallowing, her cheeks still aching, she shook her head and blotted the tears from her lashes. She looked down and gulped her brandy, and though it wasn't enough to intoxicate a humming bird, she felt emotional and hot and tipsy and turned-on. "Nothing. Nothing...only how much of our time together I've wasted."

His gaze touched every part of her face and neck. He couldn't fail to see the pounding of her heart near her throat.

He cleared his throat. His voice was low, almost a whisper. "It will be a waste, Joanna, if you make this decision based on Beth's loss." He looked away, toward the moon rising higher into the sky. She would have sworn he knew exactly what Beth had said to her.

She could hide behind that. Take refuge in Beth's plea. But all she had ever wanted from him was the truth of his feelings for her, and she couldn't deceive him about hers. "This isn't about Beth. I'm very sad for her. It breaks my heart for her sake that Phil is lost to her forever. But this is about me. About us. I want it to happen. I want...to make love with you."

Between one breathless phrase and the next his blood heated and pooled in his groin. The speed of his reaction, the magnitude of his need, staggered him. His tongue locked in the pit of his mouth, he took a jagged breath. "Are you sure, Dish?"

She met his gaze. His eyes hid nothing from her, not the intensity of his physical reaction or the naked pain of it or the desire. "I'm sure."

He took the cordial glass from her shaking fingers and dipped his thumb into the dregs of the liqueur. Her attention fixed in fascination on his thumb.

He put down her glass and brought his hand to the nape of her neck. She shivered. His thumb touched the dregs of sweet, warm brandy to the base of her jaw . . . to the pulse point at her throat . . . to the tender hollow above her collarbone. His hand closed tight around one edge of the open placket of her blouse.

The breath was already gone from her when he pulled her closer still and met her look and then tilted his head and took the first taste of brandy from her heated skin. "Tell me again," he commanded.

"I want to make love with you." His beard stubble scraped her skin; his tongue laved the drying brandy. The clashing sensations of small stabs and the soothing, wet, erotic strokes at her collarbone undid her.

His hand threaded into her hair. He cupped her nape and took her mouth and made love to her lips. His tongue touched hers. Fire leapt in her belly and she kissed him back, nipping at his lips, opening hers, begging to be parted.

"Dish . . ." He let go an uneven breath and rested his forehead on her shoulder, then turned her in his arms and splayed his hand low against her so that her bottom was pulled tight against him and she could feel what she'd already done to him.

Exhaling sharply, harsh with pleasure, he spoke into her ear. "Feel that, Joanna." With his other arm he encircled her shoulders so that his forearm first grazed and then rested above her breasts. "Feel me against you and remember this. It's flesh and blood and instinctual, but strong as it is, I swear to you, it doesn't compare to what's happening in my soul."

She lay her head back on his shoulder, breathless by his admission, touched at the core of her being, scorched inside, in her soul where she needed most to be persuaded that what he felt for her was true and forthright and wholehearted, holding nothing back.

"Believe me," he urged her. He let his arm descend onto her breasts, and he caressed them, brushing over her nipples back and forth, time and time again with his forearm while with the palm of his other hand he rubbed in small circles on her belly, descending with each circle until, through her skirt, his fingers curled into her and he touched her most sensitive flesh. "Believe in me."

Dimly she heard his voice. Pleasure more intense than anything she had ever felt in her life swamped her, as much for his words as his bold touch. She cried out and took hold of his arm and drew it aside until his hand could cup her breast. His breath came in hot bursts at her nape. "Do you believe me, Joanna?"

"Yes ... Brad ... yes."

He groaned with pleasure and pain. Through her clothing his fingers closed on her breast and, below, into her, and he stroked her, drawing her irrevocably toward arousal as great as his.

She lost all track of thought, all notion of time. The night breezes grew cooler, the harvest moon brighter, the pitch of her senses higher, the sound of water lapping against the shore more compelling.

Her head lolled back against his shoulder and he whispered urgently in her ear even as he created wave after wave of pleasure. When she cried out he wrapped his arms around her and held her tighter, and he was holding her still when she began to come down a bit from the mind-numbing pleasure.

His flesh still pressed rigidly against her lower spine, and there was never a moment—no matter how mindless, how pleasured, how unaware of anything else—that she wasn't aware of his words, his promise.... *I swear to you, it doesn't compare to what's happening in my soul.*

She turned in his arms and lay her head on his chest. The thunder of his heartbeat pounded in her, then echoed in her. She backed up, and he let her go because she met his fevered eyes and asked him to undo his shirt for her.

She watched him pull the tails of his shirt from his slacks. His movements were slow, deliberate, torturously so. He stripped the knot from his tie and the ends hung loosely to his waist. Joanna shivered. He began at the second button—he'd long ago undone the first. She forgot—again—to breathe.

She knew what his chest looked like—how broad, how muscled, how the dark hair whorled—but in the moonlight, revealed by inches, her anticipation simply soared.

At last his shirt hung loosely open, and his tie lay against his chest. The visual images left her gaping, longing, her throat pulsing. In some way she didn't question, the image meant far more to her, excited her more deeply than the visual impact of a man's primal, naked breast overlaid with the trappings of civilization. He had bared himself for her, laid himself open, revealed himself as much as in his promise, and she could believe that he had nothing to hide from her, nothing to conceal.

She dragged in a ragged, haunted breath and turned away, bent her head, exposing her nape, and began to unbutton her blouse.

His breath caught in his throat. He stood back, watching her, his heart hammering now. When she had undone all the buttons on her blouse, she looked back at him, a siren call he suspected she had only this moment discovered in herself.

His mouth went desert dry, his groin tight as sunblistered skin. He couldn't breath. She knew it and smiled and dropped her gaze with the innocence of a girl and the grace of a courtesan.

She eased her blouse off one shoulder, then the other, and lowered her arms, letting the silk fall around her waist, baring her back but for the soft white, unadorned cotton camisole. The simplicity of the garment nearly drove him to his knees.

"Dish..." The sight of her back slammed his thready equilibrium to the wall. The long, sexy, womanly curves of her back, the deeply feminine flare of her hips, the sweet guile of her seduction.

She took the bottom edges of the camisole and drew it over her head, and turned, bare breasted in the generous moonlight, returning his gesture of trust.

He would remember it all, because when she drew him to the double chaise longue with her, she opened more than her body to him. She opened places in her heart that had been sealed shut with a deeply skeptical wariness a very long time ago.

But mostly he would remember because Joanna demanded far more of him and his vaunted integrity than he had ever been tempted to give.

Lying naked in the moonlight, intimately entwined with Joanna, sated for the first time in months, he knew her mistrust of him was waning. But he knew it wouldn't be that easy. She would need the space to catch up with her own feelings, to be certain that her trust wasn't misplaced. She was not a one-night-stand woman, or a weekender or an affair to remember. She just didn't know it yet.

All she needed was time. And to uncover a murderer. And maybe, homemade peanut butter cookies.

Chapter Eleven

On Saturday morning Brad drove her to the police station to give her statement. Detective Dibell wasn't even there, but another detective, a worse-for-the-wear, pot-bellied former jock, a man with a florid complexion and sour breath named Sanger, introduced himself to Joanna and escorted her to an interrogation room.

Sanger sat down and motioned her into the chair across from him. He flipped open a notebook and switched on the recorder, then established the date and time, his identity and Joanna's. "You understand," he said, "that this interview is for purpose of making your statement of the events in question on the night of Dr. Stonehaven's murder."

"Yes."

He proceeded to ask her the questions Dibell had asked when Joanna had arrived at the pathology offices. When she'd last seen Phil, what time he called, had he seemed threatened? Anxious? Tired? Aware that the door leading to the soup kitchen complex was open?

She realized how little she really knew of what was going on around Phil only moments before his murder. "I can't say whether or not Phil knew that door was open. He was extremely focused. He'd seen something on a slide or several slides that troubled him. If a bomb had gone off near him, I don't think he would have noticed.''

"And what was the purpose of his call to you?"

"He wanted me to know that he thought Dr. Brungart's findings might have been incomplete. Phil—"

"Dr. Stonehaven, you mean?"

"Yes," Joanna said impatiently, "Dr. Stonehaven was tired and irritable, but working on evidence of generalized circulatory collapse of the kind we might expect to see in a massive blood infection."

"But overall, you would say that Dr. Stonehaven was tired, irritable and not paying attention to his surroundings."

Joanna sat back, taking Sanger's measure. It was fruitless to try to make the point that Phil's activities had threatened anyone. Brad had been right. Nothing she said would make a difference if the detectives were determined to make the vagrant case stick.

The only thing she knew for certain was that Phil had been convinced something was amiss in Brungart's sudden-cardiac-death finding and that he had intended to stay until he found the answer, but Sanger was no more interested in that than Dibell had been.

"Anything else at all you remember, Dr. Cavendish? Any unusual noises?" Sanger asked. "Any sound of potential intruders?"

Joanna took a deep breath and forced herself to think about Sanger's slanted question. If the only thing she could do now was to make it clear in her statement that she disagreed with the detectives' conclusions, then that was what she would do.

She focused a moment on her memory of her conversation with Phil. "Yes, I remembered hearing Phil clattering away at his computer keys. We were talking, but he was bringing up something on his computer. He might have been checking on lab results—in fact, that must have been it."

Phil had commented on Vine's white cell count being far too low to indicate an overwhelming blood infection. "I remember, then, that his chair squeaked in the background," she went on. "At the time I thought he'd sat up straight. The squeak is kind of distinctive. Then he said something like, "what the devil," told me he'd see me in the morning and . . . he hung up."

"So it was your conclusion at the time," Sanger said, "that 'what the devil' had to do with whatever he saw in the computer, and not an intruder?"

Joanna stiffened with the sudden perception Sanger's question provoked in her. Phil had been tapping away at the computer keyboard all the while he was speaking to her, and something must have come up on his monitor that snagged his attention and made him cut short their conversation. "I didn't think anything about it at the time . . . but, no. I didn't have the impression at all that anyone had intruded into his office."

"So it is possible that Dr. Stonehaven was distracted by some piece of information he found in the computer?"

"Yes . . ." But what could it have been?

"And being so distracted," Sanger pressed on, "it's plausible that he never heard his assailant coming?"

"Yes."

Sanger nodded and checked his notes, then his watch. "Anything else, Doctor?" She wanted desperately to know what Phil had seen in the computer, but the information would be superfluous as far as Sanger was concerned. She shook her head. "That will be all, then, I guess. Thanks for your time, Doctor."

He stood and escorted her from the interrogation room to the waiting area. Brad shook hands and introduced himself. Sanger smirked. "No need for introductions, Mr. MacPherson. Your mug's been on the TV news every time I manage to tune in."

Brad gave a long-suffering grin. "I take it you haven't identified any suspects in the murder of Dr. Stonehaven?"

Sanger shook his head wearily. "Not so far. But we'll let you know."

The desk sergeant bellowed, "Sanger! Line seven," and the detective stalked off, muttering to himself.

Walking outside into the unseasonably brisk morning air, Joanna told Brad about the question Sanger had asked, and why it seemed suddenly so relevant. "Do you think there's any way the information systems people can trace Phil's movements through the computer files that night?"

"Three days later? I don't know." He pulled his keys from his suit coat pocket to unlock Joanna's door on the Bronco, but as she climbed in he snapped his fingers. "Remember what Chip said? Dibell had asked him what he thought Phil could tell him about his father's autopsy report."

"Yes." Joanna sank into her seat. "He said he'd been hanging around the central computer room. He knew Phil had logged onto the computer and brought up Brungart's report. He wanted to ask Phil what he found."

"Exactly." Brad closed her door and went around to the driver's side. Joanna unlocked his door with her control switch. "Think about this, Dish," he went on, buckling his seat belt. "We know Chip was waiting around. He admitted that much. By that time, he already knew Phil had been asked to review the autopsy findings." Brad switched on the Bronco engine and pulled out into the Saturday-morning traffic. "Suppose Chip was sitting around the computer rooms," he continued, "just waiting for Phil to log on."

"Could he really get away with that?"

"Why not? Information Systems is his department. If somebody walked in on him, all he'd have to say was that he wanted to catch up on his work. Or that he needed to take his mind off his dad's death."

"Okay. I can go along with that. He could set things up so that the moment anyone logged onto his dad's chart, he'd know about it. But he explained that. He admitted that he wanted to know what Phil had come up with—and that's when he went looking for him."

"I know that's what Chip claimed." Frowning in concentration, Brad checked his rearview mirror and switched lanes. "But he also said Phil wasn't there when he arrived. Where did Phil go? To stretch his legs?"

"No," Joanna mused. "It's a security risk to leave the computer with your user code still in. I don't think Phil would have done that."

Brad shook his head. "I don't think so, either. He was on the phone with you. You were aware that he was into the computer files. Chip knew it at the same time. Phil was so caught up in whatever he saw that he practically hung up on you. He wasn't going anywhere."

"So Chip had to have been lying.... Could he have known anything more than that Phil was logged onto Brungart's report?"

"You bet he could," Brad answered, stopping for the traffic light. "Every end user can be monitored from the central information systems complex. Chip would know how to do that. It's even possible to monitor keystrokes—they have to be able to do that to troubleshoot when the computer is down.''

''So every screen Phil pulled up, Chip would have seen at the same time?''

''Yes.''

Joanna sat twisting a strand of her hair, trying to come up with some reason that it would have been useful to Chip to follow the course of Phil's meandering through Elliott Vine's computer file. Chip may have had the expertise to follow along, but he had none of the medical knowledge it would take to make sense of what Phil was seeing.

''The problem,'' she said at last, ''is we're making the huge assumption here that Chip did sit there in the computer room following Phil's progress instead of going to see him personally. It's just as likely Chip was just sitting there at his desk, staring at the computer, wondering how the surgery could have come off so badly, and when Phil signed on, it occurred to Chip then to go ask Phil if he'd come up with anything.''

Brad grimaced. ''That may be true, Dish. But either way, if something caught Phil's attention, Chip knew about it.''

Only three blocks from his building, Brad pulled a U-turn and backtracked to the hospital. It was a long shot that there would be anyone on duty in the hospital computer complex on a Saturday morning who could help them and be discreet about it, but they agreed it was worth their time to find out.

They got what seemed like their first break. Lauren Bristol, Chip's boss and the head of hospital information systems, was at her desk, buried in daunting stacks of printouts. Her office reeked of cigarette smoke, and fast-food wrappers littered every space not already taken up with the reams of tractor-feed paper. But Lauren herself, a sickly thin woman with a grayish complexion, in her mid-forties, was up for an interruption of any kind.

"Brad, hello. None the worse for time in the trenches, it would appear. Dr. Cavendish, have a seat. What can I do for you?"

"Hi, Lauren," Brad returned, sitting next to Joanna in the wooden, tweed-covered chairs across from Lauren. "We're really happy to find you here. We could use some help. Two things."

"Name it," she said, pulling yet another cigarette from a near-empty pack.

"On the evening after Dr. Vine died in surgery, Chip says he was here. That he couldn't go home while the verdict was still out on what had caused his dad's death. Were you here that night?"

"No." Lauren lit her cigarette, took a quick drag and expelled the smoke. "That was what? Last Wednesday night?" Joanna confirmed the day, and Lauren nodded. "I thought so. I play duplicate bridge on Wednesday nights. I would have been out of here by no later than four o'clock that afternoon. But I can check the work schedule and see who was on duty that night, if that would help."

"It might," Brad agreed. Lauren stabbed at the intercom key on her telephone and asked her secretary to find the work schedules and bring them in.

"Is it possible to tell when was the last time Chip was logged on to the computer?" Joanna asked.

Lauren frowned. "Yes. But I'm not sure it's strictly ethical to discuss. Can you tell me what you're looking for?"

Brad deferred to Joanna. She took a deep breath and plunged in. "Chip indicated to the police investigating Dr.

Stonehaven's murder that he'd been sitting around in here, and he noticed that Dr. Stonehaven had logged on to Dr. Brungart's autopsy report in the computer."

Lauren's lips tightened. "If he was, he was breaching ethical behavior himself." She dragged on her cigarette. "Chip has special clearance, of course, because he has to be able to troubleshoot problems anywhere in the system, but he knows better than to access a patient file—especially his own father's." She tapped ashes into an already overflowing ashtray. "I'm not naive. I know it's done all the time, but I don't like it. Anyway, I'm not certain I understand your question."

"The question," Brad said, sitting forward, "is whether or not Chip only noticed that Dr. Stonehaven had logged on to the autopsy report, or whether he was sitting here waiting for it."

"Does it make a difference?"

Brad nodded. "We think it does, Lauren. If he was innocently sitting around in a daze, that's one thing. But if he was waiting for someone to come on-line in his father's file, that seems a little more premeditated."

Lauren nodded, quick to see Brad's point. Joanna knew nothing irritated her more than illicit use of files. She had implemented many ways over the course of time to stop the wrong people accessing sensitive information, but nothing was truly fail-safe.

"The truth is," she muttered, "waiting for someone to come on-line in a particular file would be the moral equivalent of an ambush—but I'm afraid there's no way I can tell now whether it was innocent or not. Let me see what I can pull up."

She pulled the keyboard drawer from beneath the top of her desk and stared at the console while her fingers flew through their tasks. In a moment she was able to bring up a log of the past five times Chip Vine had logged on to the computer. When she was satisfied, she turned the screen so that Joanna and Brad could see it.

"There you go. The last time Chip was into the computer was last Wednesday night. He logged on at 7:57. Does that help?"

Joanna gave a sharp sigh. "No. It doesn't jive with what Chip told the police detective at all. It was very late, almost ten-thirty by the time Dr. Stonehaven accessed Dr. Brungart's autopsy report."

"You're certain of that?" she asked.

"Check it out," Brad suggested.

She turned her monitor back. It took her less than a minute to locate Phil's access code and determine that he had not been on the computer at all between three in the afternoon and 10:32 the night he died.

"The only possibility remaining is that when he noticed Dr. Stonehaven accessing that report, Chip wasn't using his own code."

"Is that possible?"

"It's possible," Lauren glowered. "Again, it would be a serious infraction of the rules, but he could have used one of the HIS departmental codes. It may take me a few days to check that out."

"Lauren," Joanna said, more confused than ever, "what do you make of all this?"

She heaved a raspy breath and reached for another cigarette, but only held it between her fingers. "It may all be entirely innocent. Chip might have been doing legitimate work under another code—I doubt it, considering that his father had died in the OR only hours before, and considering how erratic his work has been in the past several days. I'm willing to cut him some slack for the family pressure, but if he was trying to cover his tracks, if he *was*

spying on whatever Dr. Stonehaven was doing, he suc-
ceeded. And frankly, I'm unamused even at the possibility—not to mention the fact that Chip was brought into
the ER under restraints."

Joanna sympathized. Everything about Chip Vine's
behavior seemed suspect to her. Apparently, his boss had
found the quality of Chip's work substandard for days.
"Lauren, is there any way to know what were the last
screens Phil Stonehaven saw?"

"No. The best I can do for you is to give you a print-
out of everything in Elliott Vine's file. Will that help?"

"If it's all we've got, it'll have to do," Brad answered.
"Do you mind if we talk to Chip about all of this?"

"Good luck," Lauren replied darkly. "I haven't been
able to reach him at home at all."

They went away with two complete copies of the chart
generated for Elliott Vine from the moment he admitted
himself until the moment the files were transferred to ar-
chival records.

But Joanna suspected it would be like looking for the
proverbial needle in a haystack to discover what had
caught Phil's attention, and whether it was anything
meaningful at all to Chip Vine.

ON THE WAY HOME from the hospital, Joanna thumbed
silently through the pages of Elliott Vine's chart. Con-
centrating on the details, looking for something, anything, that might have caught Phil's attention, she was
surprised to look up and find that Brad had pulled to a
halt in a supermarket parking space.

"What are we doing here?"

"The cupboards are bare at my place, Dish. Not to
mention the refrigerator. Besides." He grinned. "I
thought it wouldn't hurt my campaign toward your com-

plete surrender to ply you with homemade peanut butter cookies and milk."

"Now you've gone and done it," she replied, feeling warm with pleasure, summarily dumping the chart copies on the floor of the Bronco and opening her door. "I won't be able to function properly now until I've had my fix."

She got out and met him at the back of the vehicle. Walking together toward the busy supermarket entrance, he put an arm over her shoulders and let his fingers come quite purposefully into contact with the top of her breast.

"Actually, I was hoping you would give up proper functioning altogether." His voice hit the lower, seductive registers. "Think of it. A whole afternoon devoted to nothing more than passionately shameless behavior."

Joanna smiled up at him. She could think of nothing more desirable than to kiss peanut butter cookie dough from his lips, or... wherever. A part of her wanted to get back to Vine's chart. The greater, less sensible part wanted to while the afternoon away. She pulled a grocery cart from the back of the line. "How fast do you think we can collect the goods and get out of here?"

"Not fast enough to suit me," he answered. She thought by the look in his eyes that she was already half-undressed.

She laughed at him, flirting madly. "Hold that thought."

"The one in which you're naked first or the one where I'm naked first or the one—"

"Brad!" she gasped, silencing him with her fingers. That would teach her to taunt him. "We're in the middle of a grocery store."

"We better hurry, then, huh?"

They beat what they considered to be land-speed record in a crowded grocery, but then they only took time to stock up on the cookie essentials, milk and a steak to throw on the grill should the need of protein sneak up on them.

They made it so far as the door of the master bedroom before she was truly half-undressed, and onto the bed before her skirt and panties came off.

THE COOKIES didn't get made that afternoon. They came in a distant third to the more urgent lovemaking, followed by the steak to allay their suddenly ravenous appetites. But distant third though they were, Brad's cookies got made, the first batch coming out of the oven at nearly eleven o'clock. Joanna sank down into the cushions on the sofa in the living room with a handful of soft, warm cookies and a glass of milk.

Thirty-seven blocks away, two skid-row bums known to frequent Sister Mary Bernadette Reilly's soup kitchen got into a knock-down-and-drag-out over an eighteen-karat-gold Seiko watch and a fistful of credit cards belonging to Philip Dean Stonehaven.

One of them sank down onto the stone-cold pavement suffering a massive hemorrhage in his booze-soaked brain. The other one, known on the streets of Chicago as Lead-brick Jimmy, wound up in the squad car of a couple of particularly alert beat cops.

Brad and Joanna got the call from Detective Dibell at two-thirty in the morning. By then, at least, the cookies were just a pleasant memory, another milestone passed in MacPherson's campaign on Joanna's affections.

Joanna stayed on the telephone extension in Brad's bedroom. He threw on his white terry robe and listened in from the phone in the kitchen.

Lead-brick Jimmy, it seemed, had only been trying to take the stuff belonging to Phil off the other vagrant, an old guy so down and out he didn't even have a street moniker. Jimmy was going down for the murder, so it would have been in his best interests to spill his guts, to tell the detectives whatever he knew of the assault on Dr. Stonehaven. According to Dibell, Jimmy was smart enough to understand that things would go a whole lot easier on him if he could help them find the scum that had knocked off a doctor. Smart as he was to grasp that, Jimmy was also smart enough to produce a convincing story to the effect that the no-name guy was the one who'd knocked over the doc and taken his valuables.

Lead-brick Jimmy, Detective Dibell concluded, was probably lying. The no-name corpse didn't look strong enough to pick up Phil Stonehaven's microscope, let alone raise it high enough to crash down on the doctor's head hard enough to kill him. On the other hand, No-name could well have been wily enough to rip off the real murderer.

In any case, the fact that the doctor's possessions had turned up in the hands of street people who had on occasion had a decent meal in Sister Mary Bernadette's soup kitchen was enough for the police to put paid to the murder of Phil Stonehaven.

When Brad came back to bed, Joanna lay silently in his arms, unable to fall back to sleep. It would take more than Dibell's conjecture to convince her. Maybe it was stubborn, maybe blind, of her. But Phil's murder had been too much a coincidence itself. His possessions suddenly, conveniently, turning up in the hands of a dead soup kitchen vagrant would not sway her.

There was still the possibility that Phil might have been being overly protective of her, searching for a reason to exonerate her in Vine's death before Rabern could make hash of her career. But she wouldn't be convinced by anything less than Tavish McCarter telling her Ruth Brungart's autopsy findings were in perfect order.

That Phil was wrong.

Then, maybe, she would have to believe that a vagrant had wandered in and murdered Phil. But only then.

THE OFFICE of Dr. Tavish McCarter was at the end of a hallway crowded with carts, enormous jugs of preservatives and chemical solutions used in the pathology department and old metal filing cabinets specially designed to hold microscope slides. The effect was a sort of maze, except that a window at the end of the west-facing hall let in a lot of sunshine. McCarter popped his head out the door when he heard them coming.

"Joanna Cavendish? Dr. Cavendish?" he asked. He was a short man, slight build, balding, with gold-rimmed glasses that gave the impression of clinging desperately to his nose.

"Yes," Joanna answered, offering her hand. "I'm Joanna Cavendish. I want to thank you for agreeing to see us."

McCarter eyed Brad. "Who's this?"

"Brad MacPherson, director of public relations at Rose, Dr. McCarter," Brad said easily. "I hope you don't mind my tagging along. I know talking with us is ticklish for you—we also have a delicate situation on our hands, and it helps to hear the necessary information first-hand."

"Well, I'm not sure the information I have is anything relevant to your PR problems, but let's talk," he said, shrugging off his irritation. He led them into his office. The corners were piled high with pathology journals and there was only one chair—McCarter's. He cleared a bench. "So. Beth told me you all believe the slides collected at the crime scene have a special relevance to Phil's murder."

"We do," Joanna said, nodding. "Any slides, especially, that were labeled with Elliott Vine's pathology accession number."

McCarter shook his head, as if only now remembering that there were two victims involved, and he'd known them both. "Damn shame." He went off on a tangent for a minute about the pit of slime all mankind was sinking to, then sheepishly stopped himself. "Sorry. Occupational hazard of a forensic pathologist. Okay. Well," he went on, focused now. "It's interesting that you should mention the labels. There were a dozen or so miscellaneous slides collected, but only two that were intact and labeled with Vine's accession number—plus one more that was still on the microscope stage when the technicians collected the evidence. I say miscellaneous because, although I was able to reconstruct a few of them, most of the slides were broken. It almost looks as if the slides were tossed on the floor and stepped on."

"Could that have happened in the struggle?" Brad asked.

"What struggle?" McCarter returned, hands upturned. "Phil was bashed over the head—he undoubtedly went down hard and fast. My point is that the identifying labels were broken off and, in my admittedly jaundiced point of view, that was most likely intentional."

Joanna frowned. "I'm not sure I'm following you."

"Look," he said impatiently. "It's all really very simple. The slides tell a story. 'There's cancer, here,' they say. Or, 'Here we have a case of blocked arteries,' or 'This poor slob has a fulminating bacterial infection,' or gangrene or what have you. The slides tell the story all by themselves.''

"So if somebody murdered Phil to shut him up about what he saw on those slides, then it would only have made sense to destroy the slides, as well," Brad concluded.

"Precisely," McCarter said. "You see, the chain of evidence rules are very specific—without the labels, no one can say beyond a shadow of doubt that those tissues were, in fact, Elliott Vine's."

"Could you say for a fact that the slides were broken on purpose?" Brad asked.

McCarter gave a barking laugh. "The DA would make hash of such an observation." He paused. "However, I was under the impression that you were interested in my gut reactions to all this."

Joanna exchanged glances with Brad. "We are, Dr. McCarter. But this is a very important detail, because if the person who murdered Phil was just a vagrant, the slides would be meaningless."

"That's my thought." McCarter batted at a fly buzzing through the small office. "Only someone worried about what Phil was seeing on the slides would take the time to destroy them." He shook his head. "There's only one problem with a jaundiced viewpoint. You begin seeing everything in more sinister light than is strictly warranted."

Brad nodded, already tuned in to what McCarter was thinking. "If the murderer knew what was on those slides, it would be foolhardy to leave them lying around. Why take the chance that someone else would have an opportunity to look at them?"

"Just so." McCarter picked up a pathology journal and fanned it at the buzzing insect. "Personally, if I'd done this thing, I would have taken those slides and thrown them in the river.''

"So you couldn't say with one hundred percent assurance that the slides weren't just accidentally broken,'' Joanna said, frustrated by yet another factor in favor of Detective Dibell's vagrant theory. "Dr.McCarter, the timing of Phil's death seems terribly suspicious to me. I spoke with him around the time he was killed. I can't help believing that the slides from Elliott Vine's autopsy tipped Phil off. That he knew Dr. Vine hadn't died of a sudden cardiac death. So—''

"He didn't,'' McCarter said flatly. He looked at Brad. "And, yes, before you ask, I would swear to that under oath. Elliott Vine died of a systemic anaphylaxis.''

Shocked beyond speech, Joanna leaned back and drew a stunted breath.

"What's that?'' Brad asked.

"Anaphylaxis? An overwhelming allergic reaction,'' McCarter explained.

"Of course!'' Joanna murmured, her thoughts racing.

McCarter blinked owlishly behind his glasses. "You knew this already? It is a very obscure finding.''

"Not specifically,'' she answered. "But Phil told me that the slides were suggestive of a circulatory collapse and not a sudden cardiac death. Wouldn't anaphylactic shock explain that?''

"In many regards, yes. But a sudden-cardiac-death finding is also consistent with circulatory collapse. Phil must have been on the verge of the correct diagnosis.''

"Wait a minute,'' Brad said. "Let me get this straight. If a sudden-cardiac-death finding is consistent, how can you say with such certainty that Vine died of an allergic reaction?''

McCarter took a quick breath and expelled it. "I'm sorry. I'm not often in the position of explaining things in laymen's terms. Let me see if I can simplify this. Say you catch cold. Your symptoms—the sore throat, runny nose, cough, achiness, sneezing—all the signs of the cold would be the same whether a virus had caused it, or a bacteria. They're not the same at all, but the way you feel is no different. The same thing is true of a circulatory collapse. The death looks the same no matter what caused it."

"Okay," Brad said, "but how do you know, when Phil didn't—or Brungart for that matter—that in Elliott Vine's case the cause of death was an allergic reaction?"

McCarter rolled his eyes and threw an arm over the back of his chair to reach for the pipe lying on his ashtray. Digging for his pocketknife, he began to scrape the bowl clean of the carbon buildup. "Let me put it this way. A whopping big allergic response such as the one suffered by Elliott Vine leaves clues behind. I'm a pathologist. It's my job to pick up on those clues. I imagine Ruth Brungart was predisposed to a sudden-cardiac-failure finding. Phil Stonehaven was also a fine pathologist, trained right here in this office, but I'm not surprised that even he had only a vague sense of something being wrong. The clues are extraordinarily subtle. But you may take this and run with it. Elliott Vine died of an overwhelming allergic reaction. I've only seen a few such cases in my career."

"What caused the allergic reaction in those cases?" Brad asked.

"One was a case in the tropics. I did a stint in the jungles in Southeast Asia for the World Health Organization. Something exotic caused it—we were never able to pin it down. The other was a drug reaction. A woman took antibiotics a friend had given her. Nowadays, there are a lot of antibiotics that use penicillin derivatives, for instance, but the common person wouldn't know that unless he or she happened to walk around with a pharmacy reference book."

"Wasn't Vine allergic to penicillin?" Brad asked Joanna.

"Yes. But he didn't receive any antibiotics during surgery. They're only given postoperatively to ward off possible infections."

But the thought was of no comfort at all, Joanna realized with a sickening jolt, because whatever had caused Elliott Vine's fatal allergic reaction in the OR had to have been administered then and there. And she was responsible for everything entering his body. "Dr. McCarter, do you know of anything that might have been given during surgery that would have caused Dr. Vine's death?"

"You're the anesthesiologist, Dr. Cavendish," he said, poking fresh tobacco into his pipe. "You tell me."

Chapter Twelve

Joanna shoved through the outside doors of the medical examiner's building, fighting the sensation of having been trapped, of having stumbled into a web she didn't understand and could never escape.

Elliott Vine was dead of something she had administered in the OR.

The thought dismantled her. Her heart beat erratically and her throat felt swollen shut. Her head pounded. She couldn't have made such a mistake. It was impossible.

Brad kept pace with her, saying nothing for half a block. "Joanna, wait." His harsh command stopped her dead in her path along the sidewalk and she stared in confusion at his hand on her arm. He was looking at her as if she'd lost her mind. Maybe she had, if she could make such a mistake.

His jaw tight with tension, he steered her across the street to his Bronco and planted her in the passenger seat. "Buckle up." Numbly, she complied. With less than an hour till Phil's funeral service in the Sacred Heart sanctuary at the hospital, Brad pulled over next to a pocket-size park and walked her to an empty bench. A flock of pigeons took refuge across the pond.

He sat sideways beside her. "Okay, Joanna. Talk to me."

She shook her head. "I don't know where to start, Brad. McCarter was fairly clear. Whatever killed Elliott Vine had to have been administered in the OR, which makes it my responsibility. What if Rabern has been right all this time and I was just too cocksure to see it?"

"Joanna, get a grip," he snapped. "You went over your medication supplies a dozen times. You checked and double-checked your blood supply. Vine didn't even begin to go into shock until you'd already begun reversing the anesthesia. So tell me. Where in this picture was it possible that you administered something that was going to kill Elliott Vine?"

She had no answer, but his reproach had the desired effect of quieting her mind long enough to begin thinking clearly. She had overreacted to McCarter's question, but the stunning revelation that Phil had been so close to seeing that Vine's death was due directly to anaphylactic shock meant that something entering his body had caused the massive collapse of his blood circulation.

But just as they had been unable to imagine any way in which Rabern could have caused Vine's death, it was inconceivable that she had done so, either. If she had, it had to have been the unwitting result of some kind of intentional sabotage.

"I'm sorry." She scraped her hand through her hair and held it combed back in her fingers, her arm resting on the back of the park bench. "I shouldn't have come so unhinged."

"But the shock of learning what really happened just sent you right over the edge?" He took her hand gently from her hair and laced his fingers through hers, bringing their palms together. A breeze sent the red and gold leaves skittering at their feet. A boomeranging paper airplane sailed perilously close.

Joanna ducked in the nick of time. The child in charge of it laughed delightedly, and the only thing left for Joanna to do was let go of her own paralyzing tension and laugh with the little girl.

Brad grinned. "At least your reflexes are intact. There's that small comfort in the midst of what appears to be an imminent mental shutdown."

"C'mon," she coaxed, fussing with the knot in his tie. "It's not really as bad as all that."

"It's worse," he assured her solemnly, his hazel-green eyes roaming her face. "But I'm consoling myself with the evidence that your spells of irrational behavior must mean you're falling crazy in love with me."

He took her breath away, took her fears and made them insubstantial as smoke and mirrors. His thumb stroked her palm and she was lost. "That must be it." She gave a shaky sigh and shivered, though the late-morning sun was hot on her shoulders. "We should go."

He broke off their eye contact, and watched a flight of geese passing over in the cloudless blue sky. "Joanna, I'd like your word on something," he said at last, looking into her eyes again. "That when this is all over you won't start heading for the nearest exit again."

She swallowed hard. Her eyes lowered. Her heart throbbed painfully beneath her breast. She was more in love with him than she dared contemplate right now, but he deserved better. "Brad, I'm not particularly proud of what I did, how I left what we had last spring. It was wrong and gutless, and Phil's death—how it's wrecked Beth—has made me realize that time is too short to be so foolhardy."

But then, he knew how Beth's warning that time was too short had affected her.

Her eyes felt suddenly too big for her face, her throat thick with emotions. "But right now, with the way things are, I don't know if I can trust my own feelings. I don't trust myself with being crazy in love with you. I don't think you should trust it. I don't know how to be in this. I think I know, and then suddenly I don't anymore."

"You think entirely too much, Dish. All I'm asking," he said, his voice low and compelling, "is that you get it in your heart and your pretty, stubborn little head to give us a decent chance. Will you do that?"

She gave a small sigh for such a momentous decision. "Yes." She wouldn't worry about how to be, because the only way she already knew how to be was alone, trusting no one, especially not any man. But smack in her face, Beth had made her see how desperately sad and lifeless alone could be.

AFTER THE MEMORIAL service concluded, the nanny took the Stonehaven children to her own home to stay with her for the remainder of the day and night. A crowd of people dropped by Beth's house with covered dishes, flowers, sympathy cards.

The turn-of-the-century house, painted a soft lemony yellow on the outside, was rich with mahogany inside. Off the expansive entry to both sides were enormous wood panel pocket doors, open now to the library on one side and the sitting room on the other—a house built for such large gatherings. Joanna stayed at Beth's side through most of the guest arrivals.

Colin Rennslaer and Erin Harper, who were going to be married in the Sacred Heart Sanctuary in November, arrived moments before Sister Mary Bernadette, and Zoe and Rafe Mastrangelo. Both couples had been the hot topic of the grapevine before Vine died. So obviously in love, they touched Beth deeply, and she came close to breaking down in Rafe's embrace.

In physical terms, Phil Stonehaven's Anglo-Saxon features would have been described as the exact opposite of Rafe Mastrangelo's dark, Latin good looks. Blond, blue-eyed, ordinary features, balding. But there was something almost spiritual about the two men, a deep, abiding gentleness that was the same, and Rafe, more than anyone, underscored the extent of Beth's loss to her.

Her own eyes misting, Joanna caught herself finding the most admirable traits of them all in Brad. Colin's polish and high energy, Rafe's strength of purpose and charisma, Phil's steadfast humanity.

Was it only an illusion, a trick of the light in her heart? Months ago she'd believed he was only a con man, a sum of the images he chose to project about himself, that he could not be depended upon or trusted. That his truth changed, chameleonlike, to suit the moment.

But by now she had seen him handle grave and ugly circumstances without compromising the truth. She'd learned his polish didn't necessarily or automatically take away from the truth.

And she knew his anger, because by now she had pushed him to it many times, was never spiteful or vengeful or poisonous or explosive. She'd unwittingly tested him over and over again, trying, she realized now, to push him away or too far. To see if he would turn on her and react as her father had, or Chip Vine, or only, finally, go away.

Brad had done neither.

No, Joanna thought. It wasn't a trick of the light; it wasn't only her heart blinding her to his faults so she could have what Beth and Erin and Zoe had. Brad MacPherson was for real, polished but genuine. She went looking for him, and found him in the kitchen pouring a cup of coffee for Sister Mary Bernadette, deep in conversation.

He sensed her approach, must have sensed the high level of her emotions, that she needed to be with him. He gave Joanna a quick encompassing glance, put his arm around her waist and drew her close to his side.

"I was just telling Sister Mary Bernadette about our conversation with Dr. McCarter."

"Terrible thing," Sister said, drawing a deep breath. "Terrible." Her old hands shook slightly, causing her cup to clatter briefly against the saucer. "If I didn't know better, I'd say Hensel Rabern poisoned Elliott Vine himself."

"Were they such deadly enemies?" Joanna asked. "I just don't understand why Vine would put himself into Rabern's hands like that if they despised each other so much."

"Oh, yes," she answered in response to Joanna's first question. "Though I wouldn't say *despised*, exactly. Elliott Vine chose Dr. Rabern because he is simply the best at heart bypass surgery," Sister said. "Whatever grudges they each held, they never let the animosity spill over into their professional lives. But I imagine you got an earful from Lucy Chavez in that regard."

Brad smothered a grin. Lucy Chavez was Mary Bernadette's Achilles' heel—the one person about whom she could not disguise her low opinion. Probably the only person about whom Mary Bernadette held such an opinion. But people were wandering in and out of the kitchen and they didn't need to be overheard having this conversation. "Why don't we move out to the patio?"

They took their coffee and a slice of angel food cake out the back door to the covered patio. Brad pulled out two chairs with floral print cushions for Sister Mary Bernadette and Joanna, then sat down himself. "You knew Lucy was having an affair with Hensel Rabern," he asked Mary Bernadette, "only to dump him and take up with Elliott Vine?"

"I suspected as much," she said, her phrases lilting in her tenacious old Irish rhythms. "Lucy is the only reason, I'm quite certain, that Dr. Rabern agreed to stay on at Rose when I retired—but there was little I could do about it by then."

"Is it true, then," Joanna asked, "that Lucy Chavez was the cause of the trouble between them?"

"Oh, in the years she's been at Rose, I suppose it's true enough. Their competition over her reduced them to little better than rutting boars. Lucy Chavez constantly played them against each other. But it's not even half the whole story."

"There were rumors floating around even before I came to Rose Memorial—at least a year and a half before Lucy—that there was bad blood between the two of them," Brad said.

"Yes," Mary Bernadette reflected. "You see, Lucy Chavez has only the most narrow perspective. She tends to believe the universe revolves around her—so she believes the animosity between them originated with her. It didn't," she said flatly. "Hensel and Elliott were the best of friends years ago, and in fact, Hensel Rabern is Chip Vine's godfather."

Joanna and Brad exchanged glances. Sister Mary Bernadette blinked. "Yes. You see it, don't you? That is why Dr. Rabern directed Lucy Chavez to remove Chip and Peggy from the emergency room post haste yesterday morning. Despite the antagonism between the two elders, Hensel Rabern is devoted to Vine's son.''

"Rabern never married, did he?" Brad asked. "Never had children of his own?"

"Aye. That is the long and short of it." Sister took a swallow of her coffee. "Over the years, Dr. Rabern sided with Chip—be it which sport he would play or which university he should attend. So much so that Dr. Vine found himself the odd man out all too often."

Joanna remembered something else. "In the ER, Peggy Vine said that her father-in-law had written Chip out of his will."

"In whose favor, I wonder?" Sister Mary Bernadette mused. "But in any case, a perfect example of the sort of mean-spirited, punishing thing that Elliott Vine was wont to do to his son," Mary Bernadette pronounced, "and a fine illustration of the sort of thing that always infuriated Dr. Rabern about his friend's treatment of his son."

A few moments passed. Joanna said at last, "Sister Mary Bernadette, Chip behaved in the ER as if he knew his father was going to die. He kept saying, 'he'—whoever *he* is—promised that things would be okay. Peggy Vine was as desperate to get him out of there as Dr. Rabern and Lucy Chavez were. I wonder . . . especially considering Chip's relationship with Dr. Rabern, if it was him reassuring Chip—but then reassuring him of what?"

"I do believe Chip would turn to Rabern with his problems. The issue of his father's will puts everything in a brand-new light, doesn't it?"

"In what sense?" Brad asked.

Clinging to her cross, Mary Bernadette shrugged and her wrinkles bunched up beneath her wimple. "Well, if Chip knew his father's will had been rewritten, leaving him a fraction of what he expected—or nothing at all—

then I should think Chip would be rather desperate to keep his father alive until he could win back his place in the will.''

Brad drew himself up. ''That would also be motivation enough for Rabern to perform Vine's heart bypass surgery despite the fact that Lucy had dumped him for Vine.''

More frustrated than ever, Joanna had to admit that Mary Bernadette's supposition reasonably addressed every question she had concerning Chip's behavior—and Rabern's. It must have been Rabern assuring Chip that his father would survive the surgery—which would have been imperative in both their minds. Chip could only be restored to his rightful inheritance if Elliott Vine survived the surgery.

Even Rabern's behavior after the fact could be excused. He would have felt a moral obligation to Chip to see his father through to a full recovery, and then, having failed at that, to intervene to the extent of getting Chip out of the Rose Memorial emergency room before he made a complete spectacle of himself.

Which, Joanna thought dismally, left no one with any viable reason for wanting Elliott Vine dead.

Sister reached out to pat Joanna's hand. ''Joanna. No matter how hopelessly mired in impossibilities it seems, Elliott Vine is dead, and you've proof now that it wasn't natural.''

Joanna shivered. ''I know. But I'm beginning to think someone pulled off the perfect murder. Elliott Vine is dead, but we don't know how, or who, or why.''

SISTER MARY BERNADETTE had suggested that Erin Harper and Colin Rennslaer could be of some help in sorting through what might have happened. Erin was a top-rated biologic researcher, and Colin knew the surgical end. Joanna checked with Beth, who was no more satisfied than Joanna with the police conclusion that Lead-brick Jimmy had knocked over No-name, who'd ripped off the vagrant who murdered Phil. Beth was all in favor of bouncing ideas around with Erin and Colin.

They polished off a plate full of ham sandwiches, then served slices of pie with fresh coffee.

There wasn't a moment, Joanna thought, that Beth wasn't fully aware they were missing Phil, but for a little while longer, the lazy, pleasant conversation was like a balm to her nerves. But now Joanna was the one lost in her thoughts.

It took Colin twice to get her attention. "What's on your mind, Joanna?"

She laid her fork down alongside her mostly uneaten lemon meringue pie and put the plate down. "Colin, I hope this isn't too sore of a subject for you since some of your patients died after Tyler Robards transfused the experimental blood, and Erin, you're the one who figured out how it was done. We're certain now that Elliott Vine didn't die of natural causes—"

"You *know* that?" Erin asked.

Joanna nodded. "We were hoping you could brainstorm with us because, frankly, we don't have a clue how it was done."

Colin and Erin exchanged glances, then put down their pie plates, as well. "Start at the beginning," Erin suggested. "How do you know?"

It took twenty minutes or so to bring Colin and Erin up to speed on what had happened, from Vine's death to the break-in at Joanna's town house to Mary Bernadette's conclusion that Rabern and Chip Vine had a powerful interest in keeping Vine alive. But this was the first time

Beth had heard about their meeting with Dr. McCarter, as well.

"So okay," Erin said, curled up on the sofa, her short blond hair tousled. "This is what you've got thus far—Elliott Vine died in the OR. By all indications, the surgery went without a hitch, but he died. The cause of death according to Ruth Brungart was sudden cardiac death, but in reality was anaphylactic shock—exposure to something he was violently allergic to?"

"Yes," Joanna answered.

"How could Ruth Brungart have missed that kind of finding?" Colin asked.

"According to Dr. McCarter, the anaphylactic shock is a rather obscure finding," Joanna explained. "Dr. Brungart noted the circulatory collapse in her postmortem examination of Dr. Vine's body, but she chalked it up to the heart failure. Phil thought there was more to it than that, and Dr. McCarter confirmed it."

"Okay," Colin said slowly. "I can believe the allergic reaction might have been missed. What's the first thing we all think of when a patient takes a dive in the operating room?"

"The blood transfusion," Joanna answered.

"Exactly." Having been in on the research project trying to develop a synthetic blood with Erin, Colin was in a position to know that donated blood could create problems.

"I don't get it," Brad said. "Our blood center is always crying for donors. If it's so unsafe—"

"It's not, really," Erin explained. "The blood is always tested very thoroughly. And doctors nowadays only order blood transfusions when it becomes a critical matter. But in a crisis situation the blood transfusions are the easiest thing to blame even though the donor blood rarely turns out to be the cause of the troubles in the OR.''

Joanna agreed. ''The only transfusion reaction I've ever personally seen documented turned out to be labeled O Positive when it was really A Positive. Even then, the patient didn't die. Still, it's ingrained in us. If a patient starts to go downhill fast, we stop the transfusion—which I did.''

''I assume you ordered a transfusion reaction work-up?'' Colin asked.

''Yes. Right away. And I checked the lab results even before I left the hospital that night.'' All the donated blood units were the correct type, and when put together with a small sample of Vine's own blood in the cross-match tests, they all proved compatible with Vine's blood, as well. ''All the tests were negative.''

''What about bacterial contamination?'' Erin suggested.

''That was a theory of Phil's, along with somebody slipping Vine a dose of strychnine, but the blood cultures all came back negative, as well.''

''Was he joking about the strychnine?'' Colin asked in amazement.

Joanna nodded. ''I'm sure he was. But he sent out a sample of Vine's blood for a toxicology screen, anyway.''

For over an hour they brainstormed on every conceivable cause of the anaphylactic shock that had killed Elliott Vine, straying even to the far-out possibilities offered by exotic, slow-acting poisons. No one prospect seemed any more or less likely than the one before it.

Erin shook her head thoughtfully. ''We're being way too smart here. There's an old bromide in science that the answer is almost always staring you right in the face. Come on, you guys! If someone asked you what one thing commonly available in a hospital was most likely to cause a severe allergic reaction, you'd have to say penicillin."

"Okay. Yes," Joanna said. "And Elliott Vine was allergic to penicillin. But even if we assume for the sake of argument that it was penicillin, how was it administered? Who got hold of it?"

"Everyone in the hospital with access to his chart would know he was allergic," Beth put in.

"That certainly narrows the field of suspects," Brad said, giving a sardonic smile.

Colin shook his head. "I think we can narrow the field considerably—but, Joanna, the first thing you have to accept is that you weren't in control of everything going into Vine's body. I'd bet any amount of money that at least three times a nurse ripped open the packaging on bags of saline, for instance."

"And the perfusionist—the tech responsible for the machine supplying oxygen to Vine's blood while his heart was stopped," Beth added.

"Here's another reality check for you, Joanna," Erin said. "If I took a twenty-five gauge needle, the smallest commonly available, I could inject a bag of saline in the rubber port with anything I chose, right through the packaging. And even if you knew it had been done, you still might not be able to find the needle hole. Not knowing, there's virtually no chance you'd have found it. You wouldn't have had to be sleeping on the job to miss it."

Joanna took a deep breath and shoved her hair away from her face. "Okay. But how do we narrow the field? There's no telling how many people knew Vine was allergic to penicillin or, for that matter, how many had the opportunity to inject the IV bags."

"The first thing to do is find out where Phil sent the tox screen," Colin suggested. "Penicillin wouldn't be on a routine screen, but if they have enough of the blood sample left over, they could sure find out if penicillin is there."

"That's right. And again," Erin said, "I'd start with the obvious. Someone who, number one, had access to penicillin and, two, had access to the IV medications and, three, had a motive for killing Vine. Is there anyone who meets all three?"

"Yeah." Brad grimaced. "Peggy Vine."

Joanna straightened. The possibility was mind-boggling. "Peggy? Are you serious?"

"Yeah. Think about it, Dish," he urged, sitting forward on the deep sofa. "She's a pharmacy tech. She delivers medications all over the hospital. And she's the one among all the others we might come up with who had not only her access but a reason for wanting Vine dead, as well."

Joanna let the possibility sink in. Peggy Vine would certainly have had ample opportunity to steal the penicillin. She had also made it perfectly clear in the ER that she hated Elliott Vine with a passion—that she'd have killed him herself if she ever got the chance.

Brad had picked up on that right away, and challenged her. *Someone did find a way, didn't they, Peggy?* Vine's open-heart surgery provided her that chance—what was there to prevent her taking it? But if she had taken that sliver of opportunity, how likely was it that she would have said anything about despising her father-in-law?

On the other hand, it might well explain why Chip had beaten her, if he only found out after the fact what she had done. If Chip knew, but hadn't confided in Peggy that his father's will had been changed to disinherit him, they would be at cross-purposes. Chip would be desperate to keep his father alive, Peggy equally desperate to kill her father-in-law while she had the chance.

Something at the edge of her consciousness nagged at Joanna, but the harder she tried, the less able she was to put her finger on it. "Peggy is certainly the most obvious choice, but the OR has its own pharmacy tech. Don't you think it would have taken a lot of finagling for Peggy to get the IV bag she injected into the OR stock, and specifically into OR 16?"

Erin shrugged. "I've seen less likely things than that happen, Joanna."

Chapter Thirteen

On the way home from Beth's house, a call came in on Brad's car phone. He punched the speaker phone key so they could both hear the call. "MacPherson."

"Brad? Is that you?"

He recognized the voice of the HIS manager, Chip's boss. "Yes, Lauren. Joanna and I are both here."

A long sigh. "I'm glad I found you. I've been ringing this line for almost two hours."

"Sorry," he said, signaling his left turn. "We've been with Beth Stonehaven."

"Well, this thing... I couldn't get it out of my mind. I've also been trying to reach Chip all day. I guess I'll have to wait. I thought I could catch him after his dad's funeral tomorrow, but I just heard they postponed. They're doing a memorial service next Friday."

"What's up, Lauren?" Joanna asked in the crackling silence. "Have you come up with something?"

"Two things. One is that Gretel Owens was on the swing-shift duty the day Dr. Vine died. She saw Chip off and on that night, but they're not pals of any kind. Neither of them spoke to the other. But Gretel says Chip was definitely on the computer after ten o'clock that night, so

I just went through our access codes until I found the one Chip used.''

Joanna glanced at Brad. "Can you tell when he logged off?''

"He didn't. After two hours, at . . . 12:43, the computer automatically booted him out.''

"Then the last time he did anything had to be 10:43?'' Brad asked, calculating backward.

The line began to break up intermittently. "Yes. But now here . . . interesting thing. Chip . . . the other code . . . at one thir—''

"Hold on a minute, Lauren, till I get past this corner.'' He sped up the Bronco a bit, turned and got beyond the canyon of glass-and-brick buildings blocking the call. "Okay. You were saying what about Chip?''

"He logged on again with another HIS code at 1:33 that night . . . the next morning, actually. I can't tell you why, but I can tell you I intend to find out.'' None of the irritation in her voice was lost in the transmission. Brad and Joanna exchanged glances.

"Anyway,'' Lauren went on, "I checked the print manager on the computer. Dr. Stonehaven did two Print Screen functions. The text was sent to printer 434, which is the laser printer in the pathology secretaries' office. You might want to stop by there in the morning.''

"Lauren, thank you so much for your help,'' Joanna said.

Lauren acknowledged the thanks, then hung up.

They rode in silence for a few moments. Joanna sighed. "This is just so . . .'' She couldn't think of a word appropriate to describe the morass of information coming together only to splinter off and go in forty different directions.

"Scattered?'' Brad offered.

"At least. I mean, think about this. We have three different doctors offering three different opinions on Elliott Vine's death. It was natural, it was unnatural, it was murder.

"We have Chip Vine," she went on, "caught dead to rights in a couple of different lies, lurking around the computer rooms until nearly two in the morning. What was he after? We have Peggy Vine with the only straightforward motive and the best shot at killing her father-in-law, but I bet you any lawyer could get her off even if she is the one. It's just too circumstantial. And to top it off, the police are now fully satisfied that Phil was murdered by a vagrant they can't find."

Joanna trailed off. It was a long speech, and something about what she'd just said troubled her. Something not quite right. But just as before in Beth's living room, she couldn't quite bring whatever it was to the foreground.

Her mind was filled with too many nebulous possibilities. She looked at Brad, at the street lamps casting shadows and light in repeating patterns over his features. She'd been in his Bronco more often in the past few days than she cared to remember. All in the name of protecting her from some equally illusory, maybe imaginary threat of harm.

If one murder weren't enough, there were two. They knew that for sure now, with McCarter's finding of anaphylactic shock. The only thing left to demonstrate was that there really was penicillin in Vine's blood, and that the drug had proved deadly, as someone had known it would.

Oddly, Joanna believed penicillin would turn out to be the cause of Vine's death. Some instinct lobbied for it, or maybe her conviction was based only on Erin Harper's assertion that the thing staring you in the face was usually what you were looking for.

It was becoming an impossible mission to separate the two murders, to think which piece of information applied to what murder, to focus on one thing long enough to arrive at reasonable conclusions. But it wouldn't get less complicated, because Phil's death had something to do with Vine's, so the two were inextricably knotted together.

The best she could hope to do was give Vine's computer-generated chart a thorough going over. She looked to Brad, whose lips were already curved in a knowing smirk.

"You were about to ask if I'd mind if you spent a few hours going over Vine's chart," he said.

"I was. Am I as transparent as all that?"

"Like cellophane, Dish." He reached over and squeezed her ticklish knee. "So long as when you're done, I can have your undivided attention."

"You'll be so tired . . ." she said, hoping it wasn't true.

"The day I'm too tired to make love to you, Dish—" He thought better of finishing that sentiment.

Joanna swallowed. "Phil would have laughed, Brad. We can't be watching everything we say."

"I know." He stroked her thigh. "I still put my foot in my mouth."

"Well . . . I don't think I've ever seen it happen before," she returned, smiling secretly. "Actually it's kind of heartening to see that it's possible even for you."

"Oh, it's possible all right. I imagine it's even possible to leave me completely speechless."

"No." She dragged out the word to six syllables instead of one. "Surely not."

He grinned. "Someday I'll tell you how it's done."

"That you're left speechless?" He nodded. "This is too cool! Tell me now," she insisted.

"Nope. Someday. Not today."

"Will pouting do any good?"

He laughed. "You want to know before you expend the effort? Dream on. I'm not telling you today. Or tomorrow, either."

"Fine."

"Fine, yourself." He whipped into his building garage, and as quickly into his space. "You just get that little photographic memory of yours working on Vine's chart. I won't be too tired," he warned her, "but I am not a particularly patient man."

SHE GOT INTO a quick shower, washed her hair and plaited her usual braid, then wrapped herself tight in Brad's sumptuous white terry robe and curled up on the master bed with her reading glasses and a copy of Elliott Vine's chart.

Brad was already minus his shirt, sitting in the chaise longue in his bedroom with the reading lamp on. He figured Joanna would find any technical discrepancies, just as Phil Stonehaven might have, while he studied the pages with the same low level of medical expertise that would have handicapped Chip Vine.

There was only the problem that neither one of them found anything amiss. Nothing. The chart was in perfect order. No entry contradicted another, no required information missing, no stone left unturned. Comparing notes with Joanna it was evident that, without fail, every step of the way the hospital staff had documented the care of Elliott Vine to an enviable level of perfection.

No metaphorical *t* was left uncrossed, no *i* left undotted. Vine would have been smugly and justifiably satisfied—except for the fact that he had died in surgery.

It would be interesting, Brad thought, to see which two pages of this chart Phil Stonehaven had found noteworthy enough to print—assuming that the pathology secretaries had kept the copies.

As advertised, he wasn't too tired to make love with Joanna. He had her undivided attention, and for an hour or so, she had his. Afterward they'd turned on reruns of "Cheers," and she fell asleep in his arms.

Months ago the prospect of a commitment had nearly paralyzed him, and in some way he didn't question but understood, Joanna had sensed that and walked away. He'd come too close with the shark woman—come too close to tying himself to a creature whose values he thought mirrored his own but were, in fact, the antithesis of what he really wanted.

It took Joanna's stunning, salient, pointed rejection of his smooth, slick, *cultivated* style to make him see that shades of gray, shades of truth and falsehood, could become one hell of a set of blinders. Some things were black-and-white. Some things were simply good and evil.

In the morning—Monday morning, 9:00 a.m. sharp—he would have to get up in front of the by-now usual crowd of news reporters and supply them with updates in the deaths of Elliott Vine and Phil Stonehaven.

He didn't have a clue what he was going to say. If he had a prayer of holding on to Joanna, it would be because he did not compromise the truth. Thursday he'd been able to turn the tide of sentiment toward the beleaguered Rose Memorial. He'd been able to say with a clear conscience that the death of Elliott Vine, while under scrutiny, was almost certainly a tragic mischance, and that

Phil's murder appeared to be the deplorable act of a soup kitchen vagrant.

He hoped to heaven that by morning inspiration would hit, and he would find a way to be faithful to the truth, whatever that was, without irretrievably damaging the reputation of Rose Memorial Hospital.

Or getting himself in so much hot water that not even the grace of Sister Mary Bernadette Reilly could salvage him this time.

THE PRESS CONFERENCE was notably missing the supporting cast Brad had recruited the prior Thursday. Chip and Peggy Vine were nowhere to be found. Ruth Brungart was taking vacation leave and Sister Mary Bernadette was off fulfilling prior commitments. Three of Brad's staff were posted at the doors. He intended to let them handle the crowd after the press conference concluded.

Joanna had gone to the pathology secretaries' office and discovered by some marvel of inefficiency that the secretaries had not yet cleared Phil's office mailbox. Inside were tucked the two pages that Phil had printed from Vine's chart.

She immediately saw what had grabbed Phil's attention, but by the time she got to the conference room, Brad was already on the riser. Wildly impatient, she would have to wait until after the press conference let out, but when he spotted her, she gave a nod to indicate that she had found the pages.

She sat in the next to the last row and tried to sit still. She knew Brad had no intention of calling her forward. Hensel Rabern walked in with Lucy Chavez and Jacob Delvecchio at the last possible moment.

The three of them, Joanna thought, made an impressive united front sitting down together in the front row just as Brad prepared to deliver his opening comments. If he was at all intimidated, he didn't show it. He looked like a million. Relaxed, composed, exchanging wisecracks with the front few reporters. Joanna decided, of the two of them, she was the nervous one.

Brad kept his comments brief and on point. The internal investigation into the death of former Chief of Staff Elliott Vine was as yet ongoing.

The death of Phil Stonehaven, as had already been reported by the news media after the press release issued by the Chicago police department, was attributed to a vagrant who had been robbed of Dr. Stonehaven's personal belongings by a second vagrant, who, in turn, had been killed in a scuffle with a third derelict, who was now awaiting arraignment in the murder of the second.

She couldn't fault a single sentence or his delivery. He concluded by saying he would entertain questions for no more than ten minutes.

"So make 'em worth your while," he joked, breaking up the tension.

The reporters laughed appreciatively, but they weren't cowed. "Mr. MacPherson," one woman called out, "you say your own internal investigation is still going on. Can you tell us why?"

"No, Ginny," he answered politely. "I'm afraid I'm not free to discuss the inquiry in progress."

"Are you saying you're not satisfied that your chief of staff received the best possible care?" another reporter called out.

"No, I'm not saying that at all. In fact, I was personally up till the wee hours last night going over Dr. Vine's patient chart. I'm no medical expert, but the chart has been reviewed in full by a physician, and I can tell you this—right up to and including the moment Dr. Vine died, his care was impeccable."

"Then why aren't you leaving it at that?" the first woman persisted.

Joanna cringed. There was simply no way to duck the question, except for Brad to say that he wasn't free to comment.

He took a deep breath, cast a glance in the direction of Rabern, Chavez and Delvecchio and delivered another line altogether. "We're unable to close our own internal investigation because we have it on the authority of an expert in the field that Elliott Vine's death is not attributable to natural causes."

Joanna's breath caught in her throat. The roomful of reporters erupted into a pandemonium like nothing she'd seen since the president committed U.S. troops to the Gulf War. The noise, the questions shouted, the studied, angry departure of the united three—all of it melded for her into a kaleidoscope of fancy colors and no sound whatever. Brad MacPherson had just laid his career, his credibility, his entire identity, on the line in favor of reporting only the truth.

In for a penny, she thought, in for a pound. She had never seen anything like it. And if she had needed proof that Brad MacPherson was a man of integrity, he'd just delivered in spades.

Brad stood back a moment, letting his gaze pass over the wild gestures, the bids for attention, the hue and cry of well over thirty news reporters, and then he looked at his watch.

The gesture worked. The ten minutes were nearly up, and they all wanted him to follow up on his bald statement of fact.

When the room had quieted, he pointed to Shelley Vance, the strident cable news affiliate who had tried to hang Joanna out to dry.

She had the good sense to make her question count. "Brad, are you saying unequivocally that Elliott Vine was murdered?"

"No," he answered. "I'm saying Dr. Vine died of circulatory collapse that was not caused by heart failure. I'm not free at this time to reveal anything further. I hope that our expert will be able to come forward in due time with a statement of his own, and I hope that when he does, we will have resolved the questions that are still unanswered—if," he said, breaking off, grinning sheepishly at the three empty front-row seats and then to the door where Rabern, Chavez and Delvecchio had departed, "I'm still here." His self-deprecating candor earned him a big laugh, to which he said simply, "Thank you all very much for coming, and have a safe day."

LEAVING HIS STAFF to deal with the media setting up for their live, on-location reports, Brad departed and went alone to his office. Joanna had agreed it would be best if they weren't perceived as being together before, during or immediately following the press conference.

Coming from separate directions, they met at his office at the same time.

His secretary looked a little stricken. "What did you do?" she asked. "Delvecchio said to tell you 'your ass is grass' and that you'd better get to his office fast."

Checking his watch, Brad grinned. "Record time." Joanna couldn't believe him. "Tell Mr. Delvecchio for me, please, Janice," he said, "that I will meet him in his office at ten o'clock." He turned to Joanna, whose beeper was going off, as well. He opened his door. "After you, Dr. Cavendish."

Carrying her briefcase, Joanna crossed the threshold, checking the phone number displayed on her beeper. Brad followed, shrugged out of his suit coat and loosened his tie and shut the door behind him, all in one smooth movement. She could tell he was jazzed.

"I had no idea hara-kari could be so exhilarating," she teased.

He laughed. "A thrill a moment, Dish." He came over to her, planted his hand in the small of her back and dragged her tight up against him right into a smoldering kiss. "Now tell me what you've got."

Feeling a little dazed by him, by his actions, his words, his boldly putting Delvecchio off and then his kiss, she ignored Delvecchio's page herself, put down her briefcase and pulled out the pages Phil had printed. She handed them to him without comment, because if he could see the difference—the discrepancy between these pages and the ones Lauren Bristol had given them—then she knew it would have been obvious to Chip Vine, as well.

It took Brad maybe fifteen seconds longer than it had taken her to spot the inconsistency. "The field where known drug allergies are recorded is screwed up."

"No doubt," Joanna said, pulling out the sheaf of papers Lauren Bristol had given them. Joanna flipped through pages until she came to the nurse practitioner's admitting notes where Vine's allergy to penicillin had been properly recorded, then to the section where her own handwritten notes had been transcribed into the record, also indicating Vine's penicillin allergy. "This is where the two reports differ."

Brad focused again on the pages that Phil had printed. On the first page, penicillin had been properly transcribed into the computer files, but on the second, where known medication allergies were compared against all physician medication orders, no allergies were noted.

"Shouldn't penicillin be entered in this field?" Brad asked.

"Yes."

"Is it a computer failure? A programming fault? Because I would think that if you logged any medication allergy anywhere in the admission workup, the information would automatically cross over into the fail-safe function."

Joanna nodded. "That's how it is supposed to work. The computer won't let you order up a medication from the pharmacy that the patient is allergic to." She pointed to the transcription of her notes. "What happens in the case of anesthesia is that I have an empty page on which I fill in the blanks and a secretary transcribes them. Sometimes, usually in outpatient surgery, I fill in the computer screens myself based on my interview with the patient. So before I even go in, I know firsthand what allergies the patient has. A lot of people are allergic to novocaine and anesthetics in that class of drugs."

"So even if a nurse has already done the medical history, you interview yourself?"

"Always," she answered flatly. "Except in an emergency, or when the patient is unconscious. But in every other instance, I do my own interviews with the patient."

"Okay. So you do the interview and you log whatever information you've gotten into the computer."

"Yes. In the first screen. And the computer is set up to transfer that information to the fail-safe function."

"So what would it take to delete the information that Vine was allergic to penicillin?"

"Theoretically, it can't be done."

"Which means it can be done, but only if you have high enough level of clearance to make changes?" Brad asked.

Joanna nodded. "Which, in turn, means penicillin was first deleted, which is what Phil saw and printed, and then put back as if it had always been there."

"Which finally means," Brad concluded, "that Chip had a few small edits to make on his father's official chart at 1:33 in the morning." His jaw tightened in anger. "Let's go have a chat with Mr. Delvecchio."

JACOB DELVECCHIO had wanted to move into the offices of the chief executive officer—plush by any standards because the last occupant had been Frank Clemenza, sole living heir of Bishop Vincente Rosario, and thus independently wealthy. Unfortunately for Delvecchio, the feds had sealed those offices pending their trial of Frank Clemenza in the attempted murder and fraud perpetrated on Centi's estate. Bishop Rosario was not dead. Clemenza was in very deep trouble.

Which left Delvecchio in his less-than-plush office, an unhappy camper to begin with, outraged now at Brad's handling of the press conference. Hensel Rabern and Lucy Chavez were also already there when Brad and Joanna arrived at 10:05.

Delvecchio was apparently too angry to speak, or else the three of them had decided Rabern would handle the initial confrontation. Two extra chairs awaited them.

Rabern sat there steely-eyed, his arms hanging over the back of his chair, staring at first Joanna and then Brad. Contempt twisted his lips. "I want to know what it's going to take to get you off this idiotic tangent."

"Which tangent would that be?" Brad asked politely. "The one concerning the death of Elliott Vine, or the one to do with the murder of Phil Stonehaven?"

"Both," Rabern snapped, "and you can cut the cute with me, sonny, because I won't tolerate it. Now if you've got something to say about either death, spit it out." He took a breath and expelled it. "We'll talk and be done with this entire unfortunate incident."

"Oh," Brad said disingenuously. "We'll talk. We'll sweep this nasty little scrape right under the ol' rug and be done with it. Is that it? Let's make a deal?"

"I don't know what you're talking about," Rabern returned, confused, or making a good show of it. "What is it that you think you have that we would even consider sweeping under the rug?"

"Elliott Vine died of anaphylactic shock," Joanna said. "Brought on, we believe, by penicillin, which makes it murder."

Delvecchio's face drained of color. Lucy Chavez stared blankly at her. Rabern answered. "That's the most ridiculous thing I've ever heard."

"Well, it get's more ridiculous," Joanna said. In her briefcase was the proof that Phil had seen the discrepancy in the allergy to penicillin data entries, but Rabern somehow made her hesitate to reveal that. "Phil Stonehaven," she said, "wasn't killed by any vagrant. He knew there was something fishy about Vine's death, and he was about to prove it when someone killed him."

Rabern looked totally befuddled. "Where are you coming up with these wild-eyed ideas?"

"They're not wild-eyed, sir," Brad said. "By chance, the medical examiner's office wound up in possession of tissue slides that evidence Dr. Vine's fatal allergic reaction."

Rabern turned his glare on Delvecchio. "Why haven't I heard about this?"

"Because no one saw fit to keep me informed," Delvecchio said, in turn glaring at Brad and Joanna. "Would you care to explain such a lapse, MacPherson?"

"Of course," Brad returned easily. "The pathologist in the medical examiner's office who looked at the slides and made the diagnosis was in the difficult position of having looked at slides that were irrelevant to the vagrant mugging case—slides that, I'm sure you realize, fall under doctor-patient confidentiality rules."

"Were you in on this fortuitous discovery, Dr. Cavendish?" Delvecchio asked.

"Yes."

"Well, even if it's true, it's a case of a monumental mix-up that can never be proven," Rabern said. "I suggest for the sake of the reputation of this hospital—"

"Why do you say it can never be proven, Dr. Rabern?" Joanna asked. She uncrossed her legs and smoothed the wrinkles from her ivory-colored linen skirt. "I know that Phil sent out samples of Dr. Vine's blood to be tested in an independent toxicology screen. He personally told me that, and that Dr. Brungart was unhappy about it."

"Penicillin," Rabern said in a tone that was condescending at best, "is not part of a toxicology screen."

"I know that, Dr. Rabern," she answered as evenly as she could muster, "but the lab can use whatever remains of the blood serum sample to test for the presence of penicillin derivatives."

"That would be convenient, but it's impossible. The lab used every drop of the sample sent by Stonehaven. Now look, this whole thing can be dispensed with—"

"Wait a minute," Brad interrupted him. "How is it that you know the outside lab has no more of Vine's blood sample?"

"Because Ruth Brungart changed her mind regarding Stonehaven's having the sample sent out."

"You mean she decided that sending out a sample for a tox screen was a good idea?" Joanna asked, skeptical.

Rabern's brows drew together in anger. "That is exactly what I mean to say. Dr. Brungart and I decided when the first set of results came back negative, in the interest of the most thorough examination of the available evidence, to pursue Dr. Stonehaven's inspiration to the fullest extent possible. We requested that the lab repeat the screen and then continue to test the sample until they came up with a positive test."

"Or until the sample was completely wasted?" Joanna demanded, leaping up from her chair.

Rabern came out of his chair, too. "How dare you imply, young lady—"

"*Doctor,* to you, sir," she interrupted heatedly, toe-to-toe with Rabern. "And I'm not implying anything. I'm stating flat out that you deliberately ordered that sample tested until nothing was left."

"I'll have your hide for this slander, *Doctor,*" Rabern roared.

Delvecchio rose, Chavez darted in front of Rabern and Brad went to Joanna.

"Hensel, calm down, for the love of God!" Chavez pleaded.

"I will *not* calm down for the love of anything!" Rabern barked, shoving Lucy aside, disregarding the warnings Delvecchio muttered. "I've had it up to my eyeballs with you, miss, and before I'm done with you, you will be penniless and without a license to practice hopscotch."

Chapter Fourteen

Brad touched Joanna's shoulders. She knew he wanted her to shut up, that this was the sort of half-witted thing she let out of her mouth without considering for one minute the consequences. But it took every ounce of self-discipline she had ever acquired to stifle her retort.

"Dr. Rabern, sir, this is getting us nowhere," Brad said, defusing the explosive climate. "I suggest that we take a breather. And we have some questions for Chip and Peggy. We'd like for you to bring them in."

"It'll be a cold day in hell," he said, shaking Lucy Chavez's calming hand from his arm. "I refuse to put those young people through this pointless display of twisted, misconstrued bull-puckey—but rest assured," he added, his steely eyes blazing, "you have started something you can't finish, and I *will* be seeing you in court. Both of you."

BY THE TIME Joanna had calmed down enough to realize that this was an instance which it would have paid her to consider the repercussions of what she said before blurting it out, they had returned to his office.

Jacob Delvecchio had followed Rabern and Lucy Chavez, so if he'd intended to fire Brad on the spot, he'd missed the opportunity.

Brad cracked open a can of Diet Coke for her and asked her nicely to sit down. She would otherwise have worn a hole in his carpet, pacing off her anger.

She shook her head, blew out a breath and accepted the can of soda. "I can't believe he did that!"

"Joanna, however tempting it may be, you cannot leap to the conclusion that he deliberately ran that lab out of Vine's sample blood."

"It's just so damned convenient," she said.

"It is. I'm not arguing with you," he answered with a maddeningly reasonable tone. He sat on the edge of his desk. "But it is in the realm of possibility that he and Brungart were exhausting every avenue to make sure she hadn't missed something. Her credibility might well have been shot to hell if Phil found something she should have seen herself."

"Okay, then," she answered smartly, "I nominate Brungart for prime suspect in the slaying of Phil Stonehaven, because he *was* about to make a fool of her."

"Joanna—"

"Don't 'Joanna' me, Brad! I'm serious. She's a big woman. She could have handled it. And no one would be the wiser. Phil would have thought nothing of her coming into his office."

"Joanna, the woman didn't kill Phil," he said flatly. "And neither did Rabern. Both of them are very smart, very savvy, and too conservative to even think of bashing Phil over the head."

"Someone did," she answered darkly. "And now, thanks to Rabern and Brungart's *exhaustive* work, we're left with virtually no proof that a murder was even committed in the OR.''

Proving there was penicillin in Vine's blood had been their only chance because, even if the identifying labels hadn't been so conveniently broken off, McCarter should still never have seen those slides. Unless he chose voluntarily to come forward, even that dubiously incriminating evidence would be buried forever.

"Look, Joanna," Brad said. "Rabern will calm down. He has to. He really can't afford to have you going around spouting off about someone pulling off the perfect murder right under his nose. And he sure doesn't want Chip to be in hot water over this whole thing, which is exactly where he's going to be when Lauren Bristol finds out that he not only ambushed Phil in the computer, he altered his father's medical records.''

"Brad, I'm not afraid of him filing a slander suit—"

"I didn't mean that he'd cool off to a point of reconsidering that. He'll have plenty of time to realize it isn't a smart thing to do. I'm talking about him calming down today—enough to listen to reason, out of any inflammatory context. I'll take him out for a drink and see how it goes with him, one-on-one.''

"What if he won't listen, or asks you to retract, or throws the poor, grief-stricken Vines on your mercy?''

"You'll just have to trust me, won't you, Dish? I promised to be covering your back and I meant it. Do you think I'd cut a deal with Rabern and leave you swinging in the wind?''

His question, or the hint of disappointment in his tone, caught her up short. She breathed in and out a few times, calming herself. "No," she answered. "At least, if I'd thought about it, I would have realized you wouldn't do that.''

He shrugged. "I know I just told you yesterday that you think too much, but try to remember that you've already thought about this. That you know I'm going to be there for you, and not to slap you around. Can you do that? Dish?"

"Yes." She wanted to erase his disappointment and to be sure she never caused it again. It felt like hell. It felt shabby of her, and she wanted to believe she could be better than that. "Yes," she said more firmly. "I can do that."

He smiled, and she knew why it was worth it to her to try to be better. To trust him. His smile lit up his handsome face, sparkled from his eyes, and the lust was definitely R-rated.

"Good. Then let's go see the chief of the pharmacy."

THE INPATIENT PHARMACY where Peggy Vine worked was off one of the basement hallways. They'd recently completed renovations to the pharmacy, but there was only so much anyone could do to make an underground facility seem bright and clean. The major purpose of the renovation had been to bump up the level of security to the pharmacy, not to improve it cosmetically.

Roger Wei was the department director. Because the doors were on locks with a series of numbered buttons to be pushed, Brad rang the doorbell to summon help. Another pharmacy tech, a woman and peer of Peggy Vine's, answered the bell.

She was the first person Joanna knew of whom Brad didn't already know. They both showed the woman their ID and asked to see Wei. Roger came to the locked door, double-checked and buzzed them in.

He shook hands with both of them and led them through a maze of library shelves stocked with pharmaceuticals to his office. The room was very small, four white freshly painted walls with only a calendar to break the monotony, and furniture salvaged from some other renovation.

"Roger," Brad began when they were seated behind Wei's closed door, "before we go into anything, I have to ask you to keep our discussion private."

Wei rocked forward in his executive chair and picked up a mechanical pencil to toy with. "Okay. You've got it. But let me guess. Based on your press conference disclosure, you're looking for drugs missing that might have induced Elliott Vine's anaphylactic shock."

"Bingo," Joanna murmured.

Wei grinned. "Doesn't take a rocket scientist, Joanna. If Vine died of anaphylactic shock, which naturally is all over the grapevine by now, the pharmacy is your next logical move—especially since Peggy works here."

"Does that mean you've already gone through your inventory?" Brad asked.

He sighed and tossed the pencil onto his desk. "I didn't have to go to any special trouble. But are you serious about thinking Peggy Vine had anything to do with Vine's death?"

"It's looking like a strong possibility, Roger," Brad answered. "Do you have a feel for what Peggy is capable of? Do you think it's possible she was involved?"

"Possible? Yes. Probable? I think it's a long shot. And if she did it, she didn't get the drugs from my inventory. See, I routinely run an inventory on Sunday nights—it's usually the slowest time, so I have whichever senior pharmacist is on run the program and do the physical count."

"Anything missing would have to have been taken in the past ten days because that's when Vine was told he'd have to get the heart bypass done," Joanna said.

Wei shook his head. "Up until last night, the only thing I've come up short on in the past month is Tylenol—and that, I suspect, is staff taking care of their headaches."

"So you don't think," Joanna asked, "that there's any way Peggy—or anyone else, for that matter—had the opportunity to pocket an allergenic drug?"

"I don't see it, Joanna. No. I'm sorry."

"Not even anything outdated?"

"I'm more careful about discarding outdated drugs than anything else. We do that once a week, and we do it in pairs and I'm usually one half of the team. I'm sorry to be of so little help. I guess if I were you, I'd get Zoe Mastrangelo or somebody from her department working on penicillin prescriptions outside the hospital."

Thinking about Wei's suggestion, Joanna knew trying to find some subtle increase in the number of times penicillin or one of its derivative drugs had been prescribed would need the wildest kind of luck to succeed. A single script written for any one of a dozen drugs would be sufficient to the cause.

Being allergic, a dose of a few thousand milligrams would be fatal to Vine. Ground up and dissolved in water, that quantity of penicillin could be gotten in as few as two or three pills.

Just in case, she would talk to Zoe tomorrow, she decided. This evening Brad would speak again to Rabern, and after that, perhaps, they would have an idea of how to proceed.

Brad walked her to the front of the hospital where she could catch a cab back to his place. They compared plans for the day again. Joanna was going to go back to Brad's place, have a bite to eat, collect her keys and meet with the repairmen at her town house by two-thirty. After that, she thought, since Brad would likely be having drinks with Rabern, she'd go to Beth's.

Helping her into the cab, in lieu of a kiss he gave her hip an intimate caress. "Please watch out for yourself," he said through her window. "Don't go into your town house until the repairmen are there, and get them to give you a lift to your car when they leave. Okay?"

They'd already been through this plan, but Joanna humored him. "I'll be very careful, I promise."

"You know where to park in my building?"

"Yes! You showed me three million times. Now go slay dragons or whatever it is you have to do this afternoon."

He gave her a wink, then tapped the roof of the cab, and Joanna was finally on her way. Looking back, watching him watch her drive off until the traffic blocked her sight of him, she got the most eerie feeling.

Like...like spending these few days with him were more than she deserved. Like it had somehow all been in a dream. Like she wouldn't see him again. Ever.

She lay back her head and closed her eyes and forced her beating heart to slow down. Rabern had really scared her, that was all. That and behaving as if the Mafia were after her. If it was going to make her feel this bad, this crazy, so frightened of never seeing Brad again, then she would have to forego moving about as if she were the prey.

She wasn't. She refused to be.

AT TWO O'CLOCK she asked Joseph, the day-shift doorman in Brad's apartment building, to call her a cab—but this would be her last. The notion that she was in any danger was based on nothing more than the break-in; since Peggy Vine's warning to her in the ER to stop interfering, not one person had so much as looked at her crosswise, unless she counted her clash with Rabern. And as Brad had pointed out to her, Rabern couldn't have murdered Phil, and he sure wasn't the one prowling through her kitchen window. She thought if someone had any intention of harming her, she would have known intuitively. Felt the vague threat, or at least been uneasy.

She knew Brad disagreed, so she would do as he had asked. Take the cab, wait for the repairmen, all that, so at no time would she be alone and vulnerable to Phil's assailant—whoever that was.

This cabbie wore a black suede vest over nothing, and a black leather fedora. Gregarious, sardonic, impressed with his own wit, he was more than willing to let the meter run in front of her town house while they waited on the repairmen. Her fare came to $31.80 before she couldn't stand it anymore. She dismissed the driver, paid him and sat on her neighbor's front porch. Five minutes later the pickup truck bearing the logo of the window company pulled up where the cab had been.

Joanna asked for ID because she'd promised Brad she would. She thought the pair of workers figured they'd landed a real nut case. She refused to give them so much as an apologetic shrug. Turning to unlock the door, she let them inside and waved in the general direction of the kitchen.

She intended to follow them in, but a sudden fear, like the one she would have expected to feel if someone were stalking her, took her in its grip. Common sense told her that the presence of the two repairmen would have driven away anyone lying in wait for her.

Berating herself for a ninny, and an easily spooked one at that, she got up, brushed off the seat of her skirt and made her legs carry her into the town house. She kept going, too, until she reached the top of the stairs and then her bedroom. She needed to collect fresh clothes to take back with her to Brad's place.

Nothing had been touched. It struck her now how little she had missed being away from her own possessions, how easily she had become accustomed and comfortable in Brad's apartment.

It wasn't that she led such a sterile, empty life. She didn't. Her photos and handmade pillows and an old jewelry box of Nana Bea's and dozens more small things like them had great sentimental value to her. But things were, after all, only things, and they were all exactly as she had left them.

The workmen clattered around downstairs, bashing out the remaining glass shards and the frame, then went outside to retrieve the replacement window. Watching them from her bedroom window, she felt a shiver go through her again.

The feeling had nothing to do with the repairmen, but she couldn't pinpoint the real cause of it. She should have felt better, more relaxed, but instead, some insistent instinct to the contrary prevailed. She stuffed her clothes willy-nilly into a suitcase and snatched up a few selections from her closet, then returned downstairs.

The open front door mocked her wariness. The only thing coming through that door was a shaft of perfectly benign sunlight and repairmen toting a new kitchen window. Still she couldn't shake her apprehension.

She should leave. Trust her instincts and just leave. The repairmen were bonded. She could leave them to do their work without fear of being ripped off. But a part of her trusted that her instincts were real and not imagined, and that if she could just keep her wits about her, she would at last uncover the cause of her nebulous anxiety.

That it was somehow vital.

She should leave. Come back later with Brad. She couldn't. She placed her belongings very deliberately on the back of her sofa and braced herself for the kitchen. Surely it—whatever *it* was—awaited her discovery in the kitchen.

The phone rang. It might be Brad. Tempted to pick up the phone, she let it ring through to her answering machine. She would only pick up the phone if it was Brad or Beth.... But the answering machine clunked awkwardly and failed to catch the call. On the forth ring, the telephone company voice-mail service intercepted.

Joanna stared at the answering machine on her kitchen counter. The small light was on, indicating that it was plugged in. Puzzled, unnerved, she punched the on-off button, but a small sensor beeped and kept beeping as the machine powered up again. Frowning, she opened the lid to the tape compartment.

Where there should have been two tapes—one with her recorded instructions, another for the caller messages—there was only one. The message tape was gone. Over the considerable noise the workmen were making, she began to hear her own pulse hammering in her ears.

This was what the break-in had been about, the reason the thief had no reason to venture farther into the town house than the kitchen. Someone needed to make sure she never heard what was on that tape.

Staring at the empty space where the tape cartridge should have been, Joanna sank onto the stool, forcing herself to keep cool, stay composed.

Call the police, she thought. But by touching the answering machine, turning it on and off and lifting the tape compartment lid, she'd already compromised any chance of getting fingerprints.

Still, she thought, this could only have to do with Phil's call to her. But she had been screening calls the night Phil was killed, and the moment she heard his voice, she'd picked up. Unless, of course, he had tried to call her back when she was in the shower. She'd left the answering machine off then, so her voice-mail service would have picked up the second call from Phil.

Her hands were shaking when she picked up the phone receiver to call Brad. The sounds signaling new, unheard messages sounded before the dial tone. She dialed the voice-messaging number, then entered her password numbers to be connected to her messages.

"First message" came the recorded voice, "left Wednesday... at 10:52 p.m." Silence. "Joanna, it's Phil again." She knew he and Beth had the same system, using their recorder only to screen calls, and voice mail otherwise, but she could barely think. Ten fifty-two.

Ten fifty-two. Dear God.

Chapter Fifteen

"Call me back, asap," Phil's recorded voice was saying.

Her palms grew sweaty. Sheer, numbing dread filled her. "It's the strawberries, Jo—" He broke off. She heard his chair squeak, imagined him bolting upright.

She heard his irritated voice. "What are *you* doing here...what the hell are you doing!" She imagined Phil Stonehaven taken off guard, confused, irate at the intrusion of someone intent on doing him bodily harm. *Someone he knew.* Someone he couldn't believe coming into his office like that.

It's the strawberries, Jo...

She tried to focus on the thought, tried to make sense of strawberries, but Phil must have dropped the receiver. The phone banged down on his desk. The awful clatter ricocheted in her ear and she couldn't think.

Her blood rushed from her head. The dread in her inflated to horror. Phil had been murdered while she showered, and she was listening to it happen as if it were taking place this very moment—Phil screaming, *"Are you crazy!"* followed by the ugly thud of what she knew now must have been Phil's own microscope bashing him in the head.

And then nothing, only the sterile feminine voice saying, "Next message left . . . Thursday . . . 1:43 p.m."

Joanna hung up the phone and wrapped her arms over her breasts. The horror refused to fade. The sounds, the desperate plea, the terrible thud, echoed in her head over the hammering of the workmen.

His assailant was someone Phil knew.

A terrible clarity possessed her. The voice-mail message from Phil pinpointed the exact moment he was murdered. Ten fifty-two p.m. Exactly nine minutes after the last keystroke Chip Vine had made on the computer in the HIS complex.

Chilled to the marrow, Joanna began to shiver uncontrollably. The thought that had been nagging at the edge of her consciousness, both at Beth's last night, and then later when she and Brad talked on the drive home, the thing that should have *leapt* out at her, damn it, was that if Peggy Vine had murdered her father-in-law with the penicillin, then it was Chip who had murdered Phil. . . .

Her breath locked in her lungs. By 10:43 p.m., Chip knew that Phil was on to the discrepancy in the penicillin data. He must have panicked when Brungart's autopsy wasn't enough, when the administration asked for Phil's opinion, as well. He must have sat around the computer room, going crazy with worry, terrified with the fear of discovery, lying in wait, hoping against hope that Phil would miss the obscure signs of anaphylactic shock. But Phil wouldn't let it go, wouldn't quit, and so Chip had murdered him to ensure that no one else would ever know what Peggy had done.

It's the strawberries, Jo . . .

The strawberries. Dear God.

Then she knew. It wasn't Peggy Vine who found a way to kill her father-in-law. It was Chip.

The strawberries finally gave it away. Months ago a pediatric patient of Beth's had required a transfusion of platelets, the clotting cells in blood, but the child had begun to get terrible hives within moments after his nurse started the transfusion.

It turned out that the little boy was allergic to strawberries, and the donor had eaten some strawberries the day before her platelet donation. Twenty-four hours later the thing that made some people allergic to strawberries was still in the donor blood.

And just like that, exactly like that, Joanna thought, horrified at the coldbloodedness of it, at the premeditation it required, Chip must have ingested a huge dose of penicillin, and the penicillin was still there in his blood when he donated a unit of blood for his father's emergency heart surgery.

THE PHONE RANG. She snatched it up. It must be Brad. It had to be Brad. But the voice on the line was thick with tears and panic, small sobs making the feminine cry nearly incoherent.

"Dr. Cavendish, y-you've...you've got to help m-me!"

Peggy Vine. Had she known?

Joanna gritted her teeth. Her hands clenched the phone receiver. She forced herself to breathe. "Peggy, what is it?"

The woman could barely speak. "Please..."

"Peggy, listen to me," Joanna ordered. "Answer me. Did Chip beat you again?"

"Yes, but—"

"Where is he now?"

She sobbed, hiccuped. "He's...we're at Hensel's house. But he's—"

"Peggy, you have to call the police. Hang up. Dial 911. Do it now," Joanna urged, trembling, shaking with emotions that were so old in her, so ingrained, so fearful, that her throat was paralyzed. In twenty-five years her mother had never once taken the simple measure to protect herself, not even once. Tears of futile outrage dribbled onto Joanna's cheeks and she dashed them away. "Do you hear me? Will you do that? Will you call 911, or should I?"

"Dr. Cavendish, no! Listen...please listen. I've got him...I mean, he's locked in the old icebox. He can't get out. I think he's passed out in there. I'll call the police, but I need someone to talk to first. Please...come. Chip... I mean, I'll tell you everything, only don't call the police yet, I'm begging you, please don't." Her words tumbled out of control on top of each other in a watershed of hysteria and dismay. "Please talk to me. Please come talk to me. You can come here—"

Joanna could barely think, hardly command herself to reason. Every instinct in her cried out to go to Peggy, to give her that much, no matter what she had done or known about her father-in-law's death. "Peggy, are you absolutely certain that Chip can't get out?"

"Yes," she answered, sniffing, crying. "It's an old fashioned walk-in icebox. There's only a handle on the outside. Will you come? I promise I'll...I'll tell you everything."

Joanna couldn't refuse Peggy Vine's desperate plea. There were things, terrible things, to come, to learn. She would never forgive Chip for what he had done to Phil, or Peggy because she had to have known, or Hensel Rabern for protecting them.

But she would go and listen and then she would call Detective Dibell, and then she would try to find a way to get beyond this nightmare and find some peace of mind in the arms of a man whose love and integrity she had only begun to appreciate.

She would call Brad, and then she would go. "All right, Peggy. I'll come on the condition that you promise me to call the police after we've talked."

Peggy heaved a stuttering sigh and her promise and then gave Joanna the address of Hensel Rabern's home.

She called Brad on his car phone, on his home phone, on his answering service. She could find him nowhere. She left messages in two places as to where she had gone and when and why, and that she knew now what had happened.

One of the workmen gave Joanna a lift to her car, which was still parked, although ticketed, at the park where she had gone to kick around a soccer ball last Thursday night.

Last Thursday. It seemed a lifetime ago. Functioning in what seemed like a jerky automatic way, as if her lips spoke and her hands and body moved through no control of her own, she thanked the repairman for the ride and wrote out a check to cover the repairs to her kitchen window plus twenty dollars for their trouble. Because she had been some trouble.

She unlocked her car door, got in and put the key in the ignition, frightened in every minute that a car bomb would explode.

How trite.

Tears eked out of her eyes again. How terribly trite to think she would go up in a car bomb. She wasn't dealing with the Mafia and this wasn't the movies. The ordinariness of it all nearly immobilized her. Chip and Peggy and Rabern and Brungart and Beth and Phil, even Lucy Chavez and Brad and Joanna herself, were only ordinary people, leading their prosaic little lives, right up until Chip had toppled the orderliness.

She drove and drove. Darkness fell, mocking the darkness in her mind. The purely numb sensation. It began to rain and the temperature dropped from a warm fall day to a cold harbinger of a harsh winter to come. She switched on her lights and windshield wipers and drove some more. Hensel Rabern lived beyond the exclusive country club suburbs. The roads were remote, the one off the interstate a lonely, potholed two-lane job. The drive seemed to take all night, but it could only have taken forty minutes or so.

She slowed to a crawl. The rain lashed the car, making it difficult to read the lane names. At last she found the one she was looking for. Hensel Rabern's turn-of-the-century house sat on Bitterroot Lane. It was the only one.

Lights shone from the curtained windows of every room of the mansion. Joanna pulled to a stop, shut off the engine and made a dash through the pounding rain for the front door. Peggy was there, waiting, staring out the long vertical window by the door. She opened the door, her tear-streaked face black and blue, her lip split, her stringy hair hanging in clumps, her heart on her sleeve.

"Oh, Peggy," Joanna cried, rushing through the door to take the poor battered woman in her arms, but the door slammed shut behind her.

Fear clawed at her throat. She started to turn around, but powerful arms clamped around her, pinning hers to her body. Filthy, snarling epithets burst out near her ear, and the sour, liquored, desperate breath of a crazed, inhumanly strong man assaulted her senses. Chip.

Time seemed to stop. Details registered as full-blown impressions, one after another. The iron grip of the arms around her. Peggy's stricken, panicked eyes. The elegant walnut staircase. The parquet, the stained-glass fixtures, the old-fashioned heat registers, the thick, cranberry-colored terry washcloth, monogrammed, soaked in ether, shoved into her face, covering her nose and mouth.

She kicked and writhed, struggling, and fought back and tried to scream, but the sickeningly sweet scent invaded her head. Her last conscious thought was not that Peggy had betrayed her or that Chip would murder her, for he surely would, but that she had fallen in love, and she would never have the chance to say it because she'd learned too late how to trust him . . . and how not to take half-witted risks. *Too late.*

BRAD PARTED COMPANY with Rabern and left the restaurant at seven-thirty. Rabern had agreed to meet him for dinner, and the story he told made Brad's blood run cold.

Chip was dangerously psychotic, Rabern said. Over the edge, around the bend, insanely unstable. At the eleventh hour, only five days before Elliott Vine admitted himself to Rose Memorial for open-heart surgery, he had gone flamboyantly about putting his affairs in order. In doing so he had not only changed his will, he'd rubbed his son's nose in it.

Chip would never inherit a single dime from his father, Rabern told Brad, and even the trust fund left by Chip's mother was left so tied up in restrictions and conditions that he would be an old man before he came into any significant sums at all.

Rabern was sick at heart, he said. Sick that Lucy had left him for Elliott Vine, sick that his old friend's true colors were now showing so hideously through, sick that Elliott had belittled and ridiculed and demeaned his son so relentlessly and for so many years that the boy was literally doomed to his psychotic fate.

Sick, in the end, Rabern concluded, to have worked so hard to save Elliott Vine's life, only to learn after what Chip had done. Falling-down drunk, loaded to the gills on some designer drug, Chip had admitted to Rabern, who was his godfather and the only human being on earth besides Peggy who understood him, to loading up his body with penicillin, donating blood for his father's surgery, knowing the minute his blood hit his father's veins, the high and mighty bastard son of a bitch would die.

And then there would be no more groveling, no more bowing and scraping and pretending and trying to please his father, who could not or would not be pleased. Chip would contest his father's will and have restored to him the inheritance he had earned simply by enduring the abuse and humiliation his father had heaped on his head his entire life.

Rabern had sat there, blithely cleansing his fingers of the scent of fresh-peeled shrimp with a hot washcloth, pleading his own case with Brad. "I know, I understand completely how morally outraged you must be. I regret the embarrassment and trouble I have caused Joanna Cavendish."

Calmly cutting into his medium-rare porterhouse steak, Rabern seemed to anticipate Brad's every question. "Yes, I did sway Ruth Brungart," he went on, "to request testing on the sample of Elliott's blood until there would be nothing left to test for penicillin. And, yes, I have harbored Chip and Peggy, and conspired to keep the extent of Chip's psychotic breakdown concealed. But don't you see?" he asked. "Elliott was already dead. There was nothing I could do about that. And in a way, he only got what he finally deserved."

Brad's steak went untouched. He had no appetite. The awkward silence hung between them as Brad refused to agree that Vine's death was in any way justified.

Rabern chewed his steak, swallowed and washed it down with a swallow of very aged, very expensive Pinot Noir, then rushed in to fill the vacuum. "So. I thought to myself, Chip would only incur horrendous expense to the community to prosecute him—in a very nasty public trial—and in the end, only be confined for life to some mental institution. So I resolved to seek out the psychiatric care he so desperately needs and pay for it myself—to make compensation, in some small way, for my part in this terrible tragedy."

Brad could stomach Rabern's self-serving bull no longer. "And how," he asked softly, his anger running so deep and hot he was afraid he might choke the life out of Rabern right then and there, "how is Beth Stonehaven to be compensated for the loss of her husband and the father of her three little children?"

For the first time, Rabern shifted uncomfortably. "A tragedy," he said, shaking his head. "A senseless tragedy—it goes to show you how desperately crazed Chip had become. If he had left well enough alone, Phil Stonehaven would not be dead, but Chip was by then bearing such an enormous load of guilt...he was frankly terrified of discovery. So he took Phil's life and then proceeded to open the door to the soup kitchen...." Rabern shook his head, apparently lost in thought. He drew a breath, shrugged and met Brad's offended, disbelieving gaze. "Perhaps some accommodation may be made to Beth Stonehaven from Elliott's estate."

"No amount of money is going to ease her loss," Brad returned. His anger only grew hotter.

"No," Rabern said, suddenly pensive. Melancholy filled his powerful voice. "It has made my life more comfortable certainly, but it can never compensate the losses of the heart. Did you know Elliott Vine married my sweetheart?" He looked for a moment as if his eyes might mist. Suddenly older, a desolate shadow of himself. "That in a kinder, gentler world, Chip would have been my own son and not Elliott's?"

For the first time, Brad felt a pang of sympathy for the wasted, empty life of a man whose best friend had betrayed him not once, but a thousand times over. But the pang was only that. Momentary. Fleeting. Hensel Rabern would have destroyed Joanna to save the skin of the son who might have been his.

Rabern put down his knife and fork in a very deliberate manner, then refolded his linen napkin, as if by doing something so physically precise, he might restore his composure. "Do this. Go home, collect Joanna, bring her to my house. Perhaps she will find it in her heart to forgive an old man. And together, we will decide what to do next."

Brad heard his car phone ringing, or thought he did, as he unlocked the Bronco. He snatched it up, but too late.

Chilled by the pounding rain, his body shivered once, hard. He jerked the seat belt into place, jammed the keys into the ignition and made the engine whine pulling out of the parking lot.

All he wanted was to get home to Joanna. Rabern's story had left him cold and tense, filled with loathing and halfhearted, unwilling sympathy. He could understand the forces that drove Chip Vine to murder. He understood the pain Rabern had endured and even the warped thinking that had led him to cover the murders his godson had committed. But many more lives had been destroyed than the one Chip had intended, and Brad refused to let him get away with it in some insanity plea.

He had no intention of taking Joanna to Rabern's place, of subjecting her to Rabern's excuses and Chip's deranged, psychotic story. He picked up the phone and dialed his place, but got no answer. Habit made him check his messages. When he heard Joanna's voice telling him she'd gone to Rabern's to be with Peggy, his chest filled with fear for her compounded by a terrible rage.

TOSSED IN A HEAP on the floor of Hensel Rabern's study, Joanna came to once, but the noise—the shouting and screaming—hurt her head. She knew where she was. She knew why. She could not have been out for more than a few minutes. Chip and Peggy were screeching at each other, and vaguely, so distantly, Joanna understood they were arguing about what they would do with her.

She forced her drugged mind to focus, to listen, to figure out what was being said…. Peggy…something about it being stupid to hurt her or bruise her or tie her up because if she was going over the cliff side of an old quarry it should look like she had missed a turn, not like someone had knocked her over the head and piled her in her car and pushed it over on purpose.

Chip was crazed, shouting in stunted, irrational phrases. He knew better. He could handle this without any of Peggy's *stupid,* hysterical, feebleminded vile suggestions.

She froze. Didn't move. Couldn't move. A shadow fell over her. Lying there on the edge of consciousness, she could smell Chip, feel his rage, and she knew it was all directed at her.

Chip kicked her in the back, Peggy screamed and then Joanna heard another voice.

"My God, what have you done now?"

She dared open her eyes, Chip jerked around in a frenzy to confront Hensel Rabern. "She's dead meat, man," he said. "If it weren't for her—"

"Oh, shut up and sit down and let me think," Rabern ordered.

"Don't you *talk* to me like that!" Chip screamed. "Didn't I have enough of that my whole damn life? Didn't you see it? Didn't you hear it? Don't you get it?"

"Chip, please settle down," Peggy begged, and Chip turned on her, backhanding her hard enough to make her fall to the floor. Joanna cringed, flashing on scenes exactly like this one, times when she was a small and helpless child and she reacted as she had a hundred other times, sitting up, backing away, clamping a fist to her mouth to keep from crying out.

But all the emotion and hatred and pent-up helpless fury she had never leveled at her father rose up in her. She was not a helpless child, and if Chip went for Peggy again, she would spring at him and scratch his eyes out.

But from the corner of her eye, Joanna saw Brad at the doorway into the study. Dressed in his thousand-dollar suit, the one that gave him such an incredible air of civilization and polish, he now looked frankly dangerous. She was the only one who noticed him standing there, and she clamped her hand tighter to her lips so she wouldn't betray his presence.

"Chip, let's just go away," Peggy moaned. "Let's just—"

"*Shut up!*" Chip screamed at her. Sweat poured off him. His eyes darted wildly around the room in a drugged and helter-skelter frenzy. He seemed not to notice that Joanna had come to.

Rabern stood warily across the room from her, and began speaking in soothing tones that Chip read as condescending and drove him into another verbal rampage.

"*You* said no one would ever *know! You* said it was the perfect execution. You said—"

"You said he could get away with it, didn't you, Rabern," Brad asked softly, the power, the danger, in his voice killing every other sound, even Chip's agitated outburst. "You fed him the penicillin. What was it, Hensel? The perfect way to get even with your nemesis? Use Chip, knowing anyone would see the boy was out of his mind blaming you?"

Chip swallowed over and over again, nodding crazily. "Yeah! That's it!"

"And then, you even betrayed Chip, didn't you, Rabern?" Brad went on, his expression betraying his utter repugnance for the surgeon. "You knew Vine had changed his will. You knew Chip was desperate to keep his father alive then, desperate to abort your little plan. You told him you'd see that the blood he'd donated the week before surgery would never be transfused—but you let Joanna transfuse all the blood."

"Don't be ridiculous—"

"It was you all along!" Joanna cried through her dismay, grasping that it wasn't Chip and Peggy, that it had never been Peggy, but Rabern's plot that Chip had gone along with. Peggy may not even have known what Chip hand done when she admitted in the emergency room that she would have killed her father-in-law herself.

And she saw that Brad was right. Rabern had let her transfuse the penicillin-loaded blood. He'd been so brutally snide about the mix-up of blood coolers the morning of the surgery. Now she knew why. Afterward, Chip had panicked, and murdered Phil. She had never felt so close to violence herself as she felt then, knowing Rabern and Chip had conspired to kill Elliott Vine. Knowing even Ruth Brungart had been manipulated into wasting the evidence, the proof of their horrible crime.

"You wanted Elliott Vine dead at all costs, didn't you, Hensel?" she asked, her voice toneless.

Rabern stared, flinty-eyed, at her, refusing to answer.

"I don't get what's going on," Chip whined.

"Tell him, Rabern," Brad ordered. "Tell him how his inheritance never mattered to you. Tell him—"

"No!" Punchy, confused, overwrought, Chip roared, "You said you'd get rid of my blood!"

"Shut the hell up, you moron!" Rabern snapped. "Don't you see what he's doing, trying to drive a wedge between us?"

But *moron* was a huge, huge mistake, obliterating the last vestiges of Chip's grip on reality. He grabbed up the fire poker and lunged at Rabern and struck with all his might, catching his godfather on the side of the head. One blow dropped Rabern to his knees. Chip raised up, crazed, maddened, incapable of stopping, and Brad threw a body slam at him that threw him to the floor, and the second, arcing blow, the poker held high above Chip's head, fell to the floor. Peggy screamed.

Brad stood over the two men and, cringing against the threat of danger Brad represented, neither man moved.

Joanna got up and dialed 911.

JOANNA AND BRAD took a very long, very hot shower together, scrubbing from their bodies the smell of ether and blood and alcohol, and the stench of murder and insanity from their hearts. Largely wordless, for a while they lay entwined together in Brad's bed, letting the dregs of anger and pain seep away. But they could not be like that together for long before desire rose up like a phoenix from the ashes, like a bloom from the muck, and they made love, sweet and tender and full-blown, then fast and hard and cleansing as nothing else on earth could do for them.

Afterward, lingering in the sensual haze, listening to Brad ramble on and on in his melodic, silver-tongued way, waxing almost poetic, almost on the verge of confessing to that wildly romantic streak Joanna had mined in him, she interrupted.

"So tell me, Mr. MacPherson, please. What trick is it that will make you go speechless so I can get a kiss in edgewise?"

He made them both sit up. The persistent harvest moon shone in the room. He cupped her face in his hands. "Will you marry me, Dr. Dish?"

She smiled. *Dr. Dish.* He made her heart throb with such ease. "I've no choice if I'm to he an honest woman, now have I?"

"Is that a yes?"

"Yes. That's a definite yes."

He grinned, looked down, said a mental thank-you to whatever powers there were that had brought her back to him and then kissed her hard and long. "Then," he said, "I am rendered positively—" kissed her again "—speechless."

Epilogue

The day came when Brad MacPherson restored the esteem of Rose Memorial Hospital with his gilded tongue alone. His gift of gab, his profound empathy, his newfound love, his unstinting integrity, together worked in concert to achieve this miracle even Sister Mary Bernadette Reilly had begun to despair of ever seeing. Her beloved Sacred Heart Hospital, transformed into Rose Memorial, beleaguered of late, now raised to an unparalleled stature of respect and regard in the community.

"Look," he had said, "at the quality of people left at Rose Memorial, the people who would not stand by and allow the abuses of an evil few destroy the fine, dedicated efforts of the many.

"Look to Erin Harper," he said, "a woman who owed Rose Memorial nothing but who risked her life and good name to expose the sabotage to our blood research project. Look to Dr. Colin Rennslaer, who despite the betrayal of his trusted associates, took responsibility and then moved heaven and earth to save the life of a child not once but twice.

"Look," he said, "at the precious lives of Stephi and Teddi Mastrangelo, at the unflinching spirit of their parents in the face of real evil—our own medical records

manager, Zoe, and her husband, Dr. Rafe Mastrangelo.
Look to Zoe's father, the beloved former bishop Vincente Rosario whose name we now bear and whose personal fortune made our survival possible many times over
our history.

"Look," he said, "to the resolute efforts of Dr. Joanna
Cavendish, without whose insight and determination to
get at the truth, the murders of Dr. Vine and Dr. Stonehaven would have slipped unnoticed and unpunished between the cracks.

"Look to Sister Mary Bernadette Reilly, whose guid-
ance and faith inspire us all.

"These are the people and this is the character of those
left to carry on the mission of Rose Memorial now and
into the twenty-first century.

"We look with humility and gratitude and awe to a future in the hands of these, our heroes and heroines, in an
unending drama of healing and service to our community.

"As Centi and Sister Mary Bernadette could say far
better than I, God bless us all in our hours of need as
much as in our hours of triumph."

Sister Mary Bernadette Reilly smiled to herself in the
tiny cell she called her office. The Lord must have been
smiling, too, the day MacPherson was inspired by her
bribe to come to Rose Memorial.

She pinched a wilted leaf from the violet plant in the
windowsill, then gave the plant a healthy dose of water.

Men and women and medicine. Such a potent combination, she reflected. Heroes and heroines abounded here.
Kisses were stolen. Love flourished. Marriages were soon
to be made in heaven in the Sacred Heart sanctuary.

Miracles, every one.

HARLEQUIN®

I N T R I G U E®

Keep up with Caroline Burnes
and FAMILIAR

This crime-solving cat has nine lives and a wicked sense of adventure. Find out how the fun began with the Familiar books. In case you've missed any in the series, here's your chance to catch up:

#215	TOO FAMILIAR	$2.89	☐
#256	THRICE FAMILIAR	$2.99	☐
#277	SHADES OF FAMILIAR	$2.99 U.S./$3.99 CAN.	☐
#256	FAMILIAR REMEDY	$2.99 U.S./$3.99 CAN.	☐

Please send me the above books I have checked. Enclosed is a check or money order, payable to Harlequin Reader Service, plus 75¢ postage and handling ($1.00 in Canada).

HARLEQUIN READER SERVICE
In the U.S.   In Canada
3010 Walden Ave.   P.O. Box 613
P.O. Box 9047   Fort Erie, Ontario
Buffalo, NY 14269-9047   L2A 5X3

Name:_____

Address: _____ City: _____

State/Prov.: _____ Zip/Postal Code: _____

Books subject to availability.
Canadian residents add applicable federal and provincial taxes.

FFORDER

HARLEQUIN®

I N T R I G U E®

HARLEQUIN INTRIGUE AUTHOR KELSEY ROBERTS SERVES UP A DOUBLE DOSE OF DANGER AND DESIRE IN THE EXCITING NEW MINISERIES:

THE ROSE TATTOO

At the Rose Tattoo, Southern Specialties are served with a Side Order of Suspense:

On the Menu for June

Dylan Tanner—tall, dark and delectable
Shelby Hunnicott—sweet and sassy
Sizzling Suspense—saucy red herrings with a twist

On the Menu for July

J. D. Porter—hot and spicy
Tory Conway—sinfully rich
Southern Fried Secrets—succulent and juicy

On the Menu for August

Wes Porter—subtly scrumptious
Destiny Talbott—tart and tangy
Mouth-Watering Mystery—deceptively delicious

Look for Harlequin Intrigue's response to your
hearty appetite for suspense: THE ROSE TATTOO,
coming in June, July and August.

HARLEQUIN®
I N T R I G U E®

Brush up on your bedside manner with...

Heart-racing romantic-suspense novels that are just what the doctor ordered!

This trilogy of medical thrillers by Carly Bishop is sure to get your blood flowing, raise the hairs on the back of your neck and bring out all the right symptoms of reading the best in romance and mystery.

Here's your chance to order any that you've missed:

#314	HOT BLOODED	$3.50 U.S./$3.99 CAN.	☐
#319	BREATHLESS	$3.50 U.S./$3.99 CAN.	☐
#323	HEART THROB	$3.50 U.S./$3.99 CAN.	☐

Please send me the above the books I have checked. Enclosed is a check or money order, payable to Harlequin Reader Service, plus 75¢ postage and handling ($1.00 in Canada).

HARLEQUIN READER SERVICE
In the U.S.   In Canada
3010 Walden Ave.   P.O. Box 613
P.O. Box 9047   Fort Erie, Ontario
Buffalo, NY 14269-9047   L2A 5X3

Name: _____

Address: _____ City: _____

State/Prov.: _____ Zip/Postal Code: _____

Book orders subject to availability.
Canadian residents add applicable federal and provincial taxes.   PUL-ORD

ANNOUNCING THE

FLYAWAY VACATION SWEEPSTAKES!

This month's destination:

Beautiful SAN FRANCISCO!

This month, as a special surprise, we're offering an exciting FREE VACATION!

Think how much fun it would be to visit San Francisco "on us"! You could ride cable cars, visit Chinatown, see the Golden Gate Bridge and dine in some of the finest restaurants in America!

The facing page contains two Entry Coupons (as does every book you received this shipment). Complete and return *all* the entry coupons; **the more times you enter, the better your chances of winning!**

Then keep your fingers crossed, because you'll find out by June 15, 1995 if you're the winner! If you are, here's what you'll get:

- Round-trip airfare for two to beautiful San Francisco!
- 4 days/3 nights at a first-class hotel!
- $500.00 pocket money for meals and sightseeing!

Remember: The more times you enter, the better your chances of winning!*

*NO PURCHASE OR OBLIGATION TO CONTINUE BEING A SUBSCRIBER NECESSARY TO ENTER. SEE REVERSE SIDE OR ANY ENTRY COUPON FOR ALTERNATIVE MEANS OF ENTRY.

VSF KAL

FLYAWAY VACATION
SWEEPSTAKES
OFFICIAL ENTRY COUPON

This entry must be received by: MAY 30, 1995
This month's winner will be notified by: JUNE 15, 1995
Trip must be taken between: JULY 30, 1995-JULY 30, 1996

YES, I want to win the San Francisco vacation for two. I understand the prize includes round-trip airfare, first-class hotel and $500.00 spending money. Please let me know if I'm the winner!

Name_____

Address _____ Apt. _____

City   State/Prov.   Zip/Postal Code

Account #_____

Return entry with invoice in reply envelope.

© 1995 HARLEQUIN ENTERPRISES LTD.   CSF KAL

FLYAWAY VACATION
SWEEPSTAKES
OFFICIAL ENTRY COUPON

This entry must be received by: MAY 30, 1995
This month's winner will be notified by: JUNE 15, 1995
Trip must be taken between: JULY 30, 1995-JULY 30, 1996

YES, I want to win the San Francisco vacation for two. I understand the prize includes round-trip airfare, first-class hotel and $500.00 spending money. Please let me know if I'm the winner!

Name_____

Address _____ Apt. _____

City   State/Prov.   Zip/Postal Code

Account #_____

Return entry with invoice in reply envelope.

© 1995 HARLEQUIN ENTERPRISES LTD.   CSF KAL

OFFICIAL RULES

FLYAWAY VACATION SWEEPSTAKES 3449

NO PURCHASE OR OBLIGATION NECESSARY

Three Harlequin Reader Service 1995 shipments will contain respectively, coupons for entry into three different prize drawings, one for a trip for two to San Francisco, another for a trip for two to Las Vegas and the third for a trip for two to Orlando, Florida. To enter any drawing using an Entry Coupon, simply complete and mail according to directions.

There is no obligation to continue using the Reader Service to enter and be eligible for any prize drawing. You may also enter any drawing by hand printing the words "Flyaway Vacation," your name and address on a 3"x5" card and the destination of the prize you wish that entry to be considered for (i.e., San Francisco trip, Las Vegas trip or Orlando trip). Send your 3"x5" entries via first-class mail (limit: one entry per envelope) to: Flyaway Vacation Sweepstakes 3449, c/o Prize Destination you wish that entry to be considered for, P.O. Box 1315, Buffalo, NY 14269-1315, USA or P.O. Box 610, Fort Erie, Ontario L2A 5X3, Canada.

To be eligible for the San Francisco trip, entries must be received by 5/30/95; for the Las Vegas trip, 7/30/95; and for the Orlando trip, 9/30/95.

Winners will be determined in random drawings conducted under the supervision of D.L. Blair, Inc., an independent judging organization whose decisions are final, from among all eligible entries received for that drawing. San Francisco trip prize includes round-trip airfare for two, 4-day/3-night weekend accommodations at a first-class hotel, and $500 in cash (trip must be taken between 7/30/95—7/30/96, approximate prize value—$3,500); Las Vegas trip includes round-trip airfare for two, 4-day/3-night weekend accommodations at a first-class hotel, and $500 in cash (trip must be taken between 9/30/95—9/30/96, approximate prize value—$3,500); Orlando trip includes round-trip airfare for two, 4-day/3-night weekend accommodations at a first-class hotel, and $500 in cash (trip must be taken between 11/30/95—11/30/96, approximate prize value—$3,500). All travelers must sign and return a Release of Liability prior to travel. Hotel accommodations and flights are subject to accommodation and schedule availability. Sweepstakes open to residents of the U.S. (except Puerto Rico) and Canada, 18 years of age or older. Employees and immediate family members of Harlequin Enterprises, Ltd., D.L. Blair, Inc., their affiliates, subsidiaries and all other agencies, entities and persons connected with the use, marketing or conduct of this sweepstakes are not eligible. Odds of winning a prize are dependent upon the number of eligible entries received for that drawing. Prize drawing and winner notification for each drawing will occur no later than 15 days after deadline for entry eligibility for that drawing. Limit: one prize to an individual, family or organization. All applicable laws and regulations apply. Sweepstakes offer void wherever prohibited by law. Any litigation within the province of Quebec respecting the conduct and awarding of the prizes in this sweepstakes must be submitted to the Regies des loteries et Courses du Quebec. In order to win a prize, residents of Canada will be required to correctly answer a time-limited arithmetical skill-testing question. Value of prizes are in U.S. currency.

Winners will be obligated to sign and return an Affidavit of Eligibility within 30 days of notification. In the event of noncompliance within this time period, prize may not be awarded. If any prize or prize notification is returned as undeliverable, that prize will not be awarded. By acceptance of a prize, winner consents to use of his/her name, photograph or other likeness for purposes of advertising, trade and promotion on behalf of Harlequin Enterprises, Ltd., without further compensation, unless prohibited by law.

For the names of prizewinners (available after 12/31/95), send a self-addressed, stamped envelope to: Flyaway Vacation Sweepstakes 3449 Winners, P.O. Box 4200, Blair, NE 68009.

RVC KAL